MIDLIFE WOLF BOND

ACCIDENTAL ALPHA • BOOK 4

CARISSA ANDREWS

CHAPTER 1

FROM THE ASHES

ELLA

An unsettling quiet wraps around me as I watch the last few embers of fire fade, like stars winking out at the end of a long night. Staring into the ashes, I can't help but wonder...

How much longer can this go on?

Where I once saw the cozy haven that was my new home, only charred remains clutch at the dark. The firetrucks are long gone, and the chaos has settled into an eerie calm.

Yet, disbelief gnaws at me, refusing to let go.

I stand here, heart heavy with loss and burning with anger, under the indifferent light of a crescent moon—so starkly different from the fiery inferno that consumed my home hours ago.

In the distance, the soft howls of my pack blend with the night, a mournful echo of our shared grief.

Part of me yearns to join them, to share in their lament, but I can't afford tears now.

No shrinking back.

Not when Troy, my ex-turned-foe and soon were-wolf, is out there plotting with Andres—the Alpha brazen enough to threaten everything I hold dear. He dared to target my children and nearly succeeded, if not for Alanna and her mysterious, destructive powers.

And as if my plate isn't full enough, a weighty prophecy looms over Stone and me, clouding my thoughts.

I need clarity.

I need a plan.

Feeling lost, as if caught in someone else's dark tale, I barely register Stone's presence until his hand rests reassuringly on my back. Silent and strong, he's always there when I need him most, reminding me we're in this together, come what may.

"We'll rebuild," I whisper, trying to convince myself as much as him. "Not just the house, but... *everything*. I won't let Andres think he's rattled us. The pack"—I sigh—"I'll protect the pack. Somehow."

"I know," Stone replies, his voice firm as resolve bleeds into his words. His hands press against my shoulders as he twists me to face him. "Andres won't know what hit him. But in the meantime, you need to rest." I open my mouth to say I have no home to rest in, but he beats me to it when he continues, "You and the kids are staying with me."

I glance into his emerald eyes and they flare, daring me to defy him.

There's no room for argument there. I get it.

I might be Alpha, but it's not like we have anywhere else to go.

Yet my stomach still flips at the idea of staying with him because I know where that puts me.

In his bed.

We've gotten so close—but not that close. Not yet.

And I still don't have a good reason why.

So, the idea that this might finally put us on a collision course...

Instead of sinking into the strangely giddy feeling that threatens to play at my heart and definitely my body, I simply nod in silent agreement.

My gaze extends past Stone to Asher. For tonight, he's being the protective older brother, as he stands close to Avery with his arm around her shoulders.

They're trying to be strong, but I can see the uncertainty in their eyes. They've grown up so much these past few months. Yet in moments like these, I'm painfully aware that they're still just kids.

Still ridiculously vulnerable. *Breakable.*

And my life is an utter mess.

A freight train of a disaster.

Big time.

Hell, my house looks like the aftermath of said train rolling through, come to think of it.

I glance at Alanna, realizing I need a word with her. Alone.

After everything she did—not only protecting my kids but the sheer scale of destruction we're only now really comprehending—I need to get a clearer picture of what she is and if she can help us with whatever else might be coming our way.

"Asher, Avery," I say, ensuring my voice remains steady—just a hint of the Alpha I need to be right now. "We'll be staying with Stone for a little while. At least until things settle down. I need to speak with Alanna, then we'll head out."

Asher gives a firm nod. While Avery tries to match his bravery, her eyes tell a story of mixed fear and determination. Her anxiety has to be running rampant under the surface, but she's doing her best not to let it win.

I turn toward Alanna, who stands slightly apart from the group, watching the embers wink out the way I had. She's stayed with us, even after my pack members left.

Her ordinarily light-hearted vibe has shifted tonight. Her posture is tense, as if she's ready to take on more adversaries at a moment's notice.

God, I hope not.

"Alanna, can I have a word?" I ask, gesturing to a more secluded area of the yard.

She nods, an air of apprehension apparent in the way she moves. It's like she's been waiting for this discussion and now that it's finally here, she's not entirely ready for it.

Hell, I'm not sure *I'm* ready for it.

We move away from the others, stepping nearer the large willow tree that looks entirely too big for the space now that the house is gone.

"Alanna, I need to understand," I begin, my gaze fixed on hers. My eyes float to the snake tattoo weaving its way up her neck and remember her description of it. About how she might look harmless but could be deadly, too. "You saved my kids, and for that, I'm eternally grateful. But the power you wielded... it's unlike anything I've seen. Which isn't really saying much, I guess." I scratch the side of my temple. I need to just come out with it. "What are you?"

She inhales sharply.

"Ella, it's not that simple," Alanna says, her eyes scanning the surroundings. "The power I have... some would kill to put it to use. Bad people. It's one thing to use it and another to say the words out loud. I can't discuss it here, out in the open. It's not safe."

Her words send a chill down my spine.

The implications of that are both intriguing and terrifying.

"But you *will* tell me?" I press gently, understanding more than most the delicacy of the situation.

Alanna nods, her expression solemn. "Of course, I

owe you that much. But it has to be somewhere private. Somewhere... *secure.*"

I nod, accepting her condition. There's a world out there, full of mysteries and powers beyond my comprehension. And it seems like I'm only starting to scratch the surface.

"Okay, we'll find another time and place. Just... be ready to explain everything."

She nods, shooting me one of her sweet, careful smiles.

I reach out, giving her arm a gentle squeeze, and hoping it relays the message that I'm not upset with her.

"We're heading out now. So, why don't you go home and get some rest, too," I say, glancing over my shoulder to where Stone and the kids are standing.

"Yeah, I suppose it's getting late," she whispers.

"Again, thank you, Alanna," I say, holding my chin high.

"It was my pleasure, Ella. I know how important family is," she replies, glancing past the house and out to the street. "Talk to you soon."

"Sounds good."

As she disappears into the shadows, leaving a trail of unanswered questions, I find myself standing alone under the large willow tree. The night is deathly quiet around me, however, my mind is anything but.

What kind of being could Alanna be?

Her abilities are beyond the scope of any supernatural creature I've come in contact with. And her caution... it suggests dangers I haven't even considered.

I don't like that. Not at all.

Then, on top of this clusterfuck is the prophecy Clementine dropped in our laps and promised to explain in the morning.

I lean against the willow, allowing myself a moment to just breathe and think.

The Moon Wolves prophecy.

Luna Scrolls.

Clementine's words echo in my mind. She said it would change everything.

What did she discover? How does it tie in with me —*with Stone?*

The uncertainty of not knowing weighs heavily on me. There are so many secrets now and so many unanswered questions.

I don't know how all of this happened, if I'm honest.

This prophecy could redefine our roles within the pack—within the world at large. Hell, our very existence.

For the first time since becoming an Alpha, ironically, I feel the weight of *destiny*—not just duty—resting on my shoulders. I can't say I'm a fan.

I turn back to Stone, Asher, and Avery, trying to steady the whirlwind of thoughts in my mind. They need me to be stable. Grounded.

Kicking off the tree, I make my way back to them. I glance at the kids, hoping to sound reassuring and calm when I'd rather be in the woods screaming my head off.

"Let's get going," I say, my voice more steady than I feel. "But first, we need to grab some essentials. Clothes, for starters."

The thought of going shopping seems ludicrous in the current scenario, but I'm nothing if not practical. Besides, the makeshift clothes I'm wearing, given to me in a blur of emergency, hang off me awkwardly and are a constant reminder of how unprepared we were for tonight's events.

The last thing I want to do is dress in them again in the morning. I'd rather toss them into the pit of my house and watch them burn, too.

Stone nods, understanding clear in his expression. "We'll make a quick stop on the way home."

Home.

The word hits different now, filled with images of Stone's place, not mine—a thought that sends a confusing thrill through me.

Focusing on Alpha duties should be my priority, not the simmering tension between us, but Stone's magnetic pull is a flame that I can't ignore—not sure if I even want to, to be honest.

With every glance, every brush of our hands, a sharp spark of awareness zips through me. My mind screams of the bigger threats—Andres, the safety of our pack, Troy's next move, the futures of my children —yet my heart stubbornly drifts toward him, tugged by a force that's getting harder to resist.

"The kids need clothes too," Stone adds, his voice breaking through my tumultuous thoughts. "We'll get everything sorted."

I nod, trying to focus on the practicalities, but my mind is like a pingpong ball stuck inside my head. Bouncing back and forth between all the insanity we're under.

We walk toward my Highlander, the only thing left untouched in the chaos, it seems. As Stone opens the rear passenger door to help Avery into the vehicle, I catch another glimpse of the protective side of him that I've come to rely on.

Come to *adore* about him.

He treats my children with such respect—such love and devotion. It makes my heart skip beats.

Asher opens his door and then takes a moment to look back at the ruins of our home. His face, usually so full of youthful confidence, now mirrors the loss we all feel. We haven't lived here long, but it was the new beginning we all needed.

And now...

I have no idea what it all means. Or what to do next.

I just know I can't take this lying down. It's not how werewolves work.

If there's one thing I've learned these past few months, it's that.

To not fight back is certain death.

Following to the Highlander, a sudden, unfamiliar scent catches my attention. It's faint, yet distinctively magical. Like the redolence of lightning right before it strikes.

A sense of unease washes over me, and I pause, sniffing the air, trying to pinpoint its origin.

Meeting Stone's eyes, I see the same alertness mirrored in his gaze. He's noticed it too.

Someone's here, watching, he says through our mental bond as he scans the shadows around us.

The revelation sends a new jolt of adrenaline through me.

Who would be watching us from the shadows?

A spy of Andres?

Or perhaps something even more sinister—unknown to us?

My jaw tightens, and I scan the dark perimeter of my property.

We need to find out who it is before we leave. If they're tracking us... His mental voice trails off, but the implication hangs heavily in the air.

The danger of leading an unknown threat to his home—where Asher and Avery would be, is too great.

We can't risk it. Not after tonight.

Just as I'm about to call out, a figure shrouded in shadow steps into a sliver of moonlight.

CHAPTER 2

TAKE A BREATH

ELLA

Seriously. Will this night ever freaking end?

If the Universe has any say in it, I'm guessing not.

The air hangs heavy with the horrible scent of charred remains and a newfound tension—the latter summoned by the unexpected presence before us.

Stone shifts into a protective stance, positioning himself between me and the newcomer. His body tenses, ready to spring into action at the slightest provocation.

A low growl rumbles through him, barely audible yet unmistakably dangerous. This is another side of him I've come to both respect and admire—the warrior lurking beneath the calm exterior.

However, the intensity of it is unmistakable. The Delta ready to defend his Alpha—and something more.

His mate.

Even though I am more than capable of taking care of myself, something in the action makes my blood sing.

As the figure steps further into the moonlight, a delicate dance of shadows and light plays across her features, revealing a woman whose presence seems as ancient as it is compelling.

Her silhouette is framed by the ethereal glow of the moonlight—her clothes whispering tales of forgotten times with their timeless design. The fabric, a blend of deep, earthy tones, moves with a grace that most couldn't replicate.

I know I couldn't.

Her dark hair cascades in loose waves, shimmering with hints of silver under the moon's caress, suggesting wisdom far beyond her serene, unlined face.

As she steps closer, my initial alarm gives way to curiosity. She's alone, and there's something about her —an air of calm authority and a touch of undeniable power—that makes me pause.

Something in me recognizes her strength.

However, I can't help but glance back at the High-lander, where Asher and Avery sit wide-eyed, watching through the partially rolled-down window of the back seat.

They both vie for space to see out, probably trying

to make sense of what they're seeing. Their pale faces are a silent reminder of what's at stake—of the need to tread carefully.

I reach for Stone, placing my hand on his arm in a silent plea to stand down.

"Who are you?" I ask, stepping around him.

"My name is Isolde." Her gaze flits between us, carrying a weight of wisdom and untold secrets. "I mean no harm," she says, and there's a sincerity in her eyes that forces an exhale of relief from my lungs. "I'm here because I felt a disturbance and felt compelled to investigate. The energy tonight was... *tumultuous.*"

I can't help the snort that escapes me. "Tumul-tuous is one word for it." I glance at the remains of my home, then back at her.

She has power—that's for sure.

"Are you a... a witch? A psychic?" I ask, hoping she says no. The last thing we need is for one of Andres' witches worming their way into things.

Isolde's lips curve into a small smile, but it doesn't quite reach her dark eyes. "Something like that. I have... *abilities.* Sensitivities to the energies of the world."

What if she's with the group that helped Andres? Stone asks through our mental connection, even though his gaze remains trained on Isolde.

I tip my chin, the movement barely noticeable to anyone but him.

I was just wondering the same thing, I respond.

Stone's still on high alert, but I can tell he's as curious as I am.

"And you just happened to be in the neighborhood?" he presses.

"I was drawn here," she explains, her gaze drifting over the wreckage. "Events like these, they send ripples through the ether. I came to see if I could help."

The idea of accepting help from a stranger, especially now, sends its own ripple through me. It's one of unease more than anything else. But then I remember Alanna, and how her unexpected aid turned the tide for us tonight.

Not everyone with powers different from my own is a danger to our peace.

"What kind of help are you offering?" I ask, narrowing my gaze at the question.

Isolde glances between us again, clearly torn.

Suddenly, the soft chime of my phone breaks the tension. A glance reveals a text from Asher, sent from the backseat of the Highlander.

> Mom, are you okay? Should we do something?

It's a small gesture, but it speaks volumes about the worry they're both feeling, cooped up and watching from a distance. Somehow, though, they're still ready to leap into action if needed.

I send a quick text back.

Stay put. We're okay.

Then I focus my attention back on the woman before us.

She eyes my movement as I tuck my phone back into my pocket."Since I can see that everyone is alright, all I can offer presently is information. Insights, I suppose. There is more at play here than meets the eye. I'm sure you feel it, too."

Stone and I exchange a significant glance. The lines on his face harden but he shrugs imperceptibly.

Information is power, especially in our world. Especially right now when it seems as though everyone has secrets.

But trust is hard to come by. After everything we've been through today, it might just be damn near impossible.

"Why should we trust you?" Stone's question is blunt but necessary. And one I was about to ask, myself.

"Because I believe we're on the same side," Isolde says simply. "And I believe I can help you understand some of the forces you're up against. Do with it as you will. I'm really fine either way."

Her offer hangs in the air between us, tempting and terrifying in equal measure.

Part of me wants to dismiss her, to protect the fragile security we have left. But another part, the part that's still reeling from tonight's revelations and the prophecy Clementine hinted at, is desperate for any shred of understanding.

"Alright," I say finally, the word feeling like a leap of faith. "Talk."

Isolde nods, stepping closer but maintaining a respectful distance. "From what I can sense, the attack tonight wasn't just about power or revenge—though there are elements of that mixed in. However, there's a deeper game being played—one that's tied to ancient magics and long-standing feuds. And you, Ella, are at the heart of it."

My mouth drops open. "H—how do you know my name?"

Isolde's smile deepens—no longer just a polite curve but a knowing, almost mischievous expression. "Word travels fast in our circles. Your rise to Alpha, the changes you've already ushered in. Your... *unique* situation with Stone." She gives a slight nod toward him, acknowledging his significance without spelling it out. "It's made you quite the topic of conversation in many circles. Mine included."

Stone's stance relaxes ever so slightly, but the tension in his jaw tells me he's far from happy about it.

"And what's your interest in all this?" he probes, the tone of his voice a mix of skepticism and curiosity.

"I seek balance, nothing more," Isolde begins, her gaze turning toward the night sky, where the moon hangs, a silent witness to our exchange. "The events transpiring here, they threaten to disrupt more than just your lives and your pack dynamic. They have the potential to unsettle the balance of this world."

I exchange a look with Stone, trying to gauge his thoughts. The idea that our pack turmoil could have such far-reaching consequences is both terrifying and kinda hard to believe.

Then again, the night's events have already stretched the limits of what I thought possible.

"Balance would be nice," I echo, my voice laced with incredulity and interest. "How do you propose to restore it?"

Isolde's eyes lock with mine, and in them, I see a depth of knowledge and pain that resonates with my own. "By offering guidance, for starters. The path you're on is fraught with danger—not just from Andres but from forces beyond him. Forces that would love to see the world plunged into chaos."

The air around us seems to grow colder, and I wrap my arms around my torso. Stone steps closer, allowing his heat to radiate into me. His protective aura is a tangible force, but Isolde's words weave a spell of their own, drawing us into her strange and disturbing narrative.

"And you just want to help us?" Stone's skepticism hasn't waned, but his interest is definitely piqued. "What's the catch?"

"No catch," Isolde assures, though her smile suggests complexities she's unwilling to divulge and we have yet to understand. "But cooperation. A mutual understanding. I can provide insights, warnings, and maybe even solutions. But I need to know you're willing to listen—to consider paths you might not have thought of."

The significance of her offer sits heavily between us. It's a strange twisted lifeline, and one that comes with its own set of unknowns. Yet, as I look at Stone, with his silent strength and unwavering support, and then back at the mysterious woman before us, I realize if she knows more about what's happening, then we don't have much of a choice.

The game has changed, and with it, the rules.

We need to take Andres down, but if there's a bigger player, then we need to know that, too. Need to be ready for them.

"Okay," I say, more to Stone than to Isolde. "We'll listen. But understand this," my gaze sharpens as I lock eyes with her, "if your help comes at a cost to my pack, or to my family, the deal's off." I release a hint of my Alpha power, ensuring the snap of the words relays the malice I'd unleash if it came to that.

Isolde nods, her acceptance of our terms almost regal.

"There's something I feel it's my duty to make you aware of," she says, her voice lowering, drawing us in.

Stone and I exchange another wary glance but stay silent, our attention fixed on her.

"It's about the *Breath of Selene*," Isolde continues, her eyes locking onto mine with an intensity that sends a shiver down my spine. She's gauging our reaction by the looks of it—testing to see if we've heard of it. "It's reemerged, and its power is... *formidable*."

The name sends a shiver of confusion through me.

"The Breath of what now?" I ask, my frown deepening.

This is the first I'm hearing of it, and from the look on Stone's face, he's just as in the dark.

Isolde's gaze softens, as if she understands our perplexity but knows this is information that holds power. "The Breath of Selene is an ancient artifact—one of immense power and deep connection to the moon's energies. It was once a very important source of power for the wolves. It's been lost for centuries, but recent... disturbances suggest it's resurfaced. It's possible others have been hunting for it if this energetic disturbance isn't coming from you two."

"Who's been hunting for it?" I press, my heart beating like a drum in my chest. *Andres?*

She shrugs. "That I do not know. Only that it's possible others are on the move."

The weight of her words settles over us like a cloak, heavy and ominous.

An ancient artifact—powerful and tied to the moon? Is this part of the prophecy?

"I still don't understand why you're telling us any of this?" Stone's voice is guarded.

"Because," Isolde says, turning to leave but not before giving us a look that's both warning and plea, "as I stated before, we are on the same side. Whoever controls the Breath of Selene could wield untold power. I would hate for it to end up in the wrong hands."

"How do you know we're the right hands?" Stone asks, his question pointed enough for Isolde to take a small step back.

"I don't," she whispers. Then, as if receiving a thought from outside herself, she takes another step back. "I really must go—but I'll be in touch."

With that, she disappears into the shadows, almost as if she controls them, leaving us with a brand new pile of questions and a new, uneasy awareness.

Stone and I stand in silence for a moment, the implications of her words sinking in.

The Breath of Selene—an ancient artifact with untold power.

Would it be a game-changer? Could acquiring it help us win the fight against Andres and ensure no other pack tried to make a move on my territory—*or my kids?*

"We need to learn more about this Breath thing," I say finally, the resolve in my voice somehow quelling the turmoil inside. "Before Andres—*or anyone else*—gets hold of it."

"We will," he assures me, his gaze scanning the darkness where Isolde vanished. "Tomorrow."

"Tomorrow," I agree.

As we head back to the car, the night feels different

—charged with a daunting realization that there's so much more about this supernatural world than meets the eye.

The Breath of Selene, whatever it is, has just added another layer to an already complex puzzle.

And, as always, we're right in the center of it.

CHAPTER 3

THE HUMAN WAY

STONE

Stone knew the only way to keep Ella safe was to allow her to sort through the bombshells they'd been delivered in her own way.

But it didn't mean he liked it.

The male part of him—or maybe it was his wolf—wanted to tear apart the world for putting them in the middle of this mess.

From Andres to the prophecy—hell, to this surprising news about the Breath of Selene—it was as though the entire world was vying for a piece of her.

And *he* hadn't even had the chance to claim her as his own.

His soul cried out to bond—to claim her officially as his mate and let the world go to hell around them if that's what it wanted.

Instead, he'd had to find a way to put all of that

aside—*continue* to put it aside—as he took care of them in the way he knew would mean most.

The *human* way.

Now, both Asher and Avery were situated in his home—likely sleeping by the sounds of their breathing—and Ella was pacing in his bedroom, refusing to lie on the bed with him.

"What are you thinking about?" Stone asked, tracking her movements back and forth.

Ella whimpered softly. It was a small, almost imperceptible sound, but he picked up on it. Like the way her heart rate just ratcheted up a notch as her worried gaze slid to his.

Concern flooded his mind as he narrowed his eyes and waited.

"It's just—" Her eyes slammed shut and she took a deep breath. "We'll be sleeping together. For like, the foreseeable future."

He couldn't help it, he had to laugh. "That's all?"

She leveled him with a glare. "What do you mean *'that's all?'* It's enough."

"We've already slept together, Ella," he reminded her. In fact, it had only been a couple of days since she asked him to stay at her place.

Her gaze rose to the ceiling as if she was praying to any god who might listen. "I know. It's just—"

He shook his head and stood up to walk to her. "You're making too big of a deal out of this. Stop over-thinking things."

She stopped pacing to face him and he slid his hands over her bare arms.

No longer in the baggy shirt offered to her at the site of her destroyed home, she wore instead, a black tank top and sleep pants he'd purchased for her at the store this evening.

The whole outfit suited her.

In fact, it accentuated her ample curves in a way that had his blood screaming at him to stop being so damned sensible.

Maybe she could pick up on that?

She inhaled a sharp breath and settled her shoulders. "This is different, Stone. You can't get rid of me—*of us.* At least, not until I get my house rebuilt. And who knows how long that's going to take. It could be a while and—"

He bent down and pressed his lips to hers just to shut down her rant. For a moment, she stiffened against his lips, then slowly, she settled into the kiss, allowing him to gain access to her mouth. He slipped his tongue inside, sweeping it slowly against hers.

A soft growl unfurled itself from the back of his throat but he mastered himself enough to break off the connection and take a small step back.

Ella's eyes remained closed as if the kiss had dragged her into a dreamy realm and away from whatever worries had held her in their grip.

"What was that for?" she asked, eyes still closed.

"To silence your craziness," he confessed with a chuckle.

Her eyes snapped open, a fire burning in them now as they connected with his. "What?"

"Ella, there is nowhere else I'd rather you be. I'm not worried that you're here with no end in sight. I'm aware that the kids are here and will be staying, too. I want it that way. Now, will you stop worrying and just lie down? It's been a long, intense day and you need your rest," he continued, sweeping his hand out to suggest she get in the bed.

She watched him with a predatory expression—like the Alpha ready to defy anyone who might challenge her authority by telling her what to do. He supposed that was more accurate than he knew.

However, she stalked over to the same side of the bed she'd claimed the other night at her house and slid beneath the covers.

Stone watched her for a moment, the light from his nightstand casting a serene glow over her features. He could sense the whirlwind of emotions churning within her—the same storm that raged in his own heart.

He knew that offering platitudes wouldn't soothe her turmoil, nor would empty reassurances quell her fears. What she needed was a connection, something to anchor her to the moment—*to him.*

After sliding into bed beside her and clicking off the light, he watched her silently, noting how the moonlight played across her features, deepening the lines of worry that didn't belong there.

Turning fully to face her, Stone reached out, brushing a stray strand of hair from her forehead.

"Ella," he said softly, "I know today has been... *a lot*. But there's something I've wanted to say to you."

Ella's eyes, shimmering with unshed tears, met his. In their depths, he saw a blend of strength and vulnerability that only made her more endearing to him. This was a side she didn't let slip through often—and yet she felt safe enough to let him see her this way.

"What is it?" she asked, her voice barely above a whisper.

Stone took a deep breath, searching for the right words. "Before I met you, I thought I understood my world, my purpose. I was going to be alone—*packless*—for the rest of my life. But you... you've turned everything upside down. In the best possible way." He paused, his gaze never leaving hers. "You've made me see things differently, feel things I didn't know I could. I know I act strong—like I have all the answers... but the truth is, I'm worried, too. Worried of not being able to protect you and the kids, or the pack, from what's coming. I've never felt this way before. It's like battling shadows—you don't know where the next strike will come from."

There was more Stone wished he could say—about his pull to bond with her. About how it's consumed his mind every waking moment and has intensified every day. But he knew that would only continue to set off her fears and concerns. He'd have to work around it.

Ella's hand found his, her grip tight, as if holding onto him could anchor her in the storm that raged around them. "Stone, I..."

He placed a finger on her lips, silencing her. "Let me finish. Being with you, feeling this bond grow between us... it's given me something to fight for— more than I ever had. But it's also opened up fears I never knew I had. Fears of losing you, of failing in the face of this... *chaos.*"

Ella nestled closer, her head finding a comfortable spot on Stone's chest. "I feel the same way, Stone. I've been so caught up in trying to be strong for everyone that—"

She paused as the moonlight streaming through the window enveloped them in a soft, silver glow. Stone lifted his gaze to the window, taking in the beauty of its radiance and fascinated by the way it's always been a symbol for them.

He pulled her closer, wrapping his arms around her in a protective embrace. "You don't always have to be strong, Ella. Not with me. It's okay to just be yourself, to let your guard down. I won't ever hurt you."

For a long while, they lay in silence, each lost in their thoughts but comforted by the other's presence. It was a rare moment of peace in a world that seemed to be spiraling out of control.

Finally, Ella spoke, her voice soft but steady. "I'm scared of what's coming, Stone. But knowing you're with me... it makes it all seem bearable. Even from the beginning—before knowing what you are. What you'll mean to me when we—"

He knew what she meant.

The bond.

Perhaps she felt its call, too. He hoped so.

Yet, she wasn't willing to break what fragile peace she had just yet.

Stone kissed the top of her head, a gesture of comfort and reassurance. "Whatever comes our way, we'll face it together. And we'll come out stronger on the other side. I promise you that."

"I know," she said, wrapping her arm around his torso as she settled in close, her scent permeating everything around him.

For what it was worth, there seemed to be a newfound sense of connection between them as they drifted off to sleep. A bond that went beyond duty or destiny. It was a bond of heart and soul, unbreakable and true.

And Stone marveled at the beauty of it.

STONE WANDERED THROUGH A DENSE, *misty forest—the air thick with an otherworldly energy that seemed to pulse with the rhythm of an unseen heart. The night sky above was dominated by an unnaturally large moon, its glow* casting an ethereal light that gave the woods an almost dreamlike quality.

Despite the serene beauty, a palpable sense of anticipation hung in the air, as if the very fabric of the night was bracing for something momentous.

Whispers wound through the trees, a familiar voice woven into the rustling leaves.

Stone strained to listen, taking note of each syllable as he tried to make sense of the words.

It was Doug's voice, he realized, fragmented—like echoes from a forgotten dream.

"Seek the essence... under the eye of Selene... where shadows and light converge..."

The words were cryptic, yet they resonated within Stone, stirring a deep, primal understanding.

As he moved forward, symbols began to glow softly on the ancient trees, casting a gentle luminescence that lit his path. These symbols, intricate blends of runic and celestial designs, were reminiscent of those Doug had once passionately discussed—mysterious markers tied to lunar energies and age-old rites.

At the time, Stone had thought it was just a curiosity of an eccentric Alpha. But perhaps it wasn't. Maybe he had been trying to understand his place in the world.

Suddenly, Stone was standing in a clearing bathed in moonlight, where the beams converged to spotlight a hovering crystal orb.

This crystal, radiant and pulsing with life, seemed to be

the heartbeat of the forest, drawing him closer with an irresistible magnetism.

Reaching out, Stone's fingers nearly brushed the crystal when its energy and glow intensified, wrapping him in a blinding light.

Doug's voice surged with urgency, "The balance teeters... the Breath stirs... only the chosen can wield... beware the shadows that lurk..."

His words plunged Stone into a sense of foreboding as darkness crept at the edges of the clearing—a malevolent force seeking to smother the crystal's light.

Doug's warnings echoed louder, a desperate plea that cut to the core of Stone's soul.

JOLTED AWAKE, Stone lay in the darkness with Ella's frame still wrapped around him. However, Doug's cryptic messages and the haunting symbols lingered in his mind, causing his pulse to race.

The urgency from his dream clung to him, pushing everything else aside. He hadn't understood it last night, but it was crystal clear now. Nothing mattered more than unraveling the mystery of the Breath of Selene with Ella.

They had to get to it before anyone dangerous did —everything else, even their vendetta against Andres, would have to wait.

CHAPTER 4

THE ESSENCE OF TRIALS

ELLA

Morning sunlight filters through the windows, casting a soft, golden hue across the Stone's kitchen counters.

It's downright serene.

In the quiet of early dawn, I slipped out of Stone's bed and quietly padded my way downstairs. There were just too many thoughts brewing in my mind to lay still—even if laying next to him is incredibly enticing.

God, being surrounded by his scent—it was heavenly.

Of course, I found myself seated at the kitchen table—a place that feels like a refuge in the never ending storm called my life. For the past twenty minutes, I've been nursing a mug of coffee, the steam swirling like the thoughts in my mind.

My sleep last night wasn't great—too many anxious dreams to feel truly restful. However, I must have gotten enough because I do feel clearer about what my priorities are.

Or at least, what they *should* be.

While all of this stuff about prophecies and ancient artifacts has a certain kind of allure, they also feel like distractions keeping me from my main objective: *retaliating against Andres and putting the rest of the werewolf community on notice.*

I am not to be trifled with.

Especially if they think they can go after my kids.

Moving to Black Crater was never supposed to be like this. It was supposed to be my place of peace after the vitriol of my divorce.

Instead, I don't even recognize my life.

And my ex?

Hell, things with him have gotten far, *far* worse.

I didn't even think that was possible.

I pinch the bridge of my nose and sigh.

I still don't know what I'm going to do about him but something tells me that situation is going to continue to get worse before it gets better.

Closing my eyes, I inhale a deep breath and contemplate adding some booze to my coffee.

Clementine is supposed to come over sometime this morning and I'm not entirely sure I'm ready to face whatever she has to say. After the revelations from Isolde last night, I don't know that I can handle more surprises—or *distractions*.

I can only hope Clementine's discoveries with the Luna Scrolls will help me connect a few dots. Hell, maybe there will be something in there about how I can defeat Andres and protect my kids from any further attacks.

Wouldn't that be nice?

"Hey, you," Stone says, entering the kitchen with a sleepy expression.

His dark hair is mussed in a way that makes my insides flip and his tight-fitting white t-shirt that hugs his muscles in all the right places only adds to the sentiment.

God, he's gorgeous.

And so damn patient.

He's given me space to process everything, knowing all too well the storm that's been brewing inside me. His ability to innately know when I need that space has been astounding. It's something I still have trouble at times believing.

Especially after my previous disasters called relationships. None of them have ever been what you'd call, *empathetic*.

I smile softly, my shoulders relaxing at his close proximity. "Hey."

It's like simply being around him is enough to take the edge off my particular brand of anxiety.

"Did you sleep okay?" he asks, reaching into the cupboard and pulling out his own mug.

I watch his back muscles move under his shirt and my eyes snag on the way the shape of his backside is highlighted in his faded denim jeans.

"Yeah, for the most part." I nod, hoping like hell he doesn't press further. "You?"

He pauses briefly, almost as if he's about to say something. Instead, he simply nods and then brings his mug to his lips.

The kids are still asleep and the house is wrapped in a rare, peaceful silence that belies the turmoil of our current lives. The last thing I need to do is bring up the fragments of panic that managed to worm their way into my dreams all night long.

As if sensing my apprehension, he takes a seat at the table beside me and places his palm over mine, giving it a gentle squeeze.

I can't help but let loose a sigh of contentment at the contact. I didn't realize how much I needed it until his skin touched mine.

Stone watches me for a moment, his gaze probing, as if he's trying to peer directly into my thoughts. However, I have them locked down tight, putting a wall around my mind so I don't carry the panic into this new day. Or pass it over to him.

He takes a slow sip of his coffee, his eyes never leaving mine. "You know, Ella," he begins, his voice low and steady. I can tell he's weighing his words carefully. "With everything going on—Troy, Andres, and now these cryptic messages from Isolde—it feels like there's no end in sight to all of the craziness."

I nod, feeling the weight of his words. It's a relief, weirdly enough, to hear him articulate it. In some small way, it makes it feel less like I'm drowning in my own head.

"Things are definitely crazy," I mutter, huffing a humorless laugh.

It feels like it's all just there to keep me from having my eye on the prize—*Andres.*

Yet, I can't explain it—there's also a strange pull to uncover the mysteries. Like it's worth my time to explore them, even with everything else going on.

I feel bipolar.

"What are you thinking about?" Stone asks, likely sensing my shift in thought.

I narrow my eyes and exhale slowly.

If there's one person I trust to help me work through this, it's him.

So, I whisper, "Do you feel like all the talk of prophecy, Moon Wolves, and now the Breath of Selene —are they just distractions from the real threat Andres poses to my family and the pack? I mean, how does all this lore help me when Andres is out there—a clear and present danger to everything I hold dear?"

Stone settles back in his chair, giving himself a moment to think through everything I just threw at him.

Finally, he says, "I understand why it feels like these things are pulling us away from our main focus, Ella. But remember, knowledge is power. The more we understand about the prophecy, the Breath of Selene —and even the idea of being Moon Wolves—the better equipped we'll be to face Andres and any other threats. Maybe it amounts to nothing. But maybe it ends up saving our asses. The way I see it, it's not just about direct confrontation—it's about being strategic and using every piece of information we have to our advantage. I don't think we should dismiss these elements as distractions. They might just be the advantage we need."

I inhale sharply and nod. "There's sense in that. Thanks, Stone. See? This is why you're my Delta."

His green eyes sparkle with humor when he says, "Is that all I am?"

"Of course not," I find myself saying without thought.

His forehead scrunches as if he's debating whether or not to unleash his next few words. "Despite everything going on, there's something that keeps nagging at me."

"What's that?" I ask, trying not to hold my breath at his sudden intensity.

"It's *us*, Ella. Us navigating through this together. I know we haven't known each other all that long—at least, not in the grand scheme of things. But it feels like we've been in this fight side by side for a lifetime.

Hell, *longer*." He pauses, searching my face. "Please don't take this the wrong way, but sometimes—I can't help but wonder if you're as committed to seeing where this leads. I know it must be a lot."

His words catch me off guard. It's something I've been pondering too, but have been too afraid to voice. The uncertainty, the fear of what the future holds for us, it's been a giant, silent specter in the room.

I take a deep breath, trying to gather my thoughts. "I've been thinking about that too, Stone. I know this hasn't been easy for you. It's like we're in the eye of the hurricane, trying to hold onto something real, something solid. But for me"—I hold his gaze, hoping to relay all of the emotion I really do feel for him—"that's been *you*."

He reaches across the table, his hand again covering mine in a gesture of solidarity and warmth. "I feel the same, Ella. But I guess I need to know, are we on the same page? Is this"—he gestures vaguely between us—"something you see lasting beyond the immediate threats? Forget the bond and all of the fated werewolf bullshit. Because if you don't—"

His question hangs in the air, heavy with implications. For some bizarre reason it feels like crossroads moment, and I know my answer will set the course for whatever comes next.

"I want it to be, Stone. More than anything," I say, my voice barely above a whisper. "But with everything that's been thrown at us, I'm just a big fucking mess.

I'm scared of what it means to commit to this—*to us*—when our world feels like it could come crashing down at any moment. I know it must seem selfish..."

Stone shakes his head, understanding flashing in his eyes. "I get it, Ella. The fear, the uncertainty—it's all valid. But know this—whatever happens, I'm here. For you, for the kids—for our pack. And when it's all said and done, I still want to be standing by your side. In whatever way you'll have me."

His declaration warms me from the inside out, offering a glimmer of hope. It's a promise of a future, however uncertain, that we can build together. And in this moment, it's everything I need to hear.

The doorbell rings, yanking us from the heaviness of the conversation.

Stone releases my hand and stands up, pressing a kiss to the side of my head. Then, he strides out of the room and to the front door to answer it.

Honestly, I hadn't even registered Clementine's arrival until she rang the bell—no small feat, considering my werewolf hearing and my pack awareness that's always thrumming through me. But I guess when you have your heart in your throat and your mind tossed in a sea of tumultuous waters, being aware of her arrival wasn't high on my to-do list.

Clementine breezes in, her presence as commanding as ever. She's dressed in her usual style that somehow blends *'pack leader's widow'* with *'boho chic.'* Her green eyes scan the room, landing on me with a warmth that's come to signify our burgeoning friendship.

I shoot her a lopsided smile and wave. "Morning."

"Morning, guys," she says, her voice carrying that distinctive tone of someone who's about to drop a gigantic knowledge bomb. In her hands is a long, slender tube. "I hope you're ready for some revelations. The Luna Scrolls have been quite chatty."

I can't help but smile despite the swirling vortex of anxiety in my stomach.

"I don't think we have any other choice," I say, trying to sound more confident than I feel.

Clementine settles into one of the kitchen chairs with the grace of a seasoned diplomat.

"Buckle up, then. What I'm about to tell you is going to take some processing," she begins.

Stone and I lean in, our coffees forgotten, already hanging on to her every word.

She opens the tube and unfurls a set of ancient, parchment-like papers across the table. Their edges are worn and their surfaces filled with cryptic symbols and writings that seem to pulse in the morning light.

Stone inhales sharply as he stiffens beside me. I raise an eyebrow in question, but he shrugs it off.

"These scrolls," Clementine gestures, her fingers tracing the lines of text as if she could read them like a book, "speak of a time when the moon's essence was woven into the very fabric of our reality. A time when the Moon Wolves weren't just creatures of myth but guardians of a balance we've long forgotten."

I exchange a glance with Stone, trying to mask my skepticism.

Guardians of balance?

It sounded more like the tagline for a cheesy super-hero movie than anything resembling reality. But the earnest look in Clementine's eyes holds me back from voicing my doubts.

I mean, who am I to talk anyway? My life is practically a superhero movie as it is.

"The prophecy," she continues, her gaze locking onto mine, "isn't just about power or destiny. It's about restoration. About bringing back a harmony that's been lost to the ages. And you, Ella, with Stone by your side, are central to this. At least, if I'm reading the scrolls right."

The weight of her words settles over me.

Restoration?

Harmony?

While both would be great, I somehow doubt that sort of thing is even possible.

Hell, I can't even manage to do that with my ex-husband. How am I meant to accomplish a feat this big for the werewolf community?

I've only been Alpha for a couple of months but it's pretty damn clear to me that our kind can't seem to get their heads out of their collective asses long enough to trust one another.

Or anyone else, for that matter.

It's each pack for themselves.

Stone leans forward, his elbows on the outer edge of the scrolls as he looks them over. "How exactly are we supposed to do that? What does this *restoration* entail?" His voice carries the weight of his protective nature, always seeking clarity—always looking to shield.

"I'm not entirely sure yet, but there's more," Clementine adds, a hint of hesitation in her voice. "The scrolls hint at a series of trials. Tests that the Moon Wolves must undergo to prove their worthiness and to fully awaken some sort of *power* within them."

My eyes widen as I glance up at her.

This is starting to sound less like a destiny and more like an obstacle course from hell.

I let out a nervous chuckle. "What kind of trials are we talking about here? Because if it involves math, we might be in trouble."

Clementine smiles, a brief flicker of amusement crossing her features. "Not math, Ella. These are trials of the spirit, of courage, and of heart—everything that matters to wolves. My guess is, they'll challenge you in ways we can't yet imagine, but they will also reveal strengths the two of you never knew you had." Then, she leans in, lowering her voice as if sharing a sacred secret. "From what I can tell, the ultimate goal of these trials is to guide you both toward something ancient and incredibly powerful. I've only been able to translate it as the *Essence*. It's an entity or force, deeply connected to our very existence as wolves, believed to be lost or hidden for centuries. Understanding the Essence might just be the key to fulfilling the prophecy and truly restoring balance. It won't be easy, and the path to it is what these trials are designed to illuminate."

The room falls silent as the weight of her revelation sinks in.

The Essence... Could this be the Breath of Selene?

The timing is just too... coincidental.

It all sounds so daunting, yet a part of me—a part I wasn't fully aware of until this moment—thrums with excitement at the prospect.

"How do the trials work? Like, how will we know they've begun?" I ask.

Clementine makes a face. "I knew you were going to ask that."

Stone's eyes narrow and he stands up to pace.

"See," Clementine's gaze shifts, a serious note underlying her next words, "the trials—Ella, they're not just arbitrary challenges. They're deeply intertwined with the events shaping our world. The destruction last night, your confrontations with Andres, even your internal struggles as Alpha—I think they're all part of the trials."

I feel a shiver run down my spine. "So, everything that's been happening... it's all connected? It's all part of these trials? They've already begun?"

Clementine nods, her expression serious. "Exactly. The trials are meant to evolve you—to prepare you for what's to come. And yeah, I think you're already in it."

Stone looks at me, his expression one of determination mixed with concern. He's likely thinking the same thing I am—that the fears and worries about this being a distraction were unfounded.

If everything is connected, then it's all intertwined —whether we like it or not.

Clementine leans back, a thoughtful look on her face. "I hate to say it, but there's *one* more thing," she says, her voice dropping to almost a whisper. "The scrolls speak of a final trial, one that will demand the greatest sacrifice and offer the most profound revelation. It will be the key to unlocking the full power of the Essence and put the Moon Wolves on their ultimate path."

I exchange a worried glance with Stone.

Well, shit. This can't be good.

"What kind of sacrifice?" I ask, my heart pounding with a mix of fear and anticipation.

Clementine's eyes lock onto mine, a grave intensity in them. "It's unclear."

I run my fingertips across my forehead. "Of course it is."

The gravity of her words hangs heavy in the air. Stone and I sit in stunned silence, absorbing the magnitude of what lies ahead.

In the silence, an awareness that we're about to

have more company filters in. Then, a firm tap on the door confirms it.

Stone moves to the door, to let Marta in while I settle back in my chair, wondering if her arrival is a sign that our troubles are ramping up, and our next big challenge is literally knocking at the door.

CHAPTER 5
DEADLINES

STONE

Stone stood in the now silence of the kitchen with the weight of the morning's revelations pressing heavily on his shoulders. As he watched Ella, her focus intently on Clementine and the papers spread across the table, he felt a surge of protectiveness.

It was partly the bond, he knew. But it was also partly because of the way he felt about *her*.

It would be the same whether she was his Alpha, his mate, or just the woman she was.

Marta's unexpected arrival, just moments after Clementine had unfurled the ancient Luna Scrolls across his table, added a new layer of urgency to the already tense atmosphere.

Stone hoped the tension that had been building would ease, but somehow, after all they'd learned, he doubted it.

If these trials were already in motion, there would be no stopping them. They'd play out until they had overcome them—or succumbed to them.

The energy he sensed from Marta was fraught with worry—a clear indication that the news she brought was far from comforting. As pack Beta, he knew she'd been tasked with ensuring their territory was clear of Andres' and his pack.

So, whatever she had to say, it was clear to Stone it wasn't going to be good news.

Stone's mind raced with strategies and contingencies, his role as Ella's mate compelling him to shield her and their pack from the gathering shadows. Even if he didn't know if he could.

Marta stepped forward, her eyes locking onto Ella. There was a seriousness in her demeanor and it drew the room's attention—a shared sense of urgency thrumming in the air.

"Ella, we need to talk," she began.

Ella straightened, her expression hardening into the mantle of the Alpha she was. "What's happened?"

It was amazing, but somehow, she was still ready to face whatever new challenge was thrown her way.

Marta hesitated, a glance at Stone betraying her concern before she refocused on Ella. "While scouting the area, following Andres' pack's scent," Marta began, her gaze shifting between Ella and the ancient scrolls that lay open on the table, "we stumbled upon something... *unsettling*."

Stone's chest tightened, the words 'unsettling' sending a ripple of apprehension through him. He moved closer to Ella and took her hand in his. She squeezed his hand in return.

"What is it?" Ella pressed before shooting Stone a concerned look.

"It looked like an abandoned... *ritual,*" Marta continued, her eyes dark with the memory. "The remnants of it anyway. There were symbols—ones I've never seen before—scorched into the earth, encircling what I can only describe as an altar. But it was unlike any alter I've seen before. It gave me the creeps."

Ella's brow furrowed, her focus razor-sharp. "Are we talking about witches?"

Marta nodded grimly. "Yes, I believe so. And not just any witches. These symbols... if I had to guess, they're tied to dark magic—magic that I've only heard of in the oldest of our pack's tales. Our verbal histories."

A chill ran down Stone's spine. The implications of what Marta was suggesting were not lost on him. This could very well be another layer tied to their current predicament. And who knows what else?

If witches were out there performing a ritual, was it possible they were trying to locate the Breath of Selene? Is this the disturbance Isolde had felt?

"Do you know if these were the same witches Andres employed to hide his pack from us?" Stone found himself asking, the idea knotting his stomach.

"Maybe?" Marta's said with slight shrug. "But, I have to admit, my memories of the witches' scents who held us captive are a bit fuzzy. My mind doesn't want to fully process it. It's strange."

"I feel the same," Stone said with a curt nod. "It must be whatever they used to drug us with."

Marta nodded in silent agreement.

Stone noticed Ella lean back again, her face hardening as she processed Marta's report. He could almost see the storm brewing behind her dark eyes—a testament to the weight of her leadership.

As he watched her, the urge to protect—*to act*—burned inside him. He wanted to go check this site out and see for himself what had occurred. It felt imperative.

Yet, he knew Ella's next words—*her next decision*—would set the course for their immediate future.

"We need to find out what this ritual was for," Ella finally said, her voice steady. "If Andres is looking to fortify his power with dark magic, we're not just dealing with a rogue Alpha anymore. This is something far more dangerous."

Stone breathed a sigh of relief.

"We'll start by investigating the site of the ritual," Ella decided, her gaze meeting Stone's. "Marta, gather a team. I want you to move out within the hour. Gather as much intel as you possibly can and report back."

Marta tipped her chin, her determination mirroring Ella's.

"And if you find any connection to something called the Breath of Selene—or perhaps the Essence, let me know immediately," Ella said, shooting a sideways glance at Stone.

Marta's eyebrows tugged inward but she didn't voice her question. Stone sensed that she trusted Ella's judgment and felt no need to press it. As Beta, she likely knew she'd be looped in when Ella had more information.

He felt a surge of pride for their pack, for the strength and resolve they all shared. They were more than just a pack—they were a family, ready to face the darkness together.

As Marta turned to leave, Clementine, who had been silently contemplating the scrolls, finally spoke up. Her voice carried an unease that matched the tension in the room.

"I don't like this," she said, her eyes moving from Marta to Ella and then to Stone. "It feels like everything is tied together—the witches, the ritual, Andres, and now these trials from the Luna Scrolls. Shit's about to hit the fan."

Stone nodded his agreement. The interconnectedness of their challenges seemed too coincidental to be anything *but* deliberate.

"It's as if we're being maneuvered into position,"

he added, his thoughts aligning with Clementine's intuition.

It certainly played into the idea that they were simply pieces in a prophecy much bigger than any of them could fathom.

Ella's lips set in a grim line. "We'll keep our eyes open. And Marta," she said, turning to her, "keep us posted on everything you find out there. No matter how small or seemingly insignificant. Something tells me this is going to get more complicated before things start to make sense."

Marta gave a firm nod. "I will. We'll be thorough."

With that promise, she turned and left, her steps quick and purposeful.

The moment Marta exited, the tension in the room seemed to momentarily lift, only to be replaced by a new source of worry as the sound of footsteps descended the stairs.

Stone turned to see Asher and Avery entering the kitchen, their expressions groggy but quickly turning to concern at the sight of their mother's troubled face.

"What's going on?" Asher's voice was thick with sleep but underscored with a protective edge that made Stone proud.

Asher's instinct to protect his family was strong and it was a testament to his growing maturity. If he became a wolf, Stone was beginning to appreciate the pack member he might be.

Ella exchanged a quick glance with Stone before responding.

"We have a new situation," she started, her tone carefully neutral and Stone knew it was to avoid alarming her kids. "Marta found something... *concerning* while following after Andres and his pack. We're looking into it."

"Can I help? I want to do something," Asher said, stepping beyond his sister and into the center of the room.

Ella gave him a soft, yet firm look, one that spoke volumes of her love and concern. "When we know more, we'll discuss how you can help. Right now, we need to gather more information. We don't know enough."

"There's so much—" Avery bit her lip and shook her head. "What about school? It's starting soon."

The room quieted at her question. Stone could feel the weight of their responsibilities pressing down. The balance between protecting their pack and maintaining a semblance of normal life for the kids was a delicate one.

Stone noticed his sister suddenly sit up straighter as she removed her phone from her pocket, her thumbs moving across the screen frantically.

Ella took a deep breath. "Avery, your safety, and making sure you both can lead as normal lives as possible, is—*and has always been*—my top priority. We don't know what's going to come from any of this—maybe nothing."

Asher nodded, seemingly reassured by his mother's words, but Avery still looked uncertain. Stone understood her worry—the unpredictability of their situation was daunting, even for them as adults. He couldn't imagine what it must be like for them.

"We have another reason to ensure our investigations are thorough and swift," Clementine said, setting her phone down and drawing everyone's attention. "The Supermoon. If I'm reading the scrolls right, it's not just a celestial event coming up—it's a hard deadline for us."

Ella's eyes narrowed, a clear sign of her confusion and growing concern. "The Supermoon? I'm not sure I follow. What is that?"

Clementine leaned forward, the seriousness of her demeanor grounding the room. "Any time there's a Supermoon, it amplifies magical energies to a significant degree. Any spells, rituals, or powers exercised during a Supermoon could have their effects magnified—sometimes beyond the caster's control. If Andres and his witches are planning something for that night, it could be disastrous."

"What makes this Supermoon so important for us? I mean, beyond the concern that Andres might be using it to work against us?" Stone pressed.

His sister huffed a laugh. "You're not gonna believe this, but it's a Super *Wolf* Moon."

"That's a thing?" Asher commented, scratching his head.

Ella nodded, her expression showing clearly that was a question she wanted to ask as well.

"Oh, yeah," Clementine said with concerning conviction.

Stone watched as Ella absorbed the information, her mind visibly racing through the implications. "So, you're saying we have until the Supermoon to stop whatever Andres is planning? That is *if* he's planning anything."

"Exactly," Clementine confirmed. "It's a deadline for us to intervene and prevent whatever they're plotting. But it also ties back to the prophecy. The Luna Scrolls speak of a time when the celestial bodies align in such a way that the veil between worlds thins—not just physically but metaphysically."

"I'm not sure I'm following, Clem," Ella pressed.

Clementine sighed. "Basically, the Supermoon is a harbinger of this alignment, amplifying the natural energies of our world and beyond. I think it's going to impact wolves—and specifically, any Moon Wolves. It's a time of heightened power, but also of great vulnerability if caught in the crosshairs."

Stone's jaw clenched involuntarily.

The thought of Andres and his cohorts exploiting such a significant celestial event was unsettling, to say the least. However, the realization that they were running against a celestial clock—with the Supermoon as their deadline, lent a frantic pace to their already desperate efforts.

"We need to anticipate Andres' moves—understand what he's planning. If the Supermoon is his target, we have to find a way to counteract whatever ritual or spell he's hoping to cast," Stone interjected.

"I hate to say it Ella," Clementine began, then shifted her gaze to the two kids, "there's a good chance this is going to take us out of our territory. We need to locate the *Essence*."

"But what about *school?*" Avery gasped. Clearly, this was her fear made manifest.

Ella's gaze shifted to her daughter. "Avery, school's not for two weeks and the Supermoon is..." She turned to face Clementine for an answer.

"Two weeks away," Clem offered sheepishly.

"Shit." Ella's fingertips flew to her forehead as she tried to press out the lines. "You have to be kidding me," she mumbled.

"The moon is at its peak the evening of the twenty-ninth, specifically," Clementine said.

"That's my birthday," Asher blurted, his eyes wide.

"Of course, that's when it is," Ella said, shaking her head in disbelief. "Okay, listen up. I will do whatever it takes to ensure our family—and our pack is safe. If that means having to hunt down this Essence thing in record time and kick Andres' ass into the next freakin' universe, so be it." She inhaled a deep breath through her nose. "But so help me, I will not miss my son's birthday or the start of school. Is that clear?"

"Ella, I don't know if that's a promise you can—" Stone clamped his mouth shut at the look of determination on Ella's face.

"Good." A hint of a smirk graced her beautiful lips. "Now that we're on the same page, Clem and Stone—can you make sure these two get something to eat? I have someone I need to go talk to."

CHAPTER 6

BALANCING ACT

ELLA

"Where are you headed in such a hurry? Got another house on fire?" someone calls out.

I twist around, only to find Jinx racing up behind me in her bright red scooter.

Despite myself, I huff a laugh. Leave it to Jinx to make light of one of the biggest events in my life—and track me down in the weirdest of places.

"I'm on my way to see Alanna. What are you doing here?" I ask, glancing down the street.

After a quick text to Alanna this morning, she gave me her address, saying it was the safest place she knew to talk. Now that I'm in downtown Black Crater, about to enter a seedy apartment building near the bar district, I'm inclined to disagree.

Even in the late morning sunshine, the place

smells like last night's booze—mixed with the stench of piss and puke.

My werewolf senses aren't exactly happy about any of it.

"Mermaid class was canceled, so I was on my way to have a chat with the witchy bar owners who took it upon themselves to enter a fray they had no purpose in entering." A wide, almost feral smile slides across her lips.

No good can come from a smile like that.

I lower my eyebrows and blink at her.

She shrugs, laughing it off. "I wasn't going to say anything. Just wanted to... hang out, have a drink, and enjoy the ensuing chaos."

"Jinx," I blurt out, laughing. "As much fun as that would be—it's probably not wise to provoke them. Not right now. There are things—*big things*—going on behind the scenes."

It's her turn to quirk an eyebrow. "Is there now? And what could you possibly have learned since last night?"

I inhale a sharp breath, my eyes wide. "Oh, you have no idea."

"Well, go on then. Fill a girl in," Jinx says, shutting off her scooter and getting comfortable.

However, her gaze flits past me and down the street.

Behind me, I hear the distinct sound of trash cans banging together and someone cursing. *Loudly.*

She chuckles under her breath and focuses back in on me.

I pinch the bridge of my nose and try, unsuccessfully, not to chuckle. "I wish I could, but I really need to chat with Alanna."

"Why don't I come with? Since you won't let me have my fun, I've got nothing better to do right now," Jinx offers, getting her scooter ready to follow after me.

"I'm not entirely sure Alanna will want me to bring company. I need to have a delicate discussion—"

"About what kinda supe she is, right?" Jinx guesses.

"How'd?" I blink at her.

"Because I know you, Ella. You had your house ripped apart and burnt to the ground. You're gonna want to know why. And the only way to do that is to ask the woman responsible," Jinx says, matter of factly. "Besides, I already know what she is, so I doubt she'll care."

And the hits just keep on coming.

"You do?" I ask, my mouth gaping open.

"I read the energies of the beings around me. Of course, I know what she is. Besides, it's not that difficult to figure out if you think about it." She shrugs one shoulder and glances past me again.

I brace myself for the inevitable scream, curse, or crash—but none of it comes.

Instead, Jinx clears her throat and returns her

attention to me. "So, ya gonna take me, or what? I ain't got all day to wait in the middle of the street."

"Huh?" I mutter, following Jinx's gaze that's again focused behind me. A woman with silver hair is leaning against a lamp post near the end of the block and her gaze is locked on us. I turn back to Jinx. "Do you know her?"

Her expression sours and she mutters under her breath, "Wish I didn't."

"Why? Is she someone messed with, here for retribution?" I snicker to myself.

"Worse," Jinx blurts, rolling her eyes. "She's my sister."

My hands rise to my cheeks as my gaze lifts to the sky. "Oh, my god, there are *two of you?*"

She shoots me a *'bitch please'* sort of expression right before she says, "There's only one of me."

"Well, I *know* that. I just meant—" I cut myself off.

"Trudie's the goody two shoes of the family. So, if she's here, the only thing she's good for is to be a pain in my ass," Jinx laments.

"Well, don't you think you should go see what she wants?"

"What for?" she snorts.

I gape at her.

"Pull your jaw outta your trousers. You're the one who's a magnet for magical misfits. I haven't seen her for sixty years. So, I'm gonna blame you and whatever's going on in your camp, girly," she fires back.

"That's a bit ridiculous, don't you think? I've never met your sister, so why would she be here for me?" Taking a deep breath, I decide it's worth a shot to mediate. "Look, Jinx, sixty years is a long time. Maybe she's got something important to say to you. Besides, with the way things have been going around here, can we really afford to ignore any potential ally?"

Jinx looks like she's about to protest, but then something in my tone or maybe the resigned tilt of my shoulders gets to her.

She sighs, the sound heavy with a history I can only guess at.

"Fine," she finally grunts, "but if she starts with her 'holier-than-thou' attitude, I'm *out*."

I snicker softly under my breath. "Fine. Whatever you say."

Looks like complicated family dynamics aren't just a human thing.

As we draw nearer, Trudie straightens from her casual lean against the lamppost, her expression one of cool composure. Yet, beneath the surface, I sense a torrent of emotions—a complex web of feelings only siblings could evoke in one another.

The thought of having two Chaos Demons in town kinda fills me with dread. The potential for mayhem seems limitless. However, watching Trudie's calm demeanor as we draw near, I start to question my assumption. She's definitely got a different vibe from her sister.

"June, still causing chaos, I see," Trudie remarks dryly, her gaze flickering between her sister and me.

There's an undercurrent of affection in her voice, layered beneath years of distance and difference. Her voice is smooth, lacking the edge I've come to associate with her sister. Despite myself, the contrast only heightens my curiosity about her.

"And you're still sticking your nose where it doesn't belong," Jinx retorts, though the edge in her voice softens ever so slightly as she shuts off her scooter and studies Trudie.

Trying to diffuse the situation, I extend my hand to Trudie. "Hi, I'm Ella."

Trudie's intense brown eyes survey me before she says, "Ella, I've heard much about you."

"I wish I could say the same," I reply, trying to keep the mood light. Though, how she's heard about me is a bit of a concern. "Jinx here was just saying what a pain you are."

"Oh, sure. Throw me under the bus right out of the gate," Jinx mumbles, flicking her scooter keys with her forefinger.

A faint smile crosses Trudie's lips, and she spares Jinx a glance that's surprisingly warm. "She's not wrong. But then, I suppose we've both been pains in each other's sides for quite some time."

"Understatement of the year," Jinx grumbles, leaning back and crossing her arms over her torso.

Turning her attention back to me, Trudie's

demeanor shifts, becoming more formal, yet not unfriendly. "I've felt the disturbances here—the energies in disarray. Your presence, Ella... it's like a beacon amidst the chaos."

Jinx harrumphs, clearly unimpressed.

"You can sense that?" I ask, narrowing my gaze.

Shit, was Jinx actually right?

"Indeed. The ley lines have been speaking to me. They're in turmoil—*flux*. Something big is unfolding," Trudie says softly. "And with the Supermoon coming..."

Her gaze flits to her sister for a moment and I swear I catch a tinge of regret.

I exchange a quick glance with Jinx, whose usual confidence seems momentarily shaken by her sister's words.

But for me, there's only one word that stood out.

"You're here because of the Supermoon?" I ask, my heart hammering in my chest.

Jinx snorts, shaking her head. "Knew it was because of you."

Trudie's eyebrows tug in, as if she's trying to suss out whatever that meant. Then, her expression turns serious. "Yes, the energy it's pulling in, the way it's affecting the ley lines—it's not something to be taken lightly. I felt the disturbances from half a world away."

"Always the drama queen," Jinx blurts out.

But I'm caught on something else Trudie said. "Ley

lines? Are you saying you can sense... what, the magical energy of the Earth? How is that possible?"

"In a manner of speaking," Trudie admits. "It's part of what I do—balancing energies, maintaining harmony."

"Harmony?" The word slips out before I can stop it, a puzzle piece clicking into place. "What Chaos Demon wants harmony?"

"Indeed." Trudie's laugh is light, almost musical. "I'm not a Chaos Demon, though. I'm what you might call a Harmony Demon."

"Goody goody, more like," Jinx mutters under her breath.

Trudie's eyes flick over to her sister, but she returns her attention to me and continues, "My... *talents* lie in restoration and balance—not disruption."

The revelation leaves me blinking in surprise.

A *Harmony* Demon.

Is that even a thing?

Jinx, who had been quietly sizing up her sister, snickers. "Alright, I'll bite. What's so epic that it's got you ditching your harmony gig to play hero in my backyard?"

"The currents of energy that guided me here— your town—it's at the epicenter of something much larger." Trudie smiles softly, the warmth in her eyes suggesting layers of untold stories. "It's not just the ley lines or the Supermoon, though they play their part. They whisper to me, helping to guide me to where my gifts are best used. However, there's an artifact—a relic of sorts—that's become a focal point of concern for me."

A shiver skitters down my spine.

Isolde's words echo in my mind, the weight of her warnings suddenly crystalizing into sharp focus.

"The Breath of Selene?" I ask, the words falling from my lips like a whispered oath.

"Yes, that's it. How did you know?" Trudie asks, her eyes alight with curiosity.

I take a deep breath, glancing at Jinx. "Last night, I was visited by a witch named Isolde. She said that something was happening—something big. She mentioned the Breath of Selene and how it's tied to the moon's energy. But I think it's a part of something bigger."

Jinx's eyebrows rise, but she doesn't say anything.

Trudie's interest is piqued, her brows knitting together in thought. "She's right, of course. The Breath of Selene is ancient, a conduit for the moon's frequencies. In the wrong hands..."

She lets the sentence hang, an unspoken dread filling the space between us.

I glance at Jinx, expecting a dismissive snort or a sarcastic remark, but find her unusually silent, her usual bravado tempered by the gravity of Trudie's words.

For a moment, I close my eyes, processing all that's just been dropped in my lap. Stone was right—somehow, everything around us seems to be connecting. Like giant magnetic pieces all coming together.

"Okay, so if the Breath of Selene is real, and it's as big of a deal as it seems like it is," I start, trying to piece together a plan from the fragments before us. "Where does that leave us? I assume you're here to help us. What do we do about it?"

"That's where things get interesting," Trudie replies, a hint of a challenge in her voice. She looks between Jinx and me, a spark of determination lighting her eyes. "I believe I know where it's hidden— or at least where to start looking. And now that I realize you've been in contact with my sister, I also believe you're going to need both of us to acquire it."

CHAPTER 7

ALIGNING FATES

ELLA

"I'm sorry, run that by me again?" I squint against the sunlight, trying to gauge Trudie's expression.

The calm composure she holds contrasts sharply with the turmoil swirling inside me. How did we go from battling unknown threats to relying on a Harmony Demon and her chaotic sister?

It's like my entire world is topsy-turvy at this point.

Yet, even if that's true, there's a common thread running through all of it: *find the stupid Breath of Selene. Or Essence. Or whatever.*

Okay, Universe. Point friggin' taken.

Trudie nods, her gaze steady. "Yes, Ella. The Breath of Selene isn't just a relic. It's a beacon of power, and it's somehow entwined with the ley lines themselves. It's not something that can be found by strength alone. It will likely require balance—my domain," she says, gesturing to herself, "and disruption," she nods toward Jinx, "to uncover its hiding place."

I process her words, each one a puzzle piece in the grand scheme that's our reality. A Harmony Demon and a Chaos Demon—opposite sides of the same coin, necessary to find an ancient artifact somehow tied to the moon's energy—*and my crazy so-called life.*

It sounds like the plot of a fantasy novel, yet here we are, living it.

Jinx, who's been unusually quiet, chimes in, "So, let's say we believe you. What's the plan then? How do we start this... *treasure hunt?*"

Her usual smirk is back, but I detect an undercurrent of seriousness I haven't seen in her before.

Trudie steps forward, the morning light highlighting the white strands in her hair turning them almost golden. "First, we need to attune ourselves to the ley lines—understand their flow and disruptions. You remember how, don't you?"

"Of course, I do," Jinx snaps.

Trudie ignores the jab and simply nods. "Once we're attuned, we'll have a clearer picture of where to start looking. It's not going to be easy. The lines are in turmoil, more so with the Supermoon approaching."

I nod, the gravity of the situation settling in. There's so much hanging on this friggin' Supermoon. "Okay, you attune to the ley lines. And then?"

"And then we follow them," Trudie says simply.

"They'll guide us to the Breath of Selene. But be prepared—we're not the only ones who might be seeking it. Its power during the Supermoon would be... irresistible to many."

"Yeah, I know," I say, resisting the urge to rub the tension from my forehead. Instead, I glance between Trudie and Jinx.

Allies.

Unlikely as they may be, they're my best shot at navigating the chaos that's rapidly encroaching on our lives. "Fine. We'll do it your way. But we'll need to move quickly. Time isn't exactly on our side. Shit, speaking of time," I mutter, glancing at my watch. "I have to go. I promised Alanna I'd be at her place twenty minutes ago."

As the reality of my late appointment sinks in, frustration ripples through me. Trudie and Jinx's unexpected appearance, while potentially illuminating, has thrown my tightly scheduled day into disarray.

Yet, the urgency in Trudie's voice and the promise of help leave me no choice but to pivot—to adapt to the ever-changing tapestry of our predicaments.

And, *oh boy,* I'm in one hell of a predicament.

"Go, girly. We can take things from here for a bit," Jinx offers, shooing me with her hands.

"I'm really sorry to cut this short. Can the two of you start the preparations for attuning to the ley lines without me? I need to understand exactly what we're dealing with—and that means talking to Alanna," I say, shifting my gaze to her building.

Trudie nods, her expression soft and understanding. She looks a lot more like her sister than I think either of them cares to admit. "We can begin the preliminary work."

Jinx, still mounted on her scooter, gives me a quick nod, her trademark smirk plastered on her face. "Don't worry, I'll keep an eye on the goody-two-shoes here. Go do what you gotta do."

"Thanks." Turning on my heel, I hurry down the street, the sense of urgency propelling me forward.

The conversation with Trudie and Jinx has left a whirlwind of thoughts swirling in my already hectic mind. It's a lot to take in, and part of me is still reeling from the revelation of a Harmony Demon in our midst.

As I navigate to Alanna's apartment, the earlier conversation echoes in my mind.

Balance and Disruption—Trudie and Jinx's roles in our quest are clear, but mine feels as murky as ever.

What power do I bring to the table? Is it merely the will to protect what's mine? Or is there something more?

Hell, what is Stone's role? Is this all tied together because of the prophecy? Or is it one giant clusterfuck?

God, I'm so confused.

I shake my head, trying to clear away my doubts. Now's not the time for existential questions. Now's the time for answers, and Alanna holds a key piece of this ever-complicating puzzle.

Reaching the seedy apartment building, I steel myself for what's to come.

The dilapidated exterior definitely makes me question Alanna's choice of a "safe" meeting place—never mind the smells and sounds assaulting my werewolf senses. But then, safety is relative when you're dealing with supernatural forces.

I press the buzzer beside Alanna's name, half-expecting a crackle of static or a gruff voice questioning my presence. Instead, a pleasant chime echoes, followed by a smooth, almost disarmingly calm voice. "Ella, you're late. But I'm glad you made it. Come on up."

The door clicks open with a soft buzz, and I step inside, the contrast between the building's exterior and the interior striking me immediately.

Gone is the grime and the smell of last night's mistakes. Instead, I'm greeted by a sleek, modern corridor, its walls lined with soft, ambient lighting.

The transformation isn't just surprising—it's a stark reminder that appearances in our world can be deceiving. A lesson, it seems, I keep learning the hard way.

As I make my way to Alanna's apartment, my mind races. The thought of leaving the kids again after such a devastating week—well, it's enough to twist my gut into knots.

But as I approach, there's a level of security and sophistication in what I'd written off as a seedy apartment building. If Alanna is somehow living in a state-of-the-art bunker, that would make asking her to protect my kids in my absence so much easier.

I reach her door, pausing for a moment to gather my thoughts. Inside, Alanna might have answers. I need her to be an ally, but more than that, I need to know if I can trust her with the most precious part of my life.

Taking a deep breath, I knock.

The door swings open almost immediately, revealing Alanna's concerned expression. "Ella, with everything going on, I was starting to worry. Please, come in."

Stepping inside, I'm struck again by the sheer contrast of her living space compared to the facade outside. It's like stepping into a different world—a meticulously organized, high-tech command center disguised as a cozy living space.

Screens displaying various surveillance feeds line one wall, while another section seems dedicated to what can only be described as a mini-lab, complete with an array of mystical and technological gadgets.

"Sorry, I'm late," I begin, my gaze wandering over the space. "Ran into Jinx—and apparently, her sister."

Alanna's eyebrows raise slightly, a mix of curiosity and concern crossing her features. "I see. And how did that go?"

I shrug, trying to mask the anxiety bubbling inside. "Informative. Turns out we're going to need all the help we can get. Which brings me to you." My tone is more blunt than I intend, but the stakes are too high for subtlety.

Alanna watches me for a moment, then smiles—a warm, genuine smile that seems to fill the room with a sense of ease I didn't expect to find. "Well, then, I suppose it's time we had that conversation."

She gestures for me to take a seat on a comfortable-looking couch, its modern design juxtaposed against the ancient tomes and artifacts that decorate the coffee table and bookshelves.

As I sit, I can't help but think about the kids, about the safety and security this place seems to exude. It's a fortress hidden in plain sight, and the realization that Alanna might be capable of protecting them in ways I can't is both comforting and a tad bit terrifying.

Hell, it makes me wish I had sent them here instead of having her come to my home the other night. Maybe it would still be standing.

"First things first," I say, leaning forward, the curiosity practically jumping out of me. "Jinx mentioned something about knowing what kind of supernatural being you are, which honestly has me at a bit of a loss. Because up until a very, very recent point in my life, I thought *'Supernatural'* was just a TV show with two hot guys."

Alanna chuckles, a light, easy sound that somehow

makes the room feel warmer. "I can imagine this has all been quite the adjustment for you."

"Oh, you have no idea," I reply, running a hand through my hair. "So, let's rip this bandaid off. What exactly are you? And please tell me it's not something that's going to make me regret asking."

Her smile widens, a spark of mischief in her eyes. "I'm a Berserker."

I blink.

Once.

Twice.

"A... *what now?* As in, the Norse warriors who went into battle without armor and scared the hell out of everyone? That kind of Berserker?"

"Not exactly," she says, clearly enjoying my bafflement. "Though, I assure you, while I do wear a *special* kind of armor when it's called for, I generally try to avoid scaring people. Or destroying property." She winces slightly, an apologetic expression taking its place.

I let out a laugh, the tension easing from my shoulders for the first time since stepping inside. "Well, that's reassuring, I suppose. While I had no idea what you might be, can safely say, Berserker wasn't even on my bingo card."

"It usually isn't." Alanna leans back, her gaze thoughtful. "It's a rare designation these days, and not without its challenges. But my abilities prove useful in protection—it's what I do. My main job, anyway."

"When you're not slinging drinks at the coffee shop for your cousin?"

She grins. "Yeah, when I'm not doing that."

The room falls silent for a moment, the weight of her words settling between us.

"Speaking of protecting what's important," I start, the laughter fading as the gravity of our situation reasserts itself. "I need to ask a huge favor. Stone and I —we're going to need to leave town for a bit. And after everything that's happened... I can't just leave the kids with anyone."

Her expression softens, understanding coloring her features. "You want me to look after them again? After what happened to your house?"

I nod, feeling both relief and apprehension at voicing the request. "Yes. I... I wouldn't ask if it weren't important. And after seeing this place," I gesture around the room, "I know the safest place they can be is still with you. Regardless of what you are."

Alanna stands, crossing the room to place a reassuring hand on my shoulder. "Ella, consider it done. It would be my honor."

The gratitude wells up inside me, nearly overwhelming. "Thank you, Alanna. Honestly, I don't know what we'd do without you."

As I rise to leave, pausing at the doorway, a sudden, inexplicable tug at the fringes of my consciousness catches me off guard.

It's a sensation I've come to recognize in the short

time since my life took a turn into the supernatural—the connection I share with Stone.

His energy hums with a frequency that signals concern, maybe even distress. It's not overpowering, but there, in the background. For all I know he's mulling things over with Clementine.

"Is everything okay?" Alanna's voice, tinged with concern, pulls me back from the edge of my worry.

I offer her a slight smile. "Yeah, it's just... *Stone*. I'm picking up on something, but I'm not sure what."

My admission feels like a confession—the realization that in the whirlwind of crises and revelations, I've neglected to consider how Stone is handling all this—how *he's* feeling.

Alanna nods, her expression understanding. "It's easy to get caught up. But from what I've seen, the two of you are stronger together. Whatever is waiting out there," she gestures vaguely, encompassing all the unknown challenges we face, "you'll face it as a unit. Check in with him. You'll feel better."

Her words, though meant to reassure, only deepen the knot in my stomach.

"You're right." I force a more genuine smile this time. "Thanks, Alanna. For everything. I'll keep you posted on timelines as soon as we have some."

"Okay," she says, tipping her head in acknowledgment.

I exit her apartment, walking the hallway to the outside in a daze.

Stepping out into the bright light of the street, the contrast from Alanna's bunker-like sanctuary to the now bustling sidewalk of our town is jarring.

The bond between Stone and I pulses again—a silent beacon urging me to reach out, to bridge the gap I've allowed to form between us thanks to all the crazy.

As I make my way back through the maze of streets, my thoughts are a tangle of concern for my kids, the looming quest for the Breath of Selene, and the uncertainty of what we're heading into.

But above all, there's Stone—my partner in almost every sense, facing his own set of challenges as we navigate this uncharted territory together.

Stone? I reach out through our mental connection. *Is everything okay?*

While our connection feels intact, he doesn't answer and that doesn't sit well with me.

The need to hear his voice, to share even a moment of normalcy before we plunge into the unknown, overpowers my senses.

I fish my phone from my pocket, dialing his number with a sense of urgency.

The phone rings, a lifeline stretching out between us, and I find myself holding my breath, waiting for him to answer. The connection we share, a mix of magic and something far more mundane—*love*—insists that whatever we face, we face it together.

As I wait for his voice to fill the silence, I'm

reminded that no matter how far we venture into the darkness, it's the light we carry with us—the love, the bonds, the connections—that will guide us home.

And right now, more than anything, I need to feel that light.

But it doesn't come.

Instead, I go into voicemail.

I end the call and try to focus on the path ahead.

Allies are gathering, pieces are falling into place, and the battle lines are being drawn.

First, we find the Breath of Selene.

And then, we prepare for war.

CHAPTER 8
ARE YOUR READY FOR IT?
STONE

S tone stood in the quiet of the kitchen, looking out over the expanse of his backyard and into the forest beyond.

He'd been up for hours now, and still couldn't seem to wrap his head fully around all that had transpired. Everything seemed to be mixed in a tangled web of destiny and danger that grew in intensity with each passing minute.

And in the midst of all this chaos, his desire to claim Ella—to solidify their connection in the most profound way their world knew, remained unfulfilled.

It was a longing that pulsed at the back of his mind, a silent song of connection and commitment that had gone unanswered in the cacophony of their lives.

He exhaled slowly through his nose and closed his eyes.

"You're brooding," Clementine observed, her voice cutting through his reverie with ease.

He offered a wry smile, the corners of his mouth twitching in a semblance of amusement. "Is it that obvious?"

"To me, it is. What's on your mind, Stone?" Her question was gentle, an offering of support rather than an intrusion.

He was grateful for that. His sister always had a way of bringing him out of his shell so he could see things from another perspective.

"It's... everything," he confessed, the words heavy on his tongue. "The attacks, the prophecy—hell, the kids' safety. And now, a dream I had last night—only it felt like more than a typical dream." He hesitated, the imagery and vibe of the dream still vivid in his mind—symbols that seemed to call out to him.

The whole thing was a puzzle piece he couldn't yet place.

"How so?" Clem asked, stepping away from the Luna Scrolls to lean against the kitchen island.

He thought on that for a moment before offering, "In the dream, I thought I heard Doug speaking to me." Stone's voice dropped to a whisper, as if saying it louder might disturb the delicate balance of reality and memory. "He was talking about finding the essence of something—about the path we're on. Then, this morning, you mention this Essence as part of the prophecy. I think it might be something we heard about last night. It has a different name, but... It's just—"

Too coincidental.

And the Universe is rarely so lazy.

Stone didn't bother to voice that last part.

Clementine's expression softened, a blend of sorrow and surprise flooding across her features.

"Doug?" she echoed, her voice tinged with a mixture of emotions. The mention of her late husband, their former Alpha, always stirred deep waters. "What did he say?"

Stone shook his head slightly, trying to grasp the elusive threads of the dream. "It wasn't clear—just impressions mostly. But it felt... *important.* Like there's something we're missing, something crucial to understanding all of this." He gestured vaguely, encompassing the swirling chaos that their lives had become.

Clementine tilted her head slightly, her gaze thoughtful. "If Doug's reaching out from beyond, even in a dream, then it's for a reason. We'll find the answers, Stone. We always do. What did Ella have to say?"

Stone frowned. "I haven't had the chance to tell her yet."

His sister narrowed her gaze, a slight frown tugging on her lips.

"Don't look at me like that. It's no big deal. I just didn't get time this morning," Stone said, shaking his head. The last thing he needed was for Clem to start worrying. "I've been thinking about it and I've decided I need to check out the ritual site Marta mentioned. Maybe there's something there that connects to my dream. There were strange symbols and an altar. I need to see if they match."

"You might be right. I can stay with the kids," Clementine offered immediately. "Go. Find what we need to know."

Stone nodded, a silent thank you in his gaze.

As he turned to grab his keys from the counter, Asher and Avery entered the kitchen, their presence a reminder of the stakes at hand.

"Where are you going?" Asher asked, eyeing Stone with an observant look that reminded him so much of Ella.

"Just need to follow up on a lead," Stone replied, keeping his voice even. "Clem's in charge. You guys okay with that?"

Avery gave a small, determined nod, her resilience shining through. "We'll be fine. Just... be careful, okay?"

Stone felt a sense of relief and nodded. "Always am."

With a final glance at Clementine, he left, the weight of his mission pressing down on him.

Stone drove as far as the roads would take him, the landscape transitioning from the familiar to the uncharted as he neared the ritual site Marta had spoken of. With civilization's concrete grasp firmly behind him, he pulled over. The dense forest ahead would be impassable by any vehicle.

Here, he reached out through the pack connection, seeking Marta's guidance.

Her presence, although not physically with him, was immediate and reassuring in his mind, guiding him toward the hidden path only his wolf form could traverse. There, he could follow her scent.

Quickly, he undressed, folding his clothes and placing them on the driver's seat.

Then, transforming with a smooth ease born of necessity and nature, Stone's senses exploded in a cacophony of scents and sounds as the world became even more vibrant and detailed.

As a wolf, his connection to the earth and its secrets was magnified, and he moved with purpose through the underbrush, guided by instincts—and sharpened by his dream.

It didn't take him long to arrive at the location. Marta and the rest of her team were no longer there, but they hadn't been gone all that long.

For some reason, a wave of relief washed over him. While he wasn't averse to having Marta and others at the site, the fact that he could connect with it alone somehow felt... *right*.

To his amazement, Stone found it just as it had appeared in his dream—a small clearing marked by ancient symbols. Their meanings were obscured by time yet pulsated with a power that tugged at the very core of his being.

"Seek the essence... under the eye of Selene... where shadows and light converge..."

Doug's words echoed through the recesses of Stone's mind.

The symbols on the ground mirrored those from his dream, a confirmation that set his heart racing and his mind reeling with questions.

How was this possible?

The air around him felt charged, the very earth beneath his paws humming with an unseen energy.

Still in his wolf form, Stone circled the site, his enhanced senses picking up traces of magic, remnants of rituals long past—and those recent. It was the distinct, unmistakable scent of the supernatural.

The symbols, seen through the acute perception of his animal form, seemed to glow faintly, etched into the earth and across the altar. It was as if the site itself was alive, whispering secrets meant only for those who truly listened.

Or even had the ability to, he supposed.

The longer Stone lingered, the more he felt an inexplicable pull toward the symbols. They felt like a call to action that resonated with every fiber of his being.

Just as Stone was about to leave, a familiar scent caught his attention, signaling Ella's approach. How she had managed to sneak up on him was either a testament to her shielding abilities as Alpha—or the fact that he had been so in his own head as he studied the site.

Remaining in his wolf form, he watched as she entered the clearing as her white wolf, her presence somehow fitting perfectly into the ancient, mystical scene before him.

Her arrival was unannounced, yet her timing felt like another piece of the puzzle falling into place. Like a perfectly orchestrated moment in time.

Wow, this place... she said, connecting through the bond.

Ella paused at the edge of the clearing, her eyes scanning the area.

It really is, he responded, waiting for her to make her final assessment.

She stepped forward cautiously, her gaze finally landing on the symbols that marked the ground and the altar.

The power radiating off these symbols is intense, she said in his mind. *Do you feel it, too?*

I do. In some ways, I think it was calling to me, he offered.

Under the canopy of the dense forest, the afternoon sun filtered through the leaves, casting a dappled light upon the clearing.

Stone shifted into his human form so he could see

her expression when he told her about his dream. He wanted to see her—*needed* to see her.

Ella also shifted, and as she approached him, her presence was a calming force that tamped down the rising panic inside him. Yet, seeing her this way— naked and proud—it made the wolf inside him howl to claim her.

Here—*now*.

"Calling to you? Did you sense trouble?" Ella asked, her voice laced with concern as she once again took in the ancient symbols and ritual space that surrounded them.

Stone hesitated, the magnitude of his dream pressing heavily on his mind, despite his other instincts that demanded it be set aside.

"It wasn't trouble—not exactly," he began, searching for the words to bridge the gap between his visceral experience and the reality they both faced. "Last night, I had a dream—a *vivid* one. It was unlike anything I've ever experienced, Ella. It was almost like a memory."

Ella's expression softened, a mixture of curiosity and apprehension in her eyes. "A dream? What was it about?"

If she felt the same pull to him as he stood before her without a stitch of clothing on, she hid it well. A part of him was disappointed by that. He wished he wasn't the only one feeling the intensity of this pull.

He took a deep breath, the details of the dream as clear in his mind as if he'd just awoken.

"I heard Doug's voice," Stone confessed, the mention of the former Alpha bringing a solemn weight to their conversation. "He was guiding me, talking about finding the essence of something significant. And then, this alter and these symbols," he gestured around them, "they were there in my dream, just as they are now."

Ella stepped closer. "Doug's voice? That's... that doesn't sound like just a dream, Stone. It sounds like a message."

Stone nodded, the validation of his own feelings in Ella's words bolstering his resolve. "I think so too. All morning I was thinking about what Marta said about this place and I felt drawn here. As if I was meant to see these symbols—to try to understand their significance. Only, I'm just as confused now as I was earlier."

Ella reached out, her hand brushing against his arm, grounding him—but her touch also excited him in ways he needed to shake off or things were about to get very awkward.

"You believe it's connected to everything we're facing?" she asked, her eyes never leaving his.

"Yes," Stone replied, the connection between his dream, the symbols, and their current predicament becoming clearer the more he shared. He only wished he knew why. "There's something here, something deeply intertwined with the message from Doug. I think—it sounds weird, but I think the Essence from the Luna Scrolls might be the Breath of Selene." His voice drifted off, as he thought about all of the possibilities.

"I agree. I had the same thought earlier today," Ella said, surprising him.

She turned to face him fully, her body mere inches from his own. He could feel the heat radiating from her and it spoke to him like a song that desperately needed to be sung.

All thoughts and worries that had been held in his mind drifted away—leaving only this moment. This place in time with *his mate.*

It felt sacred.

And before he could stop himself, he bent forward, raking his fingertips across her cheek. Her eyes drifted closed and he pressed his lips to hers, needing to taste her. Only a little.

The world around them seemed to pause—every sense heightened in a way that felt both exhilarating and entirely natural.

The connection between them deepened, the pull of their wolves intermingling with their human desires, creating a maelstrom of need that was becoming impossible to ignore.

To his astonishment, Ella responded with a fervor that matched his own, her hands finding their way to his shoulders, grounding him and urging him closer all at once.

He pressed his body to hers, letting his growing arousal be known as he ground it against her hip.

A soft moan escaped her lips and she dug her fingertips deeper into his skin.

The symbols, the prophecy, and the danger that loomed on the horizon—all of it melted away, leaving only the raw, undeniable, heady need to be with each other in the most primal way.

And he knew then, without a shadow of a doubt, she felt it, too.

As they broke the kiss, breathless and with hearts racing, they stood at the precipice of giving in to the compulsion that had been building between them since the moment they met. The air around them was thick with anticipation, each glance, each touch, sparking a fire that threatened to consume them both.

The forest seemed to even hold its breath—the ritual site a silent witness to the undeniable connection that pulsed and thrummed with life.

Ella, her eyes dark with desire and something more profound, something that spoke of their soul-deep recognition and an unbreakable bond, whispered his name like an oath.

His name on her lips was both a question and an answer, the last piece of resistance crumbling under the weight of their mutual attraction—their need to unite.

His wolf was ready—so ready to take what was rightfully his.

Yet, even as they stood on the edge, the reality of their responsibilities, the looming threats, and the gravity of their choices hung in the air like a specter. The significance of this moment, of their potential union, was not lost on either of them.

He could see that in her eyes.

Sex between them wouldn't just be a physical act —it would seal a bond that transcended the physical realm. It was a commitment that would tie their spirits together in a way that was irreversible.

And as Ella reached out, taking his aching cock in her hand, he was *so* ready for it.

CHAPTER 9

THE BOND

ELLA

I don't know what's come over me, but I like it—and have zero intentions of stopping it. The compulsion to give in to this pull to Stone has reached a fever pitch and the anticipation of what comes next is just as palpable.

Especially when I can feel the blood rushing through him as I hold his erection in my hand.

The masculine lines of Stone's body have mesmerized me since the first time I saw him and for some reason, right now, I can't for the life of me remember why I've been holding myself back from touching them.

He presses his forehead to mine and groans in the sexiest way as I slowly stroke his length. The velvety feel of him in my palm and the way his breaths catch in his throat are all I need right now.

All I *ever* need, if I'm honest.

He's been so patient, so conscientious, *so loving...*

"You don't want to do that too much," he warns, a predatory glint flashing in his eyes.

"And why is that?" I ask, biting the side of my lip and swirling my palm across his tip.

He bucks slightly under my touch and a shiver rolls through him as he spits out my name like a curse.

A slow grin spreads across my lips and I do it again.

Any of the thoughts that weighed on my mind moments ago have fluttered away on the breeze and I'm consumed by the urge to finally give in to the bond that's been drawing me to Stone.

My *mate.*

With a growl, he reaches out, palming my breasts with warm and attentive hands and all I can think about is how much I need him inside me, not just in my hand.

I want his warm body pressed against mine and his massive cock buried inside me.

We should have done this ages ago. Should have given in to it and trusted we were strong enough to withstand it.

I could feel it.

He could feel it, too.

He was just letting me figure it all out.

I was just so worried.

Worried about rushing things.

Worried about what this would mean to the kids —to *me*.

Scared to death he'd hurt me if I let him in fully.

I've never felt anything as intense as this connection to him.

He feels like the air I'm meant to breathe.

How can that be real?

My head lolls back and I shudder from the intensity as his fingertips pinch my nipples and his tongue grazes my neck. He drags one of his hands down my body, leaving a trail of fire across my skin.

As he peppers kisses across my chest, he dips his hand between my legs, pressing a finger to my clit and drawing lazy circles against it.

God, why haven't we been doing this all along?

A soft moan escapes my lips and I close my eyes, indulging in the moment—allowing myself to let loose and give into this alchemy.

This... *fate*.

He's proven himself time after time. And it's time I let him know how much that means to me. How much I trust him and... *love him*.

The thought makes my heart expand, like a star bursts from the center of my chest, and I let it consume me, giving into the heat, the promise, *the need* of it all.

"Fuck, I've wanted this moment with you for so long," Stone murmurs, his dark eyes glazed with the same lust and love I feel consuming me.

I lean forward, pressing another kiss to his lips, needing to show him how much I want him, too. He parts his lips, allowing me to dive in and enjoy the taste of him.

My head is dizzy and my body is thrumming as I tug on him again, feeling the moisture from his arousal pool against my hand.

"Stone, I—" I begin, pulling back enough so he can see the readiness in my eyes. "I want you, too."

His eyebrows tug inward as his fingers stop their ministrations. "Are you sure—?"

Still so caring.

"Yes, I'm sure."

I stroke him again, a smirk floating to my lips. I'm rewarded by another growl that rumbles through him. His lower half tenses and I lift onto my toes to press my lips to his.

No more discussions.

No more questions.

No more distractions.

He settles into the kiss, opening his mouth slightly—just enough for my tongue to slip inside. I brush it against his, sweeping it across his lips and back again.

He tastes so good—*smells* so good. *Feels* so good.

I don't know what it is—my hand or my kiss—but Stone unhinges. His emerald eyes glow—an unearthly, beautiful luminescent green and he lifts me right off of my feet.

My hand releases him and I let out a squeak of surprise despite myself.

Stone beams back, his hands gripping my ass as he positions us.

With my arms around his neck, I wrap my legs around his waist, feeling the pressure of his crown resting at my entrance—waiting for one final invite before plunging in.

His eyes lock with mine, the question again lingering there unspoken.

"Are you going to claim me, or what?" I taunt, letting the teasing tone slip through as I roll my hips, allowing the slickness between us to speak for me and how much I want this—want *him*.

With another low rumble, his answer is clear when his lips crush down on mine and he thrusts upward.

My eyes nearly roll back in my head as I take him in, reveling in the way he spreads me apart, filling me up in ways I've never been filled.

Heart, mind... *body*.

His strong arms surround me in the most protective, supportive way as we begin to move in tandem—slow, purposeful thrusts that gain in speed and ferocity. It's as if now that things have started, there's no way to slow any of it down.

Thank god for that because I want more.

I want all of him.

My fingertips weave through his hair, tugging and

pulling—earning me the sexiest whimper from him against my lips.

Had I known it would be like this—had I known just how good it would feel—I would never have held out this long. Had I known I could feel his heart and his love like this, I would never have been afraid.

Without consciously deciding to do so, my head falls back and his kisses trail down my neck and to my chest as I thrust upward. His mouth pulls in one of my nipples, then he swaps to the other. The sensation rockets through me and I swear I can feel it all the way to my toes.

Somehow, he's able to hold me, and fill me, and move in a way that feels like we're simply two parts of a single whole. Like we were always meant to work like this—be connected this way.

He removes one hand from my ass to palm my breast again, causing a rush of sensation to roll through my entire body, lighting it up. Every place he touches—with his kisses, his hands, or his cock feels like they come alive.

I never knew I could feel like this.

So full.

Perfect.

Blissful.

On the edge of my awareness, I feel my orgasm building, but I can't get enough. I want more—*more of this sensation.*

More of his body.

More of our connection.

The energy around us builds, becoming a physical thing in the space around us.

Gone is the woods, the ritual site, the altar.

In its place is a bubble of light and energy that feels meant for only us.

The *bond*.

It's the bond...

Like a tangible thing, I feel the bond sealing around us, locking into place in a way that expands my definition of what it means to be whole.

"Oh my god," Stone murmurs against my sweaty skin as he thrusts again, "you feel so good."

Swallowing hard, I nod in agreement, somehow having lost all sense of words or how to use them.

Instead, I'm lost in the sensation of being his. Of him being mine.

Mates.

My mate.

My *love*.

Together we move like that, thrusting up and down, our bodies slick with sweat and our hearts weaving energy that binds us together. I feel him opening, connecting with me in a way that feels absolutely euphoric.

"God, Ella, I'm so close—" his words cut off and his legs quake beneath us. "I hope you are, too."

I roll my hips again, feeling him penetrate deeper

yet, touching a part of me that has me screaming his name.

The energy heightens, expanding and drawing in something so powerful I don't even have a name for it.

Bond doesn't cover it. It doesn't even come close.

He tips his hips again and a litany of curses fall from his lips. His entire body is shaking now and I know it's only a matter of heartbeats before...

"Fuck, Ella," Stone cries out, his arms wrapping around my waist and pulling me against his chest.

Light bursts behind my eyelids and we both fall over the edge, succumbing to our bliss at the same time.

The bubble of light—our bond locks into place and I feel our hearts reach out for one another to seal the claim. The energy intertwines, like vines wrapping around each other. Wanting to connect and link with one another.

Only, as they connect, something peculiar happens. A strange sickly gray seeps into the brightness of our bond, casting its inky darkness across the beauty of it. It dampens the effect, making me shudder from the coldness in it.

Then, the darkness expands, causing the light to withdraw and wither back.

As much as I try to hold onto the ecstasy, the darkness causes a wave of panic to enter my awareness.

Before I know what's happening, it takes over

everything and I'm left with a heart-wrenching emptiness that leaves me stunned.

Something is wrong.

Terribly wrong.

My eyes fly open. With my hands still entwined in his hair, I find Stone looking at me as though he might be sick. His arms loosen and the energy between us shifts.

"Well, I'm so glad that's over," he says, his voice dripping with disdain as he drops me unceremoniously to my feet and takes a step back. "I didn't expect it would be *that* bad."

CHAPTER 10

BROKEN

ELLA

I can't even process Stone's words, let alone respond to them.

My heart is doing somersaults in my chest—and not the good kind.

"What?" I gasp out, more to myself than to him.

I'm struggling to understand, to find some kind of footing in this sudden, unfamiliar landscape opening between us.

For a brief moment, Stone looks just as lost, his hands pressing against his temples as if he can physically push away whatever's taken hold of him.

"I—I'm sorry, Ella. I don't know why I said that." His voice is laced with genuine bewilderment, but it does nothing to ease the tight knot of dread coiling in my stomach.

My mouth runs dry and I fight back tears.

Everything was perfect—so beautiful.

Until it wasn't.

I want to shift into my wolf—to run away so he can't see me cry because I feel it coming on.

Instead, I'm frozen—my old F habit deciding to make an unhelpful reappearance.

All those feelings of connection, of rightness that were so vivid just moments ago are now overshadowed by a stark, cold reversal.

My body is still tingling, the remnants of euphoria lingering in the background of what feels like betrayal. Adrenaline takes over and my body begins to shiver in the August heat.

Stone stands in front of me with a look of confusion and agitation fighting for dominance across his features. Yet, his erection is still evident—glistening in the dappled sunlight like some kind of sick joke reminding me of what we just had.

What we *almost* had.

I can still feel him inside me. I can feel the evidence of him running down my leg.

"I think I'm going to be sick," I blurt out, turning away from him.

I can't look at him, not after what he just said. I can't let it taint this for me. But I think it already has.

"How do you think I feel?" Stone retorts with a grunt, and I whirl around, my gaze sharp enough to cut.

However, any sharp words I might have said are swallowed by the sudden, overwhelming need to understand—to figure out what just went so terribly wrong.

This *isn't* Stone.

It can't be.

Something must have happened to him.

I shake my head, trying to clear it—to force some logic through the hurt and confusion.

"I need to think. I need... I need to talk to Jinx," I say, more to myself than to him.

Maybe she and Trudie have come across something like this before, something that could explain why Stone would suddenly turn like this. If nothing else, maybe they can help me fix it—*fix him.*

An almost bored expression takes hold of Stone's features and he rolls his eyes. "This isn't that big of a deal, Ella. We tried it"—he shrugs—"just didn't work out. You don't have to be so dramatic about it."

Bile rises in the back of my throat and I glare back unable to believe what I'm hearing.

This can't be real. He can't be—

"I'm not being dramatic. I need to find out what's wrong with you," I snap back, taking a step further from him.

He huffs a humorless laugh. "Nothing's wrong with me. Maybe I'm just seeing things clearly for the first time."

This is bullshit. I glance around the space, wondering if the ritual site had something to do with this.

Or was it Jinx? Did she accidentally mess with my mojo?

"I'm going to see Jinx," I repeat, unwilling to participate in whatever this is.

Stone looks like he wants to argue, to insist on coming with me, maybe. But I can't have him there.

Not when I don't even understand what I'm feeling or what I'm about to face. I need distance to work it out.

Using every ounce of willpower I have left, I lock eyes with him, my voice finding the steely edge of authority that comes with being an Alpha. "Do your own thing, Stone. I'll see you at home later."

It's a command, not a suggestion, fueled by my need for space, for time to process this heart-wrenching turmoil without the added weight of his verbal barbs and my own overwhelming emotions.

The moment the words leave my mouth, I turn away from him, not waiting to see his reaction—not sure I could bear it.

Thankfully, my command must have hit its mark because he doesn't say anything behind my back.

The need to shift, to let my wolf out, becomes an insurmountable force. I sprint, putting distance between us, until I'm far enough away, secluded by the dense embrace of the forest that has always felt like a sanctuary.

With a deep breath that feels like it's tearing my chest apart, I let go, surrendering to the shift. My body contorts, the familiar pain a welcome distraction from the chaos of my emotions. Bones realign, muscles reshape, and fur sprouts.

In moments, my human worries are overshadowed by the more straightforward thoughts of my wolf.

I run.

The forest blurs past me, a streak of colors and sensations, as I push my legs to carry me faster, *further*.

My heart still aches, but the physical exertion, the rush of wind through my fur, offers a temporary reprieve from the pain, the betrayal, and the utter confusion.

Eventually, exhaustion claws its way into my limbs, forcing me to slow down and acknowledge that I can't outrun my problems, no matter how fast I go.

Besides, the further away from the scene, the more agitated I get.

With a irritation, I make my way back to where I left my clothes, shifting back with a sigh that feels like it carries the weight of the world.

How the fuck did things go so terribly wrong?

The tears come and I let them fall. Willing them to come so I can release them and be done with it.

I can't—*won't*—let this break me. No matter how much it feels like it could.

Dressed once more, I head toward Jinx's house, my mind spinning with questions.

Each time I run through them, the further from a resolution I get.

All I know is this isn't Stone. It can't be the real Stone.

Please, don't let it be the real Stone.

Something's happened to him when the darkness crept over the bond.

As I knock on Jinx's door, I brace myself for the conversation to come. I need answers, and I need them now. But I don't even have any idea if she and Trudie will be able to help.

"Ella, 'bout time. Took you long enough to get back —" Jinx says when she opens the door. However, her expression shifts from sarcastic to concern at the sight of me. "What's wrong?"

I step inside, my face crumpling despite trying to stay calm. The tears come and I'm helpless to stop them. "Something happened with Stone. I think... I think we might be dealing with something supernatural. Something beyond my understanding. I don't know what to do."

Jinx ushers me in, and there's Trudie, sitting at the kitchen table surrounded by a mess of old books and maps.

"What in the world happened, Ella?" Trudie asks, her voice full of concern and curiosity as she stands up and walks over.

I take a deep, steadying breath, trying to gather my scattered thoughts.

"It's Stone," I begin, my voice shaking despite my efforts to sound composed. There's an edge of anger, total disbelief that I can't seem to fight off. "Something's not right. He... he's not himself."

Jinx takes a seat at the table. "Ella, start from the beginning. What's going on?"

"I don't even know if I can explain it," I spit out. "One moment, Stone and I were..." I glance between the two of them and scrunch my nose, "*close*—and then suddenly, he said something so hurtful, so unlike him. And his expression, Jinx, it was like he didn't even recognize me. Or *hated* me, even."

She narrows her gaze. "Not sure I want to know this, but for the sake of argument, what do you mean by close?"

"I thought..." The tears spring to my eyes again and I press my palms over them. "I thought we were consummating the bond."

When I drop my hands, a look passes between Jinx and Trudie.

"Did you do something, Jinx?" I ask her directly, the question hanging heavy between us. "Accidentally, maybe? With the ley lines or something else? I know your abilities can sometimes go awry."

Jinx's face softens, and she shakes her head, a firm certainty in her eyes. "Ella, I swear, I've done nothing that could cause harm to Stone or you. Our work with the ley lines has only been about understanding, not manipulation. And especially not to you and Stone. I like you crazy kids."

Trudie, who's been quietly observing, suddenly steps forward. "Let me get a look at you, Ella," she says, her tone commanding in a way that brooks no argument.

Her gaze is intense as she examines me.

After a moment, she frowns, her brow furrowing. "There's something... odd about your energy. It's as if there's a shadow hanging over you that wasn't there this morning. I've felt something similar once before, but this feels more personal, more... *targeted.*"

"What do you mean? Like a—curse?" I blurt out, my heart racing. "Did someone do this to us?"

She winces slightly. "Perhaps."

My heart sinks. "Can you help? Do you think you can see what's wrong with Stone? *Fix him?*"

I want him back.

Trudie nods slowly. "I need to see him for myself. There's a harmony I can sometimes bring—a balance to energies that are out of sync. It's worth a try."

Jinx interjects, "If little miss harmony over here senses something off with your aura, but Stone's the one acting out, then this is some serious shit. We're all going to help you figure this out, Ella."

Their support, the assurance in their voices, it's a balm to the raw edges of my emotions that seem to be fighting between terror, sadness, and anger.

"Thank you," I whisper, feeling the first flicker of

hope since this nightmare began. "I just... I can't lose Stone. Not like this. Not now. There's so much—"

"We won't let that happen," Trudie says firmly, her determination echoing around the small kitchen.

Jinx nods in agreement, her usual banter with her sister apparently forgotten in the face of my crisis. "I'll check the ley lines again. There could be something we missed—something that could explain this... shift."

We gather around the kitchen table, a makeshift war room in Jinx's cozy, cluttered home.

However, my mind begins to shut down. I'm there, but not. My heart and head are at war with each other.

We were so close...

I felt the bond. I felt my mate's love like it was a palpable thing.

And I have to hold onto that.

In the background, I'm vaguely aware of the sister's banter returning. Trudie quips about Jinx's stubbornness, and Jinx retorts with a comment about Trudie's overly optimistic view. But beneath the surface, there's a solid, unshakeable foundation of trust and respect. I don't even know if they realize it. It's their way of coping, of keeping the darkness at bay, and right now, I'm grateful for it. Because I feel like I'm going to lose my mind.

"Ella, I don't think this in the ley lines," Trudie says, shaking her head. "I need to see Stone. I need to feel his energy for myself. I don't want to alarm you, but curses are tricky and the longer they stick—the harder they are to remove."

The room falls silent at Trudie's declaration, the weight of her words settling over me like a thick fog. My heart, already fractured from the day's revelations, tightens further.

Oh my god, what if we can't get him back?

No—I can't focus on that. I have to believe we can fix this.

The thought of facing Stone—seeing him so changed from the man I love, terrifies me. Yet, the possibility of healing, of restoration, nudges me forward through the fear.

"I... I'm scared to see him like that again," I admit, my voice barely a whisper, choked with emotion. "But I'll take you to him. If there's even a chance you can help, we have to try."

Jinx's eyes meet mine across the table. "You're not alone in this, Ella. We're with you."

Trudie's nod is full of a determined kind of grace— the kind that reassures without words. It speaks of her presence and how it brings the hope of mending what's been torn apart.

"Thanks—both of you," I say, heading to the door.

I lead the way, my steps uncertain but guided by the knowledge that doing nothing isn't an option. We have so much going on—so much to be thinking about, worrying about. Stone being cursed shouldn't be one of them, but here we are.

Trudie and Jinx flank me, their presence a silent vow of solidarity.

As we step outside, the humid summer air does little to soothe the turmoil within me. In fact, the storm clouds that seem to be heading our way feel like more of an accurate representation. But with each step toward Stone, I'm buoyed by the strength of those beside me.

We won't rest until we figure this out.

As we make our way to Stone's home, the urgency is palpable, driving us to mend things before it's too late—before whatever has taken hold of Stone takes him away from me for good.

CHAPTER II

TO THE EDGE OF DARKNESS

STONE

T he evening air was thick with the promise of an impending storm—both in the afternoon sky and within Stone himself.

He stalked through the streets, the weight of his boots against the pavement echoing the tumultuous beat of his heart. His mind was a oscillating between confusion and frustration—emotions that seemed foreign... yet overwhelmingly his own.

He couldn't make sense of what was happening.

One moment he felt centered. The next, it was as if everything and everyone around him was begging to have their ass handed to them and he was the one who would gladly do it.

Then there was a small glimmer inside him that felt giddy—connected to Ella in a way he'd longed for.

They'd had sex, that much he could surmise, but every time he caught a glimpse of that joy, the darkness inside his mind took over, threatening to take him under.

Stone had been around the supernatural block all his life. He knew when something unnatural was at work within him. And now was certainly one of those times.

It felt like a possession.

But how could that be?

He didn't know what had happened back at the ritual site, but he knew it had to be the cause of whatever this was. That site must have been cursed and they stumbled right into it.

What else could it be?

And if that was the case, there was only one place that would have answers.

The hidden bar downtown, a place he associated with Andres and his stupid witches, loomed in his thoughts, an unwelcome beacon in his turmoil. Tonight, much like it was a couple of days ago, it was not just a destination but a symbol of his desperate search for answers.

He would confront the witches and make them set things right.

If he could hold onto his intentions long enough to make it happen, that was.

After the way he had spoken to Ella, he wasn't so sure he could trust himself and the words that would come out of his mouth. But he had to try.

Now that he was further from her, his head

seemed to clear a bit, allowing him to focus and feel more in control—but only just. Sometimes, the anger would come in waves and no matter what he did, he couldn't stop the vitriol from spewing.

Stone's stride was purposeful, driven by the unshakable conviction that the witches who helped Andres were behind the shitstorm of feelings threatening to engulf him.

Even though the bar was hidden from view thanks to a spell meant to keep its secrets—he knew it existed. Knew where it was now.

He'd find a way in.

As it turned out, since he already knew the bar was there—the only thing Stone needed was the ability to turn a doorknob he couldn't see with his physical eyes. After fumbling against the wall for a few moments, he located the handle and pulled open the door.

The familiar rush of noise and dimly lit chaos enveloped him as he descended the stairs. He paused, letting his eyes adjust, his senses on high alert. The scent of magic, subtle but unmistakable, hung in the air, and it was a potent reminder of why he had come.

Those fucking witches would fix him—fix whatever the hell this was.

The patrons parted before him, perhaps sensing the storm that walked in Stone's skin.

He made his way to the bar itself, hoping for a glimpse of either of the witches who had helped

Andres the other night. He knew his demeanor radiated a cold fury.

But as he approached, the realization dawned on him—the bartender and server he'd seen with Andres were nowhere to be found. The current staff, entirely unfamiliar faces veiled in shadows and whispers, glanced at him with a mixture of suspicion and disdain.

It was clear—he wasn't welcome here.

This wasn't a bar for werewolves, especially not one visibly teetering on the edge of his own darkness.

"Are you lost, wolf?" The bartender's voice was edged with a cold hostility that matched the chill in the air. He crossed his tatted arms across his broad chest and glared at Stone.

The underlying message was clear: *leave.*

Stone's jaw tightened, his eyes scanning the dim interior for any sign of the witches.

"I'm looking for someone," he replied, his voice coming out in almost a growl.

"Not about to help your kind," the bartender shot back, already turning away to attend to another patron—a pixie, by the look of her.

The patrons' eyes felt like daggers on Stone's back as he stood there, a lone wolf among a crowd that wanted nothing to do with him. The air was thick with an unspoken warning—push further, and consequences would follow.

Just one problem.

He was game.

Hell, he hoped one of them would make a move. Again, a fresh wave of rage burned inside Stone's chest and he was more than happy to let it out.

Stone's gaze swept across the room, his supernatural senses stretching out, seeking any hint of the witches' presence, but it was as if they had vanished into thin air, leaving him grappling with an enemy he couldn't see or confront.

They were probably with Andres, the bastards.

The bar, once a source of potential answers, now felt like a maze designed to trap and confuse.

A sudden laughter erupted from the other end of the bar, slicing through the tension. Stone turned, his eyes locking with a small group who seemed to find amusement in his predicament.

"No one wants what you got, pup," one jeered, a smirk playing across his lips.

Stone couldn't tell what kind of creature the guy was, he just knew he was about to go down.

"What did you say?" Stone's hand clenched into a fist at his side, the urge to strike, to unleash, nearly overwhelming.

The creature stood up, revealing himself to be a half-troll, half-something else that Stone couldn't quite place. His smirk widened as he stepped closer, the crowd parting like the sea.

"What, are you deaf? I said, no one wants you here. Why don't you go back to your pack and whimper about how the supe bar wouldn't let you drown your sorrows. Or won't they let you into the club either?" the half-troll taunted, his voice grating against Stone's already frayed nerves.

That was all it took. Stone lunged forward, propelled by a rage that felt both alien and his own. His fist connected with the half-troll's face, the impact sending a shockwave through his arm.

The fight erupted into chaos, with Stone at the center, a tempest let loose.

As punches flew and magic sparked in the air, a dangerous thrill surged through Stone. He was dimly aware of the destruction, of the panic as patrons scrambled to escape the fray, but he couldn't stop. His mind was a red haze. Every hit, every block driven by the turmoil inside him.

Then, just as he was about to deliver a blow that would surely end the half-troll's taunting for good, a flash of memory struck him—vivid and terrifying.

It was the night he had lost control and killed a human. The moment that had forever changed him— casting him out of the pack and into the life of an Omega. It was a scar upon his soul that even now enveloped him.

The memory surged through him, a cold wave that doused the flames of his rage.

His fist hovered inches from the half-troll's face, trembling with the effort to hold back. The realization of what he was about to do—what he had almost allowed himself to become again—washed over him, leaving a chilling wake.

The half-troll, sensing the sudden shift, scrambled backward, his eyes wide with shock and fear.

Stone stood there, his chest heaving, surrounded by the wreckage of his anger. The silence that followed was more damning than any words could have been.

He looked around, the reality of what he had almost done settling in. The bar was in shambles. The patrons either fled or cowered—or looked ready to fight.

He felt a hand on his shoulder and turned to see Ella, her expression one of deep concern.

When had she arrived?

"Stone, let's go. *Now*," she said, her words packing a powerful punch. There was no room for argument—not when his Alpha commanded it.

Behind her, Jinx and another woman stood—both seemed to be caught between appreciation and horror.

"Well, aren't you the life of the party, Stone," Jinx quipped, surveying the damage with a whistle. "Didn't know you had it in you, to be honest. I'm kinda impressed."

Stone couldn't muster the energy to respond, the weight of his actions and the flash of memories leaving him drained and hollow. He simply nodded, his gaze lingering on the destruction his hands had wrought.

The other woman stepped forward, her hands

glowing with a soft, calming light. She began to murmur under her breath, her voice a gentle balm in the tense atmosphere.

"Let's not draw more attention than we already have," she said to Ella, her magic weaving through the air, somehow attempting to soothe frayed nerves and mend what had been broken.

The spell, however, seemed to falter against the lingering aura of Stone's anger, the remnants of the fight proving resistant to her efforts.

"Well, it's not working as I hoped," the woman admitted with a sigh.

"What are you looking at?" Jinx said, her eyes fixed on a patron in the corner.

A young witch in a corner booth dropped her gaze to the tabletop, only to piss herself.

Stone snickered under his breath, despite himself. Then, instantly was at war for the pleasure that gave him.

He wasn't like this. This *wasn't* him.

Or was it?

Stone felt a hand squeeze his arm—a silent command from Ella to follow. He glanced at her, the concern in her eyes mirroring his own.

"I'm sorry," he murmured, the words barely audible over the ringing in his ears. "I don't know what's..."

Ella shook her head, her expression softening. "I

know. We'll figure this out, Stone. Let's get out of here."

Without a word, Stone nodded, allowing Ella to lead him away from the scene of chaos he had created.

As they turned to leave, the bartender called out, "Don't come back."

Stone's mind replayed the fight and the haunting flash of memory that had stopped him. The realization that he was walking a razor's edge, that the darkness within him was only simmering, ready to take over, was a weight heavier than any he had ever carried.

Ella didn't speak, and for that, Stone was grateful. He wasn't sure he could find the words to explain the unexplainable—to voice the fear that now gnawed at him with renewed vigor.

He might lose himself to the darkness.

He might once again become the monster he had worked so hard to leave behind.

How could this have happened? Especially when they had come so close to having it all?

As they emerged into the late afternoon, Stone took a deep breath, trying to push away the darkness, the memories, and the fear. But as the adrenaline faded, leaving behind only exhaustion and a deep-seated unease, Stone knew that this fight was far from over.

He had come to the bar seeking answers—seeking a way to fight the possession he felt tightening its grip on him. Instead, he had found only more questions and a darkness within himself that he couldn't ignore.

The storm that had been threatening before he walked into the bar finally broke and rain began to fall in heavy drops around them.

It seemed to Stone a fitting end to the day—a cleansing, perhaps, or a baptism into the battle he now knew lay ahead.

"You know, for a moment there, I thought we were going to see round two of 'Stone vs. the Supernatural World.' Gotta admit, part of me was kind of excited," Jinx joked, obviously trying to lighten the mood. However, the raindrops dampened the effect— *literally.*

The woman beside her rolled her eyes, but there was a smile tugging at her lips. "Only you would find entertainment in near-catastrophic bar fights, June."

Stone shook his head, trying to clear it. "I'm sorry —who are you?"

Jinx's grin widened as she wrapped an arm around the shoulders of the woman next to her. "Ah, right, introductions. Stone, meet my sister, *Harmony.* Though, between you and me, *'Goodie Two Shoes'* is more like it."

The woman offered Stone a small, polite smile. "It's Trudie, actually. June just refuses to call me by my name."

Jinx scoffed. "Because *'Trudie'* just screams *'I file*

taxes for fun' and we can't have that. It's bad for my reputation to be associated with that vibe."

Trudie shook her head, a fond annoyance clear in her expression. "Ignore her. She's been like this since we were kids."

Stone, despite the gravity of his situation, couldn't help but be almost amused by their banter. It was a brief, much-needed reprieve from the turmoil swirling within him.

"I wish I could say it was nice to meet you, Trudie," Stone managed to ground out, his voice still rough from the evening's events.

Trudie's gaze, warm yet assessing, swept over him.

"Ella has told us a little about what's been going on with you." Her eyes narrowed slightly as she concentrated, and then she frowned. "Oh, yeah. He's cursed and cursed *good.*"

Ella, who had been quietly observing, tensed at Trudie's words. Her silence spoke volumes, the complexity of their recent encounter in the woods and the subsequent turn of events creating a chasm that words couldn't bridge—at least not yet.

Stone felt a tug to make things right, yet, he had no idea how to.

Trudie focused on Stone and stepped closer, her hands glowing with that soft, calming light.

"Let's see if I can do something about this curse," she said softly.

As Trudie's hands moved through the air, weaving

a tapestry of light and shadows, Stone felt the edges of the darkness within him recoil, as if threatened by her magic. Yet, despite her efforts, it clung stubbornly to him, an unyielding shadow that refused to be dispelled.

After a moment, Trudie sighed and dropped her hands.

"I can't break it. This curse—it's some next-level stuff. But..." She trailed off, a spark of determination lighting up her eyes. "I might know someone who can help."

CHAPTER 12

THE PSYCHIC

ELLA

The rain is relentless as we head back to Jinx's house. It turns streets into rivers and the late afternoon into a blur. It's almost as if nature itself is throwing a tantrum, mirroring the turmoil bubbling inside me.

By the time we're inside, drenched and shivering, I can't help but feel like the storm is a bad omen.

Jinx's place is a haven from the chaos outside. Her walls are adorned with eclectic art and shelves crammed with books on every imaginable subject related to the supernatural. There are odd nicknacks and piles of tings stacked in every corner. However, it's cozy in a way that makes me want to curl up and forget the world outside—if only for a moment.

Stone has been silent beside me but it's clear a storm of his own brewing is simmering beneath the surface. Every now and then, I catch him clenching his fists, fighting whatever darkness the curse is dredging up. It's heartbreaking to see him like this, caught in the grip of something we don't fully understand yet.

Seeing him at the bar, fighting as a human—it was a side of him I've never witnessed. Battles for our pack, sure. But a bar fight?

I want to help him—go to him. But every time I get close, he pushes me away. Both physically and with his words.

"There's no point in doing more research if my friend can help us. I'm just gonna give her a call and hope she's free," Trudie says, reaching for her phone in her back pocket. "If she can't help us, no one can."

As she scrolls through her contacts, I find myself holding my breath.

Stone shifts uncomfortably next to me, a tangible sign of his own skepticism. We're both desperate for a solution, but the path to finding one seems to be narrowing with every turn.

"Di?" Trudie says, clutching her phone close. Her eyebrows scrunch in as she listens to the other end. "Yeah, it has been a while. Look, I know this is a bit out of the blue, but I could use your help. I have some friends here who I believe have been cursed. There's something off about it and we need a way to diffuse the damn thing quickly. They're on a bit of a... *deadline.*"

Again, she stops talking and listens intently.

There's a lot of nodding and pacing going on.

Jinx gives me one of her lopsided grins and shrugs.

I turn my gaze back to Trudie and she locks eyes with me. Can't lie, my heart thumps unevenly at that look.

"She wants to see the two of you," Trudie says, covering the mouthpiece of her phone. "I'm assuming you don't have time for an impromptu trip to Georgia."

I shake my head and snicker. "No chance."

The clock is ticking down to the Supermoon as it is and if the prophecy details are correct, shit's about to hit the fan in a big way. And that's saying something considering the week I've already had.

Good god, my life is a mess.

"That's what I thought. Are you okay with a video call?" she continues.

I nod emphatically, "Of course."

At the same time, Stone sputters, "Some psychic. This is bullshit."

I shoot him a look of annoyance.

The sooner we can get him back to his normal self, the better. I don't know how much of this *new Stone* I can handle without turning into a ball of female rage, myself.

He's beginning to remind me too much of Troy—and some of the other asshole men I've dealt with lately. It's not a good look on him.

"Can it, Stone. If there's one thing I agree with, it's

that this woman's the real deal," Jinx offers, nodding at her sister. "Make the video call."

Trudie returns her attention to the phone. "Would you be able to make an assessment with a video call?"

A tiny voice speaks on the other end and by all the nodding Trudie does, I presume she's agreeing to the proposition.

"Thank you. I'll FaceTime you now," Trudie says, then hangs up. Her eyes widen as she glances in our direction. "Talk about good timing. She didn't have another client. Are you ready?"

"What a pointless waste of time," Stone grounds out.

I bite my lip to keep from saying something I'll regret and opt to nod my agreement instead.

Trudie turns back to her phone and makes the call. Then, she hands me the phone.

Someone answers on the other end, but the screen is totally black.

"H—hello?" I say, peering at the blank screen.

Silence greets us and I'm about to hand the phone back to Trudie when a scratching noise blasts through the speaker.

"Is this thing on?" There's silence, then scuffling on the other end, followed by a loud thunk. "Ren, how do I use this infernal contraption?"

"Give it here." A loud sigh follows with a tut, and the video turns on. A man with darker skin and an impeccable hairstyle comes into view briefly. Then, he sets the phone down and I'm staring at a white ceiling as he says, "Honestly, woman. Apollo knows you've been alive long enough to learn how to use a phone. This should *not* be so difficult."

"Indeed, I can attest to that," someone in the background announces. He sounds like my grandpa. "You *have* been alive a very long time."

"I know how to use a phone. This is *not* a phone. It's a torture device," she fires back. Then, a woman barely older than Asher comes into view and I snort far too loudly.

Oh yeah, she's *totally* old.

I fight back an eye roll.

She has white-blond hair down to her shoulders—with the exception of a large bright pink chunk that sweeps across her forehead and vanishes behind her ear.

I shoot a confused look at Trudie. How is this the *'world's most powerful psychic?'* She's half my age and can't even use a cellphone.

I mean, I'm old, but at least I know how to use my calling apps without hunting Asher or Avery down, for crying out loud.

This does not bode well.

Maybe Stone was right.

Some psychic.

As much as I like Trudie, I'm beginning to think she's a bit gullible.

The woman on the phone peers into the screen,

her blue eyes narrowing into near slits. I hold it out so she can get a good look at both Stone and myself.

After a beat, she says, "Well, Trudie's right. You've got one helluva curse sticking to the two of you."

"No, shit." Stone huffs, rolls his eyes dramatically, and crosses his arms over his chest.

"Diana, we're hoping you'd be able to help us *break* the curse," Trudie offers from the sidelines. "Can you see anything that might help?"

Diana pauses, her eyes losing focus as if she's peering into something beyond the confines of the video call. For a moment, I swear her eyes glow slightly, but I assume it's just the phone glitching out.

The silence stretches, becoming almost tangible until she finally speaks, her voice carrying an unexpected gravity. "I'm sorry, but I can't lift this curse from where I am. It would require a ritual and sacred objects. The magic entwined in this... it's deeply rooted. Like it goes into the core of who you both are. You might need to confront the source directly—the witches who cast this would be able to undo it."

So, it *was* witches.

I let out a slow exhale.

Stone's frustration is palpable, a low snarl rumbling in his chest, but before he can voice his dissent, Diana continues, capturing our full attention. "However, that's not all I see." She leans closer, her gaze piercing through the screen. "Beyond the weave of your curse, there's a... *resonance*. Something powerful calling out to you." Diana's eyes narrow as if what she's about to say next surprises even her. *"The Breath of Selene."*

Her actually saying the name sends a shockwave through me.

Stone and I exchange a glance, our earlier skepticism faltering under the weight of her revelation. The Breath of Selene—an artifact we'd only just learned about last night and now here it is, surfacing again in the most unexpected way.

I kinda feel sick.

"This artifact," Diana's voice pulls us back, "it's not just a relic or a myth. It's a catalyst. For you both," she gestures to Stone and me, "it will not only give you tremendous power but it will elevate you both into a new status—ensure your destinies as something—uh, there's a word trying to rise up. Hang on." Again, her eyes seem to glow. *"Moon Wolves.* Wolves destined to unite the supernatural realm."

Chills race down my spine. Stone sits up straighter, his jaw set.

Whatever doubts we harbored about Diana's authenticity dissipate under the gravity of her words.

She might be young, but she certainly is more than meets the eye.

"Look—" Diana's gaze softens slightly. "I know this is a lot to take in, and I wish I could be there to help you navigate this path. Well, actually, no I don't.

But that's neither her nor there. I have some serious shit happening over here, too."

In the background, the old man mutters something that sounds suspiciously like, "Indeed."

"However," she continues, shooting an annoyed glance over the top of her phone, "I can give you something to start with—it's a set of coordinates. For some reason, I feel once you're there, you'll find the Breath of Selene. Or perhaps the path to it."

She rattles off a string of numbers that Trudie quickly jots down on a piece of paper.

"Go there. Face the source of your curse and keep the Breath of Selene in mind," Diana says, her expression serious. "It's all tied together. I think they're trying to stop you from acquiring it. There's a lot at stake in this. I can't grasp the full extent—but it's *huge*."

Stone, who had been scowling again, now looks contemplative. Evidently, the gears are turning in his head. I can almost see him piecing together our next moves as the Delta in him takes over. That is, if that part of him is even left.

"Anything else?" Trudie asks, looking at us but saying it loud enough for Diana to hear.

"That's all I'm getting right now," Diana offers. "It doesn't mean more won't reveal itself, though. So, be ready."

"Goodie," Stone grumbles, standing up and stalking away. His fists are clenched tightly by his side and I get the distinct impression, he'd like to smash something.

"Diana," I find myself saying, "*thank you*. For giving us a starting point."

She offers a small, knowing smile. "You're in good hands with Trudie and June. Just remember, destiny has a funny way of pushing us toward where we need to be. *Embrace* it and you'll do just fine. But if I were you, I'd get your asses moving."

I nod, letting her words sink in.

Where is destiny pushing us other than certain doom?

"Ren, how do end a video call?" Diana asks, glancing up.

"Oh, for crying out loud. The same way you end any other call. Hit the big red button," Ren calls out from somewhere. "*Honestly*."

"There *is* no red button," she mutters, staring at the screen and looking perplexed.

"I believe if you tap the screen, it shall appear," the old man in the background says, edging close enough to see white bushy eyebrows and hair, "like magic."

We can hear her tap the phone and a huge grin erupts across her features. "Would you look at that? Thanks, Kyros. Bye, guys!"

With that, she ends the call, leaving us in a stunned silence.

The revelations and the daunting task ahead—*to somehow face the witches responsible for our curse and find* the Breath of Selene—fill the room with palpable tension.

"We have a lot to do," I say finally, breaking the silence. "And not much time to do it."

"You sure know how to enter a prophecy in style," Jinx chides with a soft chuckle.

I huff a laugh and catch Stone's eye. "Think you can handle a road trip?"

He manages a wry smile, the first genuine one I've seen since our predicament. But then his jaw sets and he slams his eyes shut. "As long as you're driving. I don't know if I trust myself."

Jinx snorts. "Oh, no. You two are going to need more than a good playlist for this journey. Good thing we're coming with ya. And *I'll* drive."

Trudie nods, her expression serious but supportive. "We'll gather what information we can to help. You're not alone in this."

Good, because I have a feeling Stone and I will need a buffer.

I let the idea of an impromptu road trip sink in, the weight of our mission pressing heavily on my shoulders. There's so much do to.

I need to let the kids know. I need to prepare the pack. *I need...*

The road ahead feels daunting but I have to make this work.

"Okay, then," I reply, trying to muster more confidence than I feel. "Let's get prepared. We're diving into the deep end of the supernatural world, and we're going to come out on top."

Jinx and Trudie start discussing logistics, pulling up new maps, and making lists of what we'll need, but I can't help but feel a gnawing sensation in my gut.

Clementine's words have never felt truer. This prophecy has already begun. And I don't think there's any way to stop it.

As we plan our next steps, I realize that this journey isn't just about breaking a curse or finding an ancient artifact. It's about proving our worth—facing down the darkness, and maybe, *just maybe,* changing the course of the supernatural realm.

Diana's parting words also tumble around in my mind.

Embrace destiny.

It sounds like a challenge, a call to rise above everything we've faced so far. And as the storm outside continues to rage on, I can't shake the feeling that we're stepping into a larger story—one that's been waiting for us.

As if on cue, the power flickers, plunging Jinx's cozy haven into darkness. A collective gasp fills the room, and then, just as quickly, the lights flicker back to life. But it's enough to remind me that in this supernatural chess game, we're not the only players.

Someone, or something, is watching.

Waiting.

The journey to confront the witches and unearth

the secrets of the Breath of Selene is more than a quest —it's a race against forces we can barely comprehend.

Bigger than us.

Bigger than even the witches, I think.

And as we stand on the brink of this unknown adventure, I can't help but wonder...

Will we be able to embrace our destiny?

Or will we succumb to the forces trying to tear us apart?

CHAPTER 13

THE JOURNEY AHEAD

STONE

In the oddly bunker-esque interior of Alanna's apartment, Stone stood slightly apart, his arms crossed, watching Ella and her teenagers with a wariness that had little to do with them and everything to do with what was going on inside him.

They had gone through the motions. Prepped the pack—put Marta in charge. Clementine was still scouring the Scrolls. And now, they were here—the final step before heading to mysterious coordinates.

Tension knotted in Stone's chest, a constant reminder of the internal battle he waged—a fight between his nature and the dark influence that sought to alter his every reaction. He didn't know how long he could hold it back, but he was trying.

What other choice did he have?

"I promise, we'll be back before you know it," Ella said, her voice firm but layered with a softness only a mother's love could weave. "This isn't going to be easy for any of us, but I have to make sure we're all protected—and that means keeping you here with Alanna for now. She'll keep you safe."

Asher crossed his arms, mirroring Stone's posture but with a hint of simmering defiance. "I hate being human. You should turn me. At least then I'll be able to protect Avery if anything happens while you're away," he insisted, his eyes burning with the urge to protect—to prove himself.

Ella gave him a *'get real'* kind of look. "First of all, you're adorable, Ash. But you're also naive. The process of being turned isn't easy and figuring out how to embrace your inner wolf—even harder. Besides, I thought you wanted to be"—Ella raised her hands to air quote—*"whatever she was."* She tipped her chin toward Alanna with a smirk.

"Well, I mean, I—" Asher stuttered, glancing between the two of them.

"Sorry, kid. As much as I'd love to have someone else like me running around, what I am..." Alanna sighed heavily. "We're born, not made."

"Isn't one supernatural in the family good enough?" Avery fired back, her jaw working back and forth.

Asher's brown eyes flashed. "Technically, there are *two*." Avery scrunched her face in confusion but before she could say anything, Asher fired back, "Remember? Dad?"

Avery's lips tugged downward as if she still hadn't let that thought land just yet.

"Come on, Ella, they're not babies and we don't have all day," Stone spat out, his tone bordering on cruel.

Inwardly, he cringed.

He wasn't that guy, not really, but the fucking curse made it hard to remember who he was anymore. Or apparently keep his mouth shut.

Ella's eyes flashed to him but rather than even offer a response, she turned back to her kids.

Stone's gaze flickered briefly to Alanna, noting the amusement and sympathy on her face as she stared back at him.

He hated that most. The *sympathy*.

The curse inside him twisted again, a gnarled vine eager to disrupt the moment with another venomous remark, but he held it back, clenching his fists tighter at his sides.

"Yeah, well," Asher shrugged, also ignoring Stone's outburst. "Being a werewolf will have to do, then. After my birthday, right? That's still the plan?" His eyes locked onto his mother's for confirmation.

"Right," Ella confirmed with a nod. "*After* your birthday. We've got enough to deal with without adding a brand-new werewolf to the mix. Plus, I don't think coming into this mess during the Supermoon would be wise either, come to think of it."

Ashe's jaw ticked, but he nodded in resignation.

Her eyes softened as she pressed her hands to his shoulders, an unspoken promise hanging between them.

Stone's attention shifted as Avery leaned against the kitchen counter, arms crossed, watching the exchange with a skeptical eye. "So, we're just going to sit tight while you all go off on some super secret... *mission?* What are we supposed to do if something happens?"

Ella turned to face her daughter, her expression softening. "Nothing is going to happen, Avery. Alanna is more than capable of keeping you both safe. Otherwise, I'd never leave you with her. And this mission... It's something we *need* to do—to make sure our family can have a future. One without constantly looking over our shoulders."

The room fell into an uneasy silence, the weight of the situation settling heavily on all present.

Stone felt the curse clawing at the edges of his control, urging him to end this drawn-out farewell, to push them into action. He swallowed the bile that rose in his throat, refusing to let the darkness win.

He could fight this. He had to.

Instead, he found himself stepping forward—a reluctant mediator.

"We should get going," he said, his voice more even than he felt. "The sooner we start, the sooner we're back."

His eyes met Ella's, and he hoped like hell she saw

the apology in them for his impatience. Ordinarily, he'd understand this hesitation and its significance.

Deep down, he hoped Ella knew that.

Ella nodded, her gaze lingering on her children for a moment longer before she turned to Alanna. "Take care of them. Please," she whispered, a plea wrapped in a command, her Alpha nature never fully at rest.

Alanna smiled reassuringly. "You know I will. Go. Do what you need to do. We'll be fine here."

A beat of silence fell between them all—a collective breath held before the storm.

Ella's gaze swept over her children once more, a fierce tenderness etched into every line of her face—offering them each a look that seemed to convey a thousand unspoken promises.

Stone watched, feeling the tension between his desire to leap into action and the necessity of this goodbye. He dug his fingertips into the palms of his hands to remind himself he could stay silent and in control.

"Remember what I told you," she said, her voice stronger now, imbued with the authority of an Alpha and the warmth of a mother. "Stick together. Listen to Alanna. We'll be back before you know it."

Asher nodded, a semblance of his usual confidence flickering in his eyes. "We got this, Mom. Just... be careful, okay?"

Avery, for all her earlier protests, stepped forward, wrapping her arms around Ella in a tight hug that spoke volumes of the fear and bravery mingled in her heart.

"Hurry back," she murmured, her voice muffled against Ella's shoulder.

Stone felt the pull of the curse, eager to disrupt the tender scene with a snide remark, but he turned away, determined not to ruin the moment.

This was not the time for the curse's venom.

This was a time for strength and unity.

Ella held her daughter for a moment longer, then gently pulled away, her glassy eyes meeting Stone's.

It was time.

She kissed the side of Avery's head and took a deep breath. Then, she stepped back, blinking back tears.

Stone was already out the door by the time Ella followed after.

The two of them stepped into the strangely shabby hallway. Stone, a few steps ahead, turned back when he heard Ella pause. She was standing there, her back to him, her posture strong and resolute as she faced the closed door.

But as he watched, he saw her hand move to the doorframe, her fingers gripping the wood. For just a second, her hand trembled, a silent testament to the weight she carried on her shoulders.

It was a fleeting moment, gone as quickly as it came.

Ella straightened, squared her shoulders, and stepped away from the doorframe. She caught Stone's eye, offering him a nod that spoke volumes of her resolve.

Despite the uncertainty that lay ahead, despite the fear for her children's safety and the future of their pack, Ella was going to face whatever came next.

Stone felt a surge of admiration for Ella—a pride that even the curse couldn't take away from him.

He realized then, that if ever there was a time to fight against the darkness within him, it was now—to be the support Ella needed, the partner she deserved in the trials ahead.

He reached for her hand and gave it a squeeze. She returned the gesture and held on tight.

When they stepped outside, the late evening chill nipped at their skin. The rain had stopped, but it was still a stark reminder of the journey ahead.

The quiet of the evening was shattered by the roar of an engine as Jinx's bright yellow sports car screeched to a halt in front of them.

How she knew the precise moment to come get them, he'd never know.

Highlighted by the street lamps, the vehicle was as loud and unapologetic as its owner.

Jinx, with her signature wild red hair and a grin that could only mean trouble, leaned out the window.

"Hope you weren't planning on a covert operation," she joked, her eyes sparkling with mischief. "Because I only ride in style."

Stone couldn't help but grimace.

Jinx's energy was chaotic at the best of times, and today, he felt it clash with the turmoil within him as he and Ella got into the back seat.

They had packed hastily and given Jinx their luggage before heading to Alanna's—but Stone now questioned whose idea it was to ride with Jinx.

Trudie's calming presence offered a more grounded greeting as she said, "We've got everything ready. Diana's coordinates are locked into the GPS. Do you need anything else before we hit the road?"

Ella cast a wary glance at Jinx. "Maybe a less... *conspicuous* vehicle would've been better."

Jinx waved off the concern with a cackle. "Where's the fun in that? Besides, this baby can outrun anything."

Stone's body tensed, preparing for the inevitable havoc Jinx's driving would wreak on his already frayed nerves.

Ella glanced in his direction, her resolve clear, despite the uncertainty that lay ahead.

No sooner had they buckled up than Jinx hit the gas. The car lurched forward with a force that pressed them into their seats. The rush of the engine seemed to drown out the world, and for a moment, Stone's internal battle quieted, overtaken by the immediate thrill of speed.

However, the peace was short-lived.

Jinx, in her element, decided to crank up the

music, the heavy bass vibrating through the car like a second heartbeat.

Stone felt the curse stir, agitated by the noise—the *chaos*. Hell, the very essence of Jinx's presence, come to think of it. He fought to keep his hands to himself, wanting desperately to punch the radio in, so no more sound could come out.

Instead, he focused on finding the witches who did this to him.

They would find the *Breath of Selene*—and the witches. They'd force them to break the curse and then they'd elevate to—whatever the hell they were meant to elevate to.

Moon Wolves.

Prophecy players.

Whatever. He just wanted to be back to normal.

Then, they'd bring the fight to Andres.

Just as Stone began to acclimate to the cacophony and the rhythm of the road, Jinx's voice cut through the din. "Hold onto your seats, folks. I know a shortcut that'll get us there in no time. Who needs roads when you've got instinct?"

Before any of them could protest, Jinx veered off the main road onto a barely visible dirt track that wound through the dense forest. The car buckled and bounced over the rough terrain, eliciting a string of expletives from both Stone and Ella.

Ella, gripping the seat tightly, practically yelled over the music, "Jinx, this better not be one of your 'sidetracked scenic routes' that ends with us needing a tow truck—*or worse.*"

Jinx laughed, the sound almost maniacal against the backdrop of the wild ride. "Trust me, I've taken this path a dozen times. Nothing will go wrong."

Almost as if on cue, a low-hanging branch scraped against the side of the car, leaving a screech in its wake that had everyone wincing.

Clementine would've had a field day commenting on the irony of that statement, Stone thought grimly.

The shortcut, while shaving off time, did nothing for the tension that had built up in the car. If anything, it served as a physical manifestation of the unpredictability of their quest.

Yet, when they finally emerged onto the main road again, there was an undeniable sense of accomplishment, albeit mixed with relief and a touch of adrenaline-fueled exhilaration.

Ella shot Jinx a look that promised retribution, but Stone noticed her eyes also held a spark of amusement. "Next time, let's stick to the roads less likely to bounce us from the backseat."

Stone couldn't help but chuckle, the sound surprising even to him.

It was a momentary lapse, a brief respite from the curse's constant shadow. In the shared experience of Jinx's shortcut, there was a reminder of the strength they found in each other—in their unity against the odds.

As they sped down the road, the landscape blurring past them, Ella leaned over, her voice barely audible over the music. "Thank you," she said, her eyes meeting his. "For keeping it together. For being here, now. I can see you fighting it."

Stone managed a tight smile, the struggle within him momentarily easing under the weight of her gratitude.

Ella gave him a quick nod, the smile on her lips almost reaching her eyes.

The road stretched out before them, a ribbon of possibilities, of dangers untold and challenges yet to face. But in that moment, sealed within the cacophony of Jinx's making, Stone found a semblance of resolve.

They were moving forward, together, united against whatever awaited them. And for now, that was enough to keep the curse at bay—to keep him anchored to the man he wanted to be.

CHAPTER 14

ROAD LESS TRAVELED

The neon sign of the roadside motel flickers against the evening stars, casting an eerie glow on the dusty parking lot. It's one of those places that time let slip, clinging to the edges of a forgotten highway like a relic from a bygone era.

It wouldn't be my first choice—but out here, choices are hard to come by.

We've been on the road for what feels like an eternity, and the fatigue is starting to wear on all of us.

"Time to rest. My ass can't take another minute in this car," Jinx mutters, eyeing the motel with apprehension. Then, she flips the blinker on.

She's right. We're all exhausted, and with our destination still a good stretch away, pushing on through the night seems more reckless than brave.

In fact, we're still twelve hours away. Even with all

of us taking turns driving, we'll be lucky if we arrive by tomorrow evening.

Jinx pulls the car into the lot, and we all step out, stretching our legs and taking in the quiet of the night. The air is warm—a stark contrast to the air-conditioning of the car.

I catch Stone's gaze, and there's a question there, one that's been hovering between us since we left. While he's been insanely quiet—which is totally unlike him, it hasn't been a mutual sort of silence. I wish I could talk to him. Hell, hold his hand.

The curse has made everything between us so complicated, blurring lines and raising walls where there used to be open space.

"Do we get one room or two?" I ask, the words feeling heavy.

It's a practical question, but loaded with all the complexity of our current situation.

Stone looks at me, and I can see the weariness in his eyes.

"One room should be enough," he says after a moment, his voice steady. "It's just for a few hours. I'm pretty sure I can suffer through it."

I itch at my eyebrow, bristling at his words. I know it's the curse speaking for him, but it makes my heart plummet into my stomach all the same.

"Two beds, though," I say, needing to maintain some boundaries.

He agrees without hesitation, and there's an

unspoken understanding that passes between us. The curse has taken so much from us and twisted so many aspects of our lives, but right now, at this moment, it's about finding a way to coexist with it.

And apparently, that means making it through the night without wanting to stab him with a grapefruit spoon.

Trudie and Stone head into the motel office to get us rooms, while Jinx and I remain by the car. My gaze flits to the stars as I take a deep breath, hoping for some perspective.

She leans against her hood, fiddling with her phone. The night is quiet, the only sounds are the distant hum of the highway and the soft whisper of the desert wind.

"How you doing, girlie?" Jinx asks, not even looking up from her phone.

My gaze darts over to her and I swallow hard. "I don't know, Jinx."

She shoves her phone into her pocket and turns to face me. "Don't let him get to you."

"I'm not—" I begin, but clamp my lips shut at the expression on her face. "Okay, maybe a little. I just..." I sigh heavily. "Jinx, we were so close—I could feel the bond. The joy of our connection. And the sex was—"

A feline grin spreads across her face. "Good, huh?"

"It was." I fan myself, then cringe slightly, remembering those last few moments. "Until it wasn't."

Jinx pushes off the hood, her grin softening into

something more understanding. "The curse was nasty from the start?" she whispers.

"Yeah," I admit, feeling the weight of it all. "I can tell he's fighting it, but it's a struggle. He hasn't been as bad as those first few moments, but it's like walking a tightrope, and I never know when the wire's going to snap."

She steps closer, her voice dropping to a conspiratorial whisper. "Look, Ella, you guys are dealing with some heavy-duty, supernatural relationship crap. But don't forget, that connection you felt? That's real. And it's *strong*."

I chuckle dryly. "Feels like the curse is stronger."

"Maybe," Jinx concedes, leaning back against the car. "But I've seen you two. Together, you're like this unstoppable force. You'll find a way to beat it. Believe you me."

Her confidence is infectious, and despite everything, a tiny speck of hope flickers to life. "You really believe that?"

"Absolutely," she says, clapping a hand on my shoulder. "And hey, if you need a break from the brooding werewolf, you can always join me and little miss *harmony*. We can make it a girls' night—talk about all the ways we're going to kick this curse's ass."

The offer brings a genuine smile to my face, even if a part of me hopes I don't have to take her up on that offer. "Thanks, Jinx. That means a lot."

Just then, Trudie and Stone return with the keys and the moment is gone.

Trudie hands a key to Jinx with a nod, then turns to us. "They only had a couple of rooms left. Luckily, you guys are right next door to us."

"Hard to believe they're booked at all, considering this dump," Stone mutters.

He passes me our key and his hand brushes mine as he does. The contact sends a jolt through me, a reminder of how much has changed—and how much hasn't.

"We'll see you two in the morning, then," Jinx says, her tone implying an understanding of the delicate balance we're all trying to maintain. However, the look she gives me is to press home her alternative offer.

I nod and smile faintly.

Then, she and Trudie head to their room, leaving Stone and me standing awkwardly with our bags.

"Come on. May as well get some sleep," I say, leading the way.

As we head toward our room, I'm hyperaware of Stone's presence beside me. Everything feels so... *off.*

Stepping forward, I unlock our door and step inside our room. It's then that the reality of our situation settles in.

The space is cramped, with just enough room for two queen-size beds and a small table between them. Stone sets our bags down and sits on the edge of the furthest bed, dropping his head to his hands.

The room fills with a tension that begs to be broken.

I hesitate by the door, watching him. "Stone? Are you okay?"

He looks up, and I'm struck by the turmoil in his eyes. "I'm trying, Ella. To fight this... *thing*. But every time I think I'm making progress, it just..." His voice trails off and his frustration is evident.

I sit beside him, close but not touching even though a part of me longs to bridge that last gap. "I know you are, Stone. I see it, and it means everything to me."

But then, as if on cue, his expression hardens, and he stands abruptly, moving away.

"Well, maybe if you weren't so damn sensitive about everything, we'd actually get somewhere," he snaps, the harsh words slicing through the tentative peace we'd just started to build. "It's no wonder there are so few female Alphas."

His words, sharp and cold, slice through the tentative warmth that had begun to thaw some of the chill between us.

I feel like I'm on a see-saw.

My logical brain knows now this isn't Stone, but the hurt his words inflict still feels deeply personal.

Tears prickle in my eyes and I wrap my arms around myself, feeling a chill that has nothing to do with the desert night settling outside.

"Well, we should get some sleep," I murmur, getting up to go to the other bed.

Stone doesn't stop me, and the silence that follows is heavy with words best left unsaid.

In bed, I face away from him, the distance between us filled with the echo of his words. Those hurtful words spoken moments ago—and the first ones he spoke after we...

I brush away the tears, hoping like hell we can fix this before his words do irreparable damage.

Sleep is a long time coming, but when it finally does, it brings no peace.

UNDER THE CLOAK of an unnaturally vivid night, my consciousness tumbles into a realm shaped by whispers of moonlight.

I find myself wandering through a dense, mist-laden forest, where each breath I take is overloaded with a palpable, otherworldly energy.

The night sky, a canvas stretched wide and painted with the luminescence of an impossibly large moon, casts the world below in hues of silver and gold and it blurs the line between dream and reality.

Though, right now, I'm pretty sure I'm dreaming.

Despite the serene beauty that envelops me, a sense of anticipation clings to the air, as tangible as the mist that swirls around my feet. It's as if the very essence of the night is holding its breath, awaiting a moment of significant change.

In many ways, it feels similar to when Stone and I attempted to claim our bond.

The forest around me is alive with a muted symphony of nocturnal sounds, but it's the silence between them that draws me forward.

It's a silence filled with meaning—with purpose.

I'm compelled to move deeper into the heart of this dreamscape, guided by an innate understanding that something vital lies ahead.

It's calling to me and I must answer its beckoning.

As I navigate through the ancient trees, a clearing emerges, bathed in the direct glow of the moon. Here, the light converges, spotlighting a single point in the clearing that pulses with indescribable power.

Suspended within this column of light, a clear crystal orb hovers in mid-air. Its surface reflects the moon's brilliance and casts patterns of light that dance across the clearing.

Radiant and alive, the crystal seems to beat with the rhythm of the earth itself. An irresistible force pulls me toward it, a longing to connect, to understand—to possess.

My hand stretches out, fingers inching closer to the crystal, but as they near, the light intensifies, wrapping me in a brilliance that obliterates all sense of direction, time, and self.

A voiceless whisper fills my head—a message conveyed

not in words but in feelings, in knowledge imparted directly to my soul.

"The balance teeters... the Breath stirs... only the chosen can wield... beware the shadows that lurk..."

A shiver of foreboding runs through me as shadows begin to creep at the periphery of the clearing. It's a darkness that seeks to envelop—and to obscure.

It feels like the darkness that claimed our bond and stole it away.

The crystal's light, now a beacon in the encroaching gloom, stands as a solitary guard against the night's malevolent forces.

And I have no idea how to protect it.

Jolted awake, I find myself back in the dimly lit motel room, the remnants of the dream clinging to me like cobwebs.

Stone had mentioned a dream like this—one that felt more vivid and real than any other.

It was almost like a past life being remembered.

As I lie there in the darkness, the dream's message reverberating through my thoughts, a new realization dawns and it's chilling in its clarity.

The Breath of Selene isn't just a myth or a distant hope—it's *real*, and it's calling out to us. *Stone and me.*

But more than that, the dream has unveiled a truth I can't ignore. The path to claiming it—*to saving us all*

—is fraught with dangers far greater than we anticipated.

The shadows that lurked at the edge of the clearing, their presence menacing and familiar, weren't just part of the dream.

They were a warning.

CHAPTER 15

BETRAYAL & BONDS

ELLA

Dawn breaks with a gentleness that belies the turbulence of my thoughts as it paints the sky in pretty shades of pink and gold.

Birds chirp happily from a nearby tree as I sit outside on a rickety picnic table that seems as old as the motel itself. Witnessing the splendor, I cradle a cup of coffee in a tiny paper cup.

At this point, the coffee is more for warmth than taste because it's far too bitter for my liking. For all I know, it's three days old.

Because it's so early, the world around me is still hushed. I'm grateful for the quiet, for the space away from the room—away from Stone.

God, I never thought I'd feel that way.

After last night's harsh words, the distance feels necessary.

I mean, he basically told me I wasn't fit to be Alpha.

I've been out here since first light, my mind a whirlwind of thoughts about the dream, the Breath of Selene, and the ominous shadows.

It's a lot to process, and now that I'm fully awake, part of me wonders if the dream was just that—a dream and nothing more. But the intensity of it, the vividness, feels like a harbinger of something more—something *real*.

My only hope is it's not the warning I feared when I woke up.

I don't think I could take more bad news.

My phone lights up, then buzzes on the table in front of me.

It's a text from Alanna.

> Hey, Ella. Morning! I'm up, so feel free to call whenever.

I'd messaged her earlier—a habit born out of concern for the kids and the need to make sure they're safe. Especially now.

I dial her number and it only rings twice before she answers.

"Hi Ella, everything okay there?" she asks, her voice still groggy, but a welcome sound, nonetheless.

"Yeah, as okay as it can be," I reply, trying to infuse a bit of lightness into my voice. "How are the kids? How's everything on your end?"

"They're doing alright. Still sleeping, of course," Alanna responds, her voice clearing. "Asher's been a huge help around here—really stepping up. It's actually been nice. Avery... she's been a bit anxious, but given everything, it's not surprising."

I nod, even though she can't see me. "I'm glad they have you. And each other. I hope this trip goes quickly."

"They're strong kids, Ella. They're handling things in stride, all things considered." There's a pause on her end before she continues, "So, have you guys made it to your destination yet?"

I let out a sigh, my gaze drifting to the painted sky. "No, not yet. We've still got about twelve hours to go. If we're lucky, we'll be close by tonight."

"Wow, that's a long drive. Be safe, okay? And keep me posted."

"I will. Thanks, Alanna. Keep me posted, too. If you need anything, I'm just a call away," I say, exhaling a deep breath.

"You got it. Don't worry about us, though. We're good."

"I know," I say, relief and gratitude coursing through me.

Just as I'm about to end the call, Trudie steps out of her motel room, her expression serious. She makes her way straight to me. "Ella, Diana's on the line. She needs to talk to you."

My heart skips a beat. "I have to go, Alanna. I'll call you back later."

"Okay, good luck," she says, and then she's gone.

I take the phone from Trudie, my pulse quickening as I lift it to my ear. "Diana? What's going on?"

"Ella, I had a vision this morning," Diana begins without preamble. Her voice is steady, but there's an undercurrent of urgency that sets my nerves on edge. "It rocked me right out a dead sleep. I've been waiting ages for you to be ready to receive this call."

"Sorry, but what was it about?" I ask, glancing up at Trudie's concerned expression.

"It was about the Breath of Selene... and it came with a warning. A significant one."

I grip the phone tighter, bracing myself. "What kind of warning?"

Diana takes a deep breath, and I can almost hear her organizing her thoughts. "There's a magnetic quality about it now—something that's intensifying. It's waking up and wants to be found. Like it has its own consciousness."

I frown, confusion and concern knitting my brow as I glance over at Trudie, who takes a seat on the other side of the table, bathed in the soft light of dawn.

"It's part of the prophecy, isn't it? The Moon Wolf thing you and Stone seem to be wrapped up in?" Diana's question makes me sit up straighter. We hadn't discussed the prophecy with her. However, before I can say anything, she continues, "From what I got, it won't allow just anyone to acquire it. I think it wants someone *worthy.*"

I shake my head slightly. "Honestly, Diana, I don't know much about how any of this works. The prophecy wasn't exactly detailed instructions."

Diana's sigh crackles through the phone, a sound of frustration and concern mingled into one. "Typical. Well, based on what I sensed, acquiring it might involve a different plane of existence."

I blink hard, my gaze flitting again to Trudie.

"Have you ever gone to the astral realms?" Diana asks.

Astral realms?

The term is as foreign as it is intriguing and sends a ripple of curiosity through me.

"The astral plane? Diana, I'm not even sure what that means."

"Yeah, okay. It's... *complicated,*" she admits. "But it's something you might need to explore. The prophecy, this journey you're on—it's tied to powers and realms beyond the ordinary. Just keep an open mind, Ella. You and Stone might be capable of more than you realize, especially where the Breath of Selene is concerned. Hell, maybe all of it."

I nod slowly, digesting her words. It feels like we're stepping into a world that's larger and far more complex than I'd ever imagined.

It's like learning I was about to become a werewolf all over again.

"But," Diana interjects, pulling me back from the edge of my thoughts, "that's not the only reason I called. My vision... it was unsettling. There was this intense sense of... *betrayal*. Someone close is working against you. So, please, watch your back."

Betrayal?

The word sends a shiver down my spine, echoing the shadows and warnings from my own dream.

Is this a warning about Stone and the curse?

Or someone else?

"Did you see who it might be?" I ask, my heart thumping unevenly in my chest.

"No, I didn't. I'm sorry. The vision didn't reveal a face or a name. Just the imminent threat of it," Diana's voice is heavy with regret. "Sometimes that happens so you aren't derailed from your current trajectory. Or if they haven't yet made the decision to betray. However, it also means anyone could be a suspect. You need to tread carefully. This betrayal... it feels like it could unravel everything you're working toward if you're not careful."

The gravity of her words settles over me like a cold blanket of dread. My mind races, cycling through faces and names, wondering who could betray us—*and why*.

The mistrust Diana's warning sows is toxic, seeping into cracks I didn't know existed, and threatening to widen them into chasms.

I don't like the feeling. I don't like it at all.

"Thank you for telling me, Diana," I manage to say, though my voice sounds distant, even to my own ears. "We'll... We'll be careful."

"Good. That's what I want to hear. Reach out if you need anything. Trudie has my number," Diana says, then the line goes dead.

She's clearly not one to hang around when a conversation is over.

As I hand Trudie back her phone, the morning suddenly feels less peaceful.

We need to get moving.

Jinx's sudden laughter breaks through my contemplation, pulling me back to the present.

I turn to see her emerging from her room, stretching elaborately, her movements exaggerated and playful. She's donned what can only be described as a shockingly bright ensemble, even for her, as she hobbles her way over to us.

"Morning, sunshines! Ready to hit the road or what? We've got a prophecy to fulfill and a curse to kick in the crotch," she announces, striking a pose that's part superhero, part grandma in need of a cane.

I can't help but crack a smile, despite the heaviness in my heart.

"Yeah, we do," I agree, standing up. "Just give me a minute to wake Stone."

Her expression softens for a moment as she glances quickly to Trudie and back again.

"You got this, Ella. We've got your back, curse and all. And hey, if Stone gives you any trouble, just remind him who's the Alpha around here," she says with a wink, her tone light but firm.

Trudie grins, nodding in agreement.

However, her words only stir up Stone's venom from last night.

Taking a deep breath, I brace myself for the task ahead. Going back into that room and dealing with Stone right now feels like the last thing I want to do.

Yet, Jinx's words and Diana's warning—they all forge a resolve within me.

We have to move forward. *Fuck the obstacles.*

The Supermoon isn't going to wait for us and I have kids to get back to, dammit.

As I make my way to our hotel room, the key feels heavy in my hand. When I open the door, I expect to find Stone still asleep. Instead, I find him sitting on the edge of his bed, bags packed and ready by his feet.

He looks up, his emerald gaze a tumultuous sea of conflict and determination.

"Already up?" I say, trying to keep my tone neutral.

"Couldn't sleep," he replies curtly, his voice tinged with something I can't quite place.

There's a moment of silence as we both face-off, the space between us charged with unspoken words and tensions. It's like we're on the edge of a precipice and the stupid curse is a gust of wind ready to push us over.

"I talked to Diana again. She had a vision this morning," I start, hoping to bridge the gap between us, even slightly. "About the Breath of Selene... and she had a warning. She was getting vibes of betrayal and she—"

He stands abruptly, his movements sharp. "So, what? Let me guess—you think I'm going to be the one to stab you in the back?"

There's a challenge in his eyes, a defiance there begging to be called out.

"No," I answer quickly, *too* quickly maybe. Because it certainly crossed my mind. I sigh, dropping my gaze to the carpet, as I say, "But it has me on edge. It's hard to know what to believe—or who to trust."

When I look up, his gaze softens for a split second, hinting at the real Stone beneath the curse's shadow. "Ella, you know me—or at least, I thought you did. Do you really think I'd turn on you?"

I cross my arms, trying to mask the hurt. "The Stone I knew wouldn't. But this curse... It's making you say things, do things— You've turned once. How do I know you won't do it again when the time comes?"

"Fuck, that's not—" He cuts in, frustration evident in his voice. "Even cursed, I'm still *me*. Deep down, I'm me. I wouldn't hurt you or the kids. You have to believe that."

I want to believe him—I do. But Diana's warning

and my own dream cloud my judgment, casting long shadows of doubt.

"It's not just about you and me, Stone. It's about all of us. Diana's vision... it didn't specify who. Anyone could be the threat," I say, tugging my lips to one side.

He takes a step closer, his expression torn between anger and desperation. "But I'm still on the list, right?"

"It crossed my mind," I admit, hoping the honesty in my voice will bridge the distance between us.

A chuckle escapes him, bitter and laced with sorrow. "Great. Cursed and now a suspect of betrayal in my own mate's eyes. Fuck my life."

My heart aches to reach out for him—to console him.

"It's not like that, Stone," I say, softening. "We're just... on edge. All of us."

He runs a hand through his hair, tugging at the strands. "This is tearing us apart, Ella. It's only been a day and it's tearing us apart. How are we going to survive if we can't fix this? Hell, how are we supposed to fight something we can't even see?"

I sigh, feeling the weight of our situation. "Together. We fight it together. Despite the curse, the doubts, the warnings... We don't have a choice, Stone. We need to trust each other."

His gaze meets mine, intense and searching. "Do you trust me, Ella?"

The question hangs heavy in the air, charged with meaning.

After a moment of hesitation, I nod. "I do. Despite everything happening right now—*I do.*"

A small smile tugs at the corner of his lips. "Well, I guess that's something."

"Come on. We have a long trip ahead of us," I say, tipping my head toward the door.

Stone nods, picking up our bags and following me out.

As we leave the hotel room behind, my only hope is I didn't lie to Stone—that my trust for him can remain unshakeable.

Because I still feel our connection—*our bond*—nestled somewhere in the center of my chest.

I just pray I can continue to hang onto it.

CHAPTER 16

THE UNIVERSE DEMANDS AN APPOINTMENT

ELLA

Trees, cars, and cities whiz by as I rest my forehead against the cool glass and stare at it all—my gaze soft and barely registering anything but a blur of colors.

We've been on the road all day and my ass is thoroughly numb.

With the exception of the occasional pit stop to pee and stretch our legs, it's been nothing but nonstop driving.

It wouldn't be so bad if Stone weren't cursed—and if Jinx wasn't blaring heavy metal at an ear-bleeding decibel.

I mean, would it be so bad to listen to some Taylor Swift?

Instead, I've been left alone with my tumultuous thoughts and the need to recoil whenever Stone accidentally bumps into me or vice versa.

How did things get so messed up?

A week ago, his touch would have sent a flurry of butterflies through my abdomen and a surge of lust to my nether regions.

Now...

I sigh heavily.

Okay, it still does that but it's overshadowed by a layer of hurt and confusion.

"Would you stop doing that?" Stone says, pulling me from my internal dialogue and reminding me why this road trip sucks ass.

I pull my head from the glass and look over my shoulder at him. "Do what? I've barely said a word to you."

"You've been sighing like someone shot your dog," he fires back. "It's annoying."

"I don't have a dog." I blink at him with zero amusement.

He shakes his head and turns his attention to his own window. "Whatever."

That one word sends my skin crawling.

It was the same thing Troy used to say to me when he was sick of talking or just simply didn't deem my opinion worthy of discussion.

My irritation flares at his dismissal, a raw, primal part of me reacting before my mind can catch up. My voice comes out, coated with the authority I seldom use outside of pack matters—a command that slices through the tension in the car like a cold blade.

"Stone," I say, my tone sharp, demanding his attention. "Look at me."

He turns, a mix of surprise and something else—perhaps resentment—flashing in his green eyes.

But he listens, he *has* to.

That's the power of the Alpha voice, a tool I use sparingly—and never on him.

And now, in the past two days, I've done it twice.

For a moment, the curse seems to recede, leaving the man I know, *the man I love,* looking back at me. His posture straightens—an automatic response to the Alpha command.

I suppose it's a testament to the bond between us and the hierarchy that ties it all in place.

It's both reassuring and heartbreaking.

Regardless of what the curse has taken from us, at least it hasn't severed that.

I wish I could Alpha command him out of the curse. That would be handy but I instinctively know it doesn't work like that.

Eventually, the curse would take hold again and we'd be back to square one.

However, I instantly regret using that tone when I see the way his jaw clenches and the brief flicker of hurt in his eyes before he schools his expression into one of indifference.

"Sorry," I say, softer this time. "I didn't mean to snap. I'm just... *frustrated.* Not with you, but with this whole situation."

He looks away, the tension not quite leaving his shoulders, but he nods. "I know. Me too."

We ride in silence after that, the weight of the curse between us like a fifth passenger. But at least now, he seems a bit more present—a bit less asshole.

Not even Trudie tries to lighten the mood with her harmony-making skills.

Maybe we're beyond that now.

"Hey, guys, we're about five minutes out," Jinx announces as she turns down the god-awful music.

Five minutes out from *where*, exactly?

Diana's directions were cryptic at best, guiding us through coordinates and feelings rather than clear destinations.

Since we raced out as soon as we got the details, I have no idea what to expect.

Will we even know it when we see it?

As we continue down the road, the landscape shifts—the mundane blurs of cities and trees giving way to the stark, breathtaking expanses of the desert.

The air outside feels charged, even from within the confines of the car. It's a stark contrast to the heaviness that's been following us.

For a while, I almost thought we were driving to the city the kids and I used to live in. The route was damn near identical, but instead of heading to Hesperia, we kept on going.

I mean, it was a long shot, but with how weird this summer has been, anything was possible.

Trudie shuts off the music entirely as everyone focuses on the GPS navigation guiding us on the screen of Jinx's phone.

However, it doesn't take a genius to see where it's leading us.

A white, domed structure comes into view, sitting in stark contrast against the backdrop of the desert and the darkening sky.

It's so out of place, yet utterly fascinating.

"What in the world is that thing?" I murmur, leaning forward to get a better look.

"That, my friends, is the Integratron," Jinx announces, her tone now full of wonder and a hint of reverence I've never heard from her before. "I've heard of it, but never been here. Guess I can scratch it off my bucket list now."

She slows the car as we pull off the road, giving us a better view of the structure. It's unlike anything I've ever seen—part science fiction, part spiritual retreat— *if the sign means anything.*

"Integratron?" I repeat, the name feeling alien on my tongue. "Why are we here?"

Jinx parks the car, and we all step out, stretching our legs and taking in the sight before us. The air outside is alive with energy and it makes the hairs on the back of my neck stand on end.

"This is where the coordinates Diana gave us lead. There must be something about this place—the energies here... Whew, they're something, that's for sure. It must be important for whatever comes next," Trudie says, her tone coming out in hushed reverence. "I wonder if we'll find the Breath of Selene inside?"

"Yeah, because the Breath of Selene is going to be in some space age boob in the middle of the desert," Stone blurts, skepticism clear in his voice.

"There's only one boob I see here," Jinx says, giving Stone the stink eye.

He simply rolls his eyes and flips her off.

"Anyway," Jinx continues, leading us closer to the domed building. "If I remember right, the Integratron is built on a geomagnetic vortex. It's supposed to be a place of healing, rejuvenation, and... well, they say time travel and accessing other dimensions. Who knows about all that hooey without some experimentation, but one thing's for sure, it's all about the vibes."

"Time travel?" Trudie gasps, her voice tinged with incredulity, but it's clear the surrealness of it all intrigues her as much as it unnerves her. "Are we here to take a trip to the future or the past?"

"Beam me up, Scotty," Stone snickers under his breath.

Jinx claps her hands, ignoring Stone and drawing our attention back to her as she begins walking toward the Integratron's entrance. "Maybe it's not about the when but the *where*, and the *how*. This place, with its unique energies, might help us unlock or understand something crucial about the Breath of Selene. I mean, it must, since Diana sent us here. She's not in the game of wild goose chases."

I follow her, still processing the cascade of information and the potential implications. Diana did mention keeping an open mind—maybe accessing the astral realm or something. Right?

I turn back to the group and say, "But why here? She must have sensed something specific about this place. Maybe it's not just about healing or bizarre energy theories. Maybe it's about harnessing these energies for our specific needs."

Trudie nods thoughtfully, falling into step beside me. "Like a conduit or a... amplifier for whatever we're supposed to do next?"

"Exactly what I was noodling," Jinx says as we all walk up to the structure. "And there's talk about this place aligning perfectly with various celestial bodies—it amplifies geomagnetic forces which, who knows, might just be what we need to combat the curse or understand the Breath better. Especially with the incoming Supermoon thrown into the mix."

Reaching the door, Jinx's confident stride halts abruptly as she rattles the handle, only to find it firmly locked. Her brows furrow in confusion, then lift in an 'oh-well' manner.

"Well, poop," she exclaims, turning back to us with a shrug. "Looks like the universe demands an appointment. Diana could have at least warned us about that."

Stone raises an eyebrow, a smirk tugging at his lips despite the tension between us. "So much for our grand entrance into the unknown. You know I could just bust the door open."

"Let's not cause any unnecessary commotion just yet," Trudie advises with a shake of her head.

Jinx fishes out her phone with a flourish. "Fear not, my skeptical friends. This modern shaman has just the trick—*Google*." She taps away, her fingers a blur of movement. "Let's see if they're open tomorrow for enlightened visitors or if we've just hit a mystical dead end and need to rely on super-strength *boob* over here."

Trudie leans closer, trying to peek at Jinx's screen. "Do they even list 'geomagnetic vortexes' on Yelp?"

I can't help but laugh at the absurdity of the situation. Here we are, standing in the middle of the desert, banking on a building that looks like a giant's hat—because I will not call it a boob—for answers. And possibly, *solutions*.

"Good news, they're open this time of the year. Bad news, it looks like destiny has us on hold until tomorrow if we want to say on the down low," Jinx says, flipping through her phone with a frown.

"So, what's the plan? Camp out under the stars?" Trudie asks, surveying the area.

Jinx's eyes light up and she claps her hands. "Oh, that's the best damn idea I've heard you come out with."

No wonder she founded *The Sidetracked Scene.*

She's *literally* all about it.

I shoot her a look—the kind that says *'in what universe?'*

"As much as I appreciate the allure of desert stars, Jinx, I'm more of a glamping girl, and I don't see any yurts with king-sized beds and AC around here," I say, trying not to sound too harsh.

The truth is, after everything, the last thing I want is to spend a night outside, exposed and vulnerable. I might be a werewolf, but I'm not an idiot.

Stone chuckles darkly.

"Well, shoot." Trudie nods in agreement. "Let's find a hotel. There's got to be something around here. Even a motel like the last one will do."

Jinx sighs, pocketing her phone with a theatrical show of disappointment. "Fine, fine. But just so you know, we're missing out on a prime opportunity for alien encounters and mystical desert revelations."

"Aliens can wait," I say, already heading back to the car. "Right now, a shower and a bed sound about as mystical as I want to get."

However, as I get closer to the car, something makes me pause. A familiar scent that wafts by but is gone before I can place it.

God, I must be losing my mind.

I turn, eyeing the space for a moment as everyone stares expectantly at me.

"Sorry," I mutter, shaking my head.

As we pile back into the car, relief and anticipation start to settle under my skin.

Relief that we're heading toward the comfort of civilization, and anticipation for what tomorrow at the Integratron might bring. It's this strange juxtaposition of the mundane and the extraordinary that seems to define our journey.

At least now we know what we're looking for.

Jinx starts the car, and as we pull away from the Integratron, I catch one last glimpse of the dome under the rising moonlight. It stands silent and enigmatic—like a sentinel waiting for the right moment to reveal its secrets.

But as the desert fades behind us and the lights of a small town begin to twinkle in the distance, one question remains, lingering in the air like the dust we leave behind...

What are we walking into?

And more importantly...

Will we be the same when we walk out?

CHAPTER 17

PROXIMITY

STONE

S tone's agitation was a palpable force, thickening the air as they stood in the brighter, cleaner lobby of their new hotel. This place was a stark contrast to the seedy motel they had endured the previous night, with its welcoming lights and the promise of comfortable beds.

But comfort was the furthest thing from Stone's mind.

Hell, he didn't even know if it was possible to be comfortable anymore. It had only been a couple of days since this stupid curse took root but it felt like centuries trying to keep it at bay.

He was acutely aware of Ella standing close but not close enough—her presence was both necessary— like the air he breathed—and a source of deep frustration.

The curse pulsed within him like a second, discordant heartbeat. His connection to her urged him toward her, while the curse simultaneously drove a wedge of rage and resentment between them.

He knew another night loomed ahead—a night filled with the torment of being so near, yet so far.

The thought was fucking unbearable.

The clerk behind the desk offered them a smile, unaware of the tension that simmered beneath the surface. "We have a variety of rooms available. Would you two be needing one suite, or...?"

Before Ella could respond, Stone cut in, his voice sharper than he intended. "Separate rooms."

His gaze didn't meet Ella's—couldn't meet it. Not at first. The turmoil inside him was too great, the fear of what he might say—or worse, *do*—under the curse's influence was a constant shadow that loomed over him.

Ella shot him a quick look, a mix of surprise and something else—*disappointment, perhaps?*—flashing across her face before she masked it with a nod toward the clerk. "Yes, separate rooms please."

The clerk nodded, tapping away at the computer, oblivious to the charged exchange. Stone's hands clenched at his sides, each click of the keyboard echoing in the silence that had fallen between him and Ella.

When they received their key cards, Stone's were

practically thrown at him, his own agitation mirrored in the stiff set of Ella's shoulders.

That was fine. He deserved it, he supposed.

Jinx and Trudie exchanged a significant glance, but thankfully, kept their mouths shut.

The silence that enveloped them as they walked to their respective rooms was suffocating—each step heavier than the last.

Stone knew he was the problem and yet he couldn't bring himself to outwardly care. However, that didn't stop him from wishing he could kick his own ass.

When they reached their row of rooms, Jinx turned to Ella with a grin that didn't quite reach her eyes. "Hey, if you need us, we're just a scream away. *Literally*. I plan to watch every alien abduction documentary I can find tonight."

"Oh, joy," Trudie muttered under her breath, but her eyes crinkled at their edges.

Ella managed a weak smile, the strain around her own eyes softening momentarily. "Thanks, Jinx. Just make sure to keep the volume down, or you might get abducted by an angry hotel guest instead. And I'll be the first with the pitchforks."

Their laughter, a brief respite, filled the space between them. But as Jinx and Trudie headed to their room, the laughter faded, leaving Stone and Ella enveloped in the pregnant silence.

He turned toward his room, the key card heavy in

his hand, and took a deep breath, bracing himself for another night of battle against the darkness.

"Night, Stone," Ella said from the doorway of her room.

Her lips were pressed tight but she didn't linger or wait for his response before vanishing inside her room. He should be grateful because God knows what would come flying out of his mouth anyway.

Inside his room, the walls felt too close, the space too confined.

He was alone but far from peaceful.

The curse gnawed at him, a relentless presence that filled the room with its dark whispers and it was driving him insane.

A sudden need for air, *for space,* propelled him to grab his keycard and head outside. He didn't bother telling any of them where he as going. He'd deal with the repercussions later, if it came to that.

The night was cooler now, and the sky a tapestry of stars, but Stone barely noticed.

His thoughts were consumed by Ella, by the curse, and by a desperate need to find a way to break it.

As he walked, the faint buzz of the city nightlife mingled with the distant chirp of crickets, and Stone found his steps slowing, each one a deliberate movement. He wasn't sure where he was going, only that he needed to walk—*to move*—to somehow outpace the chaos swirling inside him.

This was worse than when he was ousted from the

pack with the knowledge of who and what kind of man Silas was.

It was a new kind of hell if he was honest.

Now, not only did he feel disconnected from his pack, but he was also disconnected from his alpha—*and his mate.* Even though she was right there, sometimes even within touch. That is, when she didn't recoil from it or he didn't put his foot in his damn mouth.

That was fucking unbearable. It broke his heart each and every time.

The farther he walked from the hotel—and from Ella—the lighter the oppressive weight of the curse seemed to be. It was as though he could breathe again and he wasn't sure how he felt about that.

In fact, it was a startling realization—one that halted him mid-stride.

Was it her proximity that intensified the curse's grip?

The thought twisted in his gut, both a relief and a new kind of agony.

If distance eased the curse's hold, what did that mean for them? For what they had—*or could have had*—without this damn affliction?

No, he refused to believe they'd be stuck with this curse. They'd find a way to end it.

They *had* to.

Stone's footsteps resumed, slower now—more contemplative. A small park appeared ahead, bathed in the soft glow of street lamps, offering a bench that seemed as good a place as any to unravel the knot of thoughts that plagued him. He sank onto the bench, the cool metal a sharp contrast to his heated skin, and let out a long breath.

It was strange. From here, he could feel the bond that connected him to Ella so vividly. It was a vibrant thread that hummed with life.

This connection, this undeniable bond, was what made everything so complicated. It was supposed to be a source of strength—*of unity*. Instead, it had become a twisted lifeline, pulling him in with promises of warmth only to push him away with bursts of cold fury.

Stone leaned back, his gaze lifting to the stars.

"What are you trying to do to me?" he whispered into the night, half-expecting the curse or fate itself to answer.

The silence that followed was profound. It was the kind of quiet before a storm, or perhaps the stillness of a battlefield after the fighting has ceased.

The realization that he could think more clearly and felt more like himself away from her was a bitter pill to swallow.

He loved Ella, more than he'd ever loved anyone or anything, and yet, here he was, paradoxically finding solace in the distance between them.

Was the curse designed to make him isolate himself—to push away the one person who mattered most? Or was it a twisted test, seeing how far he could bend their bond before it broke?

Stone's fingers curled into fists, the frustration at his situation, at his own helplessness, simmering just below the surface.

"How do I protect her from something I can't control?" he murmured, the question hanging in the air unanswered.

The real question was: *how does he protect Ella from himself?*

The night stretched on, and Stone remained on the bench, lost in his thoughts.

As the waxing moon climbed higher, casting long shadows across the park, Stone knew this battle was far from over. But for the first time in a long while, he felt a glimmer of clarity—maybe, just maybe, he could find a way to fight back, to reclaim the life the curse was trying to steal from him.

But as he finally stood, ready to make his way back to the hotel, a lingering fear echoed in his mind.

What if he couldn't find the answers they needed before the curse consumed him completely?

Or was he destined to lose himself—*and Ella*—along the way?

Was this a part of the prophecy?

That grand, final sacrifice it talked about?

Walking back to the hotel, the streets empty and quiet, Stone's thoughts drifted to their mating. He hadn't thought about it at all. Not once since the curse took hold.

How odd was it that the distance provided the momentary insight for that kind of reflection?

When they were in the act—it had felt like the claiming of the century. Hell, *the millennium.*

It was a moment of pure connection and profound love.

And it was all he had ever wanted.

They had been so close, not just physically, but in every way that mattered.

And then, as if someone had flipped a switch, the darkness of the curse consumed him, turning what should have been an endless source of strength and happiness for them both into his greatest source of pain.

Ella's too, if the look in her eyes was any indication.

Who would do this? Who would curse him— *and why?*

Shouldn't they be hunting them down?

Even if it had been the witches—what was the *purpose* of it?

It just didn't make sense.

Was Andres trying a new tactic? Something to unsettle and separate them so he could take control of Black Crater?

That didn't make sense either. Why not just start there?

Why do all the mind games with Troy?

The questions swirled in his mind, each one a torment of its own. The curse didn't just threaten his relationship with Ella. It threatened his very essence, *his soul*.

It was a precision strike against his happiness and his future.

Returning to the hotel, the building loomed large and unwelcoming. Stone paused at the entrance, taking a moment to steel himself against the turmoil that awaited him inside his own room—inside his own mind.

With a heavy heart, he entered the building. Inside his hotel room, the weight of his solitude and the rush of the curse's presence were more oppressive than ever.

Yet, as he lay in the dark, staring at the ceiling, an idea began to form—a desperate plan, perhaps, but one that offered a glimmer of hope.

If proximity to Ella intensified the curse's effects, then perhaps understanding the curse's mechanics, as well as its origins, could lead to a solution. Much like finding the vaccine in the ailment itself.

Maybe there was a way to turn the curse's power against itself, to use their bond—the very thing the curse sought to corrupt, as a weapon to break free.

But such thoughts were dangerous.

They carried the risk of true hope, and with hope came the potential for despair.

Yet, what choice did he have?

To do nothing was to accept defeat—to let the curse win. Stone wasn't ready to give up—not on himself, and certainly not on Ella.

He would fight.

For Ella, for their future, he would fight the curse with everything he had.

CHAPTER 18

IDGAF

ELLA

I must be entering my IDGAF era because I. Don't. Give. A. Fuck.

Caged in my hotel room alone, I've been standing in the dark, staring out the window for far too long. Thanks to our bond and my stupid werewolf hearing, I knew Stone was leaving the hotel and telling no one.

Not even me.

The moment he was no longer in the vicinity, it was like all of the air had been sucked out of my lungs. Every breath since then has been a struggle, each one a labor through thick, unseen waters, and my skin prickles with a restless energy I can't quell.

The reasonable side of me—the human Ella who calculates every decision like a mom juggling her kids' extracurriculars—has been shoved into a corner by this wild, new presence clawing its way out. The wolf inside me is prowling, snarling against the confines of my skin, and all because he *dared* to leave when every instinct screamed for him to stay close.

How very dare he?

The thought ricochets through my skull like a bullet, leaving rage in its wake. The silence in the hotel room amplifies every subtle sound, turning the clock's ticking into a taunt and the distant laughter from another room into a sneer. I can even make out Jinx's chuckles at whatever alien documentary she's watching and it makes me want to hurl my lamp at the wall.

The horrendously wallpapered walls close in, a physical manifestation of the pressure building inside my chest. Whatever this is, it's not just anger—it's a betrayal that stings sharper than any wound I've ever nursed and I can't even process why.

Instead, I give into the indignation, letting it consume me—no longer willing to play nice about all that's happening.

Fate is a fucking asshole.

As minutes morph into hours, the tension knots deeper. My pacing wears a figurative trench in the carpet. Back and forth, back and forth—a relentless metronome of rising fury.

Why isn't he here? Where the *fuck* did he go?

Each step hammers home a growing list of accusations, each more unreasonable than the last, but I can't stop them. They feed the fury, and the fury feeds the wolf.

Outside, the night deepens, shadows stretching across the ground like dark fingers. The moon hangs low, a silent witness to my unraveling. In its light, I see my reflection in the window—a wild-eyed, barely recognizable version of myself.

The sight should startle me—force me to take stock and calm down, but it doesn't.

It fuels me.

I grab my phone, a lifeline to sanity I should reach for, but my fingers tremble with such ferocity that I nearly drop it. Texts and missed calls from my kids go unchecked. The thought of speaking to anyone else, of having to pretend even for a minute that I'm not coming undone, is unbearable.

I throw the phone down, watching it bounce on the bed and crash against the lamp on my nightstand.

Good, let it break. *Let everything break.*

The sounds of drunk singing and laughter float up from the street below—taunting, *mocking*.

Envy mixes with my anger.

How can the world continue to spin so indifferently?

Don't they feel it?

I tug at my hair, desperate to release this tension. I've faced off against rivals and enemies with a cold precision, never once losing my cool like this.

What's happening to me?

This ache—this void expanding inside me with each second he's away.

My thoughts spiral, dark and uncontrollable—and even though I can acknowledge it, I can't seem to stop them.

I imagine Stone, out there somewhere, possibly laughing just like those drunk people—carefree and distant.

Does he feel this tension, this gnawing emptiness? Or is it just me, tethered alone to a curse that feels more like a noose with every breath?

I pace faster, the energy within me a cyclone that needs to wreak havoc—to explode. I'm a caged animal, and the cage is my own skin—my own failing resolve.

He should be here, *fixing this*. Not leaving me to drown in a sea of my own tumultuous emotions.

And then, as if summoned by my rage, I hear the sound of his footsteps in the hallway—his return not a moment too soon but ages too late. My heart, which should leap with relief, instead pounds with fierce determination.

This isn't over. Oh, no.

It's just beginning.

As his key card clicks against his door, I steady myself.

Tonight, I don't plan to hold back.

Tonight, he will hear everything—every raw, unfiltered truth my raging heart can hurl at him.

Because I. Don't. Give. A. Fuck.

Not anymore.

When I hear the door to his room click shut, my body tenses and my heart beats a furious tattoo against my ribs.

I should go over there.

Right now, I should—

My anger loses some of its steam and for some reason, that pulls me up short.

It's still there.

The rage.

The acrimony desperately wants to be let out to play.

But I can't move.

For minutes—hell, maybe hours, I stand there.

Then, his door opens and I sense him moving again. This time, toward me.

The sound of his footsteps approaching my door feels like a countdown—each one reverberating through the charged silence of the corridor.

By the time his knock finally sounds, it's almost a relief—*almost.*

It kicks something loose in me and I'm on the move.

I wrench the door open, and there he stands—a mix of shadow and light, his face drawn tight with lines of worry that only fuel my anger.

"What do you want, Stone?" I snap, not even bothering to hide the edge in my voice.

Stone's eyes, usually so calm and reassuring—at least before all of this bullshit—now reflect the storm brewing between us.

"Ella, we need to talk," he says, his voice a strained whisper that somehow pierces the tension.

"Talk?" I scoff, folding my arms over my chest. "*Now* you want to talk? You request a separate room, walk out without telling anyone, and *now* you decide it's time to talk?"

The disbelief and hurt tangle together, making my words sharper—harsher.

He takes a deep breath, visibly bracing himself against the barrage. "I know how it looks, but you have to understand—being close to you right now... It's not helping. This curse is—"

"Torture?" I cut in, my voice rising with each word. "You think I don't know that? You think I don't feel it too? But maybe that's the point, Stone. Maybe we're supposed to feel this, to *fight* through it, not run from it."

He steps forward, closing the gap I'd been guarding so fiercely. His presence envelops me, the familiar scent of him—pine and storm—washing over me, stirring a mix of anger and longing that I hate and crave in equal measure.

My resolve slips just a little bit.

"I'm not running," he practically growls, pushing me against the wall. I groan at the contact, but it ignites something else inside me—a fire that burns beneath the surface. Then, shaking off his flare of aggression, his hands lift to cup my face, his touch a spark to my dry tinder. "I'm trying to protect you—from myself, from this curse, and from the way it makes me want to claim you in ways that might..."

His words trail off, but his eyes burn into mine, dark and intense.

"Claim me?" I echo, my breath catching, my body leaning into his touch despite my agitation. "That's what you were doing when this stupid curse was triggered. As I recall, the thought of claiming me *disgusted* you."

Another growl rumbles through his chest and the animal in him is back as he leans in, his voice low, "Do *you* really believe that?"

He presses his hips closer, grinding his erection against my hipbone and a burst of lust rolls through me. This is not a side of Stone I've seen come out to play before and it's messing with my head.

"Maybe?" I admit, but my resolve is faltering at his proximity.

He drops his hand to mine and forces me to cup him. "I might say stupid shit, but my body can't lie, Ella. Not to you."

I huff a breath, desperate for the air to fill my lungs since he joined me in this room. My fingertips squeeze and he pulls my hand away with a low string of verbal curses.

"I just want to protect you—" he says, his voice a low whisper as his gaze drops to my lips.

"I can protect myself, Stone. I don't need you to do it for me. Alpha here, remember?" The challenge in my voice matches the defiant lift of my chin, despite the way my body warms beneath his fingertips.

A smirk slides across his lips, but he doesn't say anything.

"You don't believe me?" I spit back. "Oh, that's right. I don't *deserve* to be Alpha. I forgot."

His thumb strokes my cheek, a soft contradiction to the tension binding us. "Ella, this curse, whatever it is, it's tearing at me. One second I'm good—*I'm me.* The next, I want to fight against you and make you hate me so I can get more distance between us. When we're together, I can't always fight off the words that come out of my mouth and I hate it. It's *miserable.*"

"Being apart is miserable. It's messing with my head. It's—" I lick my lips. "I feel like you don't want me. Like everything we were building is..."

His nostrils flare and his eyes dart back to my lips. "Ella, I *want* you. I want us to—"

"Then prove it," I interrupt, my voice low, dangerous with an offer that tempts and terrifies me in the same breath.

For a long heartbeat, we stand there, locked in a stand-off of wills and desires, the air thick with unsaid words and unspent passion.

Then, impulsively, recklessly, he closes the last of

the distance between us. His lips crash against mine with a desperation that borders on possession—a claiming that has nothing to do with curses and everything to do with the desperate need we both feel.

The kiss is a clash—a storm of teeth and tongues, and a battle we are both determined to win and lose in equal measure.

Stone's hands slide back into my hair, pulling slightly, tilting my head back to deepen the kiss. The sting is sweet, sparking a thrill that shoots through my nerves as it lights up the dark corners of desire I'd forced into submission.

His other hand traces a searing path down my spine, pressing me closer against him until there is no space for doubts, just the overwhelming sense of being consumed.

Our breaths mingle, ragged and hot, feeding the flames that each touch stokes. My hands find his chest, pushing not to separate but to feel the solid reality of him beneath my palms.

God, I've missed this. Missed *him*.

The room spins slightly. The walls echo with the low growls that escape him and the soft whimpers that I can't hold back.

This isn't just a kiss—it's a battle for control, a desperate clash of lips and teeth where each retreat feels as devastating as a surrender—and every advance tastes like victory.

But as quickly as the storm rises, it breaks.

Stone's lips slow their fervent assault, the pressure easing as his kisses turn from demanding to almost stilted. The sudden shift leaves me reeling, my heart pounding against the cage of my ribs, desperate for something I can't name because I've lost all semblance of words.

He pulls back just enough to look at me, his eyes dark pools of emotion that I'm afraid to drown in.

"Ella," he whispers, his voice rough with the remnants of our storm. "I—"

"No," I cut him off, stepping away—the air between us a cold shock after the heat. "Don't."

I can't hear his excuses, not now. Not when my body is still humming with the imprint of his touch. Not when my lips still burn with the memory of his and my body wants him desperately inside me.

He frowns, the lines around his eyes deepening in confusion—or is it pain? "Ella, I'm trying to—"

"Don't you *dare* say protect me."

He takes a step forward, his hand reaching out as if to bridge the gap I've put between us. "It's not that simple."

"Make it simple," I challenge, my voice steadier than I feel. "Tell me this is what you want. Tell me you're not just reacting to whatever this curse makes you feel."

His hand drops to his side, and he looks away, a muscle ticking in his jaw. "I can't," he admits, and it feels like a blow to my chest.

"Great," I say, nodding to myself, the sting of tears prickling in my eyes.

"I don't trust myself with you," he says, his voice barely audible over the ringing in my ears. "Not like this. Not until we figure out how to break this curse. What if I hurt you? I couldn't—"

I stare at him, my heart breaking under the weight of his words. The room feels colder now, emptier.

"Then maybe you should go back to Black Crater," I say, the words tasting like ash in my mouth.

His eyes snap to mine, hurt flashing across his features before it's quickly masked. "Is that what you want?"

I want to scream that it's not, that I want him to stay, to fight through this with me. But the fear and the uncertainty hold my true feelings hostage.

"I don't know what I want," I confess, my voice breaking. "But I can't do this."

Stone nods slowly, a resigned acceptance setting into his posture. "I'll go if that's what you need."

It's not what I need, but maybe it's what *we* need.

To find our footing again.

As he turns to leave, a part of me wants to call him back, to rewind and replay this all differently.

But I don't.

Instead, I watch him walk away, each step echoing like a finality in my heart, leaving me alone with the echoes of what might have been.

CHAPTER 19
ON THE THRESHOLD
STONE

S tone woke a few short hours later to a morning draped in silence. The sunlight barely filtered through the blackout curtains of his hotel room and somehow, that seemed appropriate.

Despite the quiet, a cacophony of last night's words and actions replayed in his mind.

After the clarity from his walk, they'd all but thrown down and nearly had some sort of hate-sex. Hell, he'd been so close to stripping her bare and showing her exactly why she should stay away.

But something odd had happened.

She'd met his anger, his volatility with her own. She'd been upset—*pissed*.

And she was right there with him.

She wouldn't have hated it. He could see it in her eyes.

She *wanted* it.

She would have *enjoyed* it.

Somehow, that scared him enough to pull back.

Then he had offered to leave if she needed him to, but the proposition now hung between them like a specter.

Is that what she'd be expecting today?

As he dressed, thoughts of departure tangled with a deep-seated reluctance to untwine his life from hers. The impending visit to the Integratron was supposed to give them answers, and yet for Stone, it loomed as a battleground for hidden truths and suppressed feelings.

This thing between him and Ella was reaching a breaking point. He just wasn't sure which one of them would break first.

Exiting his room, the corridor stretched out as he walked to the lobby. It was a physical manifestation of the distance he felt growing between him and Ella.

He spotted her by the coffee counter, her posture stiff as she conversed with Jinx and Trudie. The mere sight of her tightened something in his chest—a blend of longing and regret.

Jinx caught him in her gaze as he approached. Her expression bordered on concern and her usual sharpness that missed nothing.

"There you are, Stone," she called out, her voice cutting through the stillness. "Ready for a day of energy realignment or whatever they claim happens at that dome?"

Stone glanced from Jinx to Ella, the unspoken question settling between them.

Does she want him to go?

Ella's nostrils flared and her jaw set but she didn't say anything. Instead, she simply watched him in expectation.

Jinx's eyes flicked between him and Ella, then back again. "You two okay?" she teased, her voice light but her gaze sharp. "You're giving off some serious doom-and-gloom vibes. And while you know I love a bit of doom, I don't think that's the vibe we want amplified at the Integratron."

Trudie, holding her coffee to her chest, gave Jinx a look of agreement. "Jinx is right. What's going on? You both look like you've been through the wringer and feel like you need me to take you out back for a Reiki session."

Their differing approaches to the situation brought Stone a brief, wry smile, but it quickly faded as he focused on the matter at hand.

"It was a rough night," he admitted, his voice heavy with the weight of his thoughts and the memories tangled in Ella and their explosive tension.

Jinx leaned in, her eyes gleaming with mischief. "Oh, rough night, huh? Do tell. We've got all the time in the world, and I've got all the curiosity."

Trudie gave Stone a sympathetic look, her voice soothing as she said, "You don't have to share, Stone.

But if you want to, remember, talking things through can help clear the air. Maybe we can help?"

Stone took a deep breath, the battle inside him evident. "Ella and I are trying to navigate some... complicated dynamics."

Ella nodded slightly. "Exactly. This curse is exhausting, and we're just trying to figure out if there's a way through it."

Her eyes found his and held them for a beat. The intensity in their depths made Stone uneasy.

What was she trying to say without saying it?

He wished she'd use their mental connection to fill him in.

Jinx clapped her hands together. "Well, this sounds like a proper curse conundrum! Makes my old chaos heart flutter."

Trudie shot Jinx a disapproving glance before turning back to Stone with a comforting smile. "I'm sure today's visit to the Integratron will help, even if just a little. It's a place meant for healing, right? Maybe it will offer some insights, or, at the very least, some peace."

Jinx chuckled. "Or stir up more chaos if they don't untuck their chins from their drawers. But I guess, sometimes things need to get worse before they get better."

Trudie huffed a soft laugh, shaking her head as they all fell into a yawning silence.

Ella finally spoke up, her voice steady but carrying

an undercurrent of something fragile. "Stone," she began, her eyes holding his in a direct gaze that didn't waver. "I think you should come with us today. We need to figure this out. The Integratron might help us understand the Breath of Selene better and maybe the curse, too. I mean, that's why we're here, right? We can't lose sight of that."

Stone felt a flicker of surprise, mixed with a cautious relief. Her invitation was a bridge, however tentative, and he took a moment to consider it.

The thought of spending another day in close proximity to her was both daunting and necessary. It was a chance to see if the mysterious healing properties of the Integratron could offer them any insight.

"Are you sure?" he asked, his voice low.

The last thing he wanted was to impose more tension on an already strained situation.

Ella nodded. "Yes, I'm sure. Whatever is happening between us, we can't ignore it. Maybe today will give us some answers."

Trudie smiled warmly at them both. "That's the spirit. Sometimes, facing things head-on is the only way to find peace."

Jinx grinned mischievously.

"And I'll be there to watch it all unfold. For emotional support, of course," she added with a wink.

"I'd be surprised if you weren't the one causing all the drama just to see it happen," Stone fired back, unable to stop the words before they were launched.

Ella gasped softly, but Jinx just laughed him off.

"Ah, there's that cursed guy. Knew you'd come out to play again. Come on, let's go," she said, slapping Stone on the back and walking out the door.

Stone's jaw ticked, but he pressed his lips tighter. He needed to maintain better control of his damn mouth.

As the rest of them gathered their belongings and headed to the car, the air between him and Ella still felt charged.

Today was about more than just seeking healing or experiencing an architectural curiosity. It was about unraveling the mysteries of the Breath of Selene. Once they had it, maybe they'd be able to find a way to mend the fraying edges of their bond.

The drive to the Integratron was quiet, each mile a meditation on the unresolved tensions and potential of the day ahead. Stone hoped like hell they could finally get some answers inside the dome. All of this would be worth it if they did.

The desert landscape spread wide and empty around them.

Arriving at the Integratron, the structure stood resolute under the midday sun, its white dome glaring brightly against the deep blue sky. Unlike the mysterious allure it held under the cloak of night, the daytime view rendered it a more historical landmark than a mystical portal, or source of deep revelations.

The four of them joined a small group of tourists

and locals milling about, waiting for the next guided tour. The air buzzed with casual conversation, a stark contrast to the significant purpose that brought Stone and Ella back to this place.

They exchanged a glance, acknowledging the impossibility of exploring privately with so many witnesses.

As they entered the main chamber for the sound bath, the guide's voice echoed off the smooth walls, explaining the structure's acoustic properties and historical significance. However, even without her rundown, Stone could feel a tingling sensation that prickled against his skin and beckoned him in the back of his mind.

Stone watched Ella's determined face as she looked around and a surge of tentative admiration rose within him. The curse had strained them to their limits, and yet here she was, steadfast and brave.

As they settled into the echoing resonance of the Integratron's chamber, Stone felt the gravity of their task. He wasn't sure how meditating with a sound bath would help them accomplish their mission.

They should be looking around, testing the integrity of the building or looking under floorboards. Anything but closing their eyes and going all New Age.

Suddenly, a low, resonant hum of the Integratron's sound bath enveloped the chamber, and Stone felt the vibrations seep deeper into his consciousness than before.

It tilted him off his axis and made a part of him sit up straight and take note.

The sounds were not just auditory but visceral—pulsating through his very being like the heartbeat of the earth itself. Each tone seemed to resonate with a forgotten frequency within him, calling forth memories and sensations that were both alien and intimately familiar. It made his skin hum and his heart race.

He glanced at Ella, who had her eyes closed and seemed to be focusing intently on the sounds. Their hands found each other's, and a subtle communication passed through their touch—a recognition of something significant happening to them both.

Ella's hand tightened around his, her pulse a rapid staccato against his palm. Their breathing synchronized, and as the soundscape deepened, the chamber seemed to dissolve around them. The walls, the floor, and even the presence of others in the room faded into a misty periphery. Stone had never felt anything like it.

As the session deepened, the sounds of the Integratron induced a trance-like state, where the physical boundaries of his body felt increasingly irrelevant.

He sensed Ella's presence intertwined with his own, their mental and emotional barriers dissolving in the shared experience.

No sounds, no words.

Just *knowing*.

He could rest here forever.

Their spirits, unburdened by the physical constraints of their bodies moved freely. It was a profound peace and connection he hadn't felt since the curse began—a glimpse of what could be.

What *should* be.

Suddenly, they were no longer in the Integratron—they were adrift in a vast, starlit expanse that existed somewhere between dream and reality.

Here, the heavy shroud of the curse that had clung to their spirits like chains was absent.

Amidst this shared experience, a vision flickered into clarity—the shimmer of a large, faceted crystal hovering in the space between them. It pulsed with a soft light, rhythmic and soothing.

Stone understood instinctively that this was the Breath of Selene, the source they had been searching for—now tantalizingly within their spiritual grasp. It was just as he had seen in his dream.

But how could they acquire it?

Yet, as the vision of the Breath materialized between them—a shimmering crystal orb of light cradled in the essence of the moon itself—their time was running out.

Stone reached out, desperate to grasp the fading orb, his heart pounding with the fear of losing their only chance to change their fate.

Unfortunately, as quickly as the vision appeared, it faded. The resonant tones of the sound bath slowed, and the tactile sense of the floor beneath them returned.

As the light of the vision waned, Stone felt a sense of impending loss, as if the answers they so desperately sought were dissolving before them.

Their eyes opened almost simultaneously—the immediate world of the Integratron's dome returning with a sharp focus.

Stone and Ella exchanged a look, each recognizing the significance of what they had just experienced.

"We need more time," he whispered urgently to Ella as the last notes of the sound bath ebbed away. "We have to come back. Alone."

Ella nodded, her eyes glowing with intensity. "I agree."

At least they were on the same page. They needed to return—to explore this vision space without the distractions of a public session.

Jinx, who had been hovering nearby, chimed in with a grin. "Looked like you two were about to levitate or something. What did you find out?"

Trudie observed them with a more understanding gaze.

Ella took a deep breath, then said, "We... I think we saw the Breath of Selene. We need to come back when it's just us."

"I knew it." Jinx grinned, half-teasing, half-serious. "We should have busted through the door last night, then camped out here, eh? You might have solved all your mysteries by now."

Trudie smiled but gave a gentle shake of her head. "The right moment comes when it's meant to," she said thoughtfully. "Tonight will be your time."

They decided they would return after dark. This time, they would bypass the constraints of a public tour to dive deeper into whatever mystical properties the Integratron held.

Stone had to admit, even he was a convert to its magic.

As they walked toward the exit, plotting their return, the air felt charged with potential. Outside, the daylight was a stark contrast to the dim, resonant chamber.

As they approached the parking lot, ready to regroup and prepare for their nocturnal excursion, a familiar scent caught his attention. Before he could say anything, a voice stopped them in their tracks.

"Leaving already?"

CHAPTER 20

CURSES & PROPHECIES

ELLA

I solde's question hangs in the air, tinged with an edge that cuts through the momentary peace that had settled over us inside the Integratron.

Stone stiffens beside me, his arm brushing against mine. His touch is a silent question. One that I'm not ready to answer—not until I understand the full extent of what Isolde is implying.

"No, we're not leaving so soon," I reply, my voice more steady than I feel.

The mid-afternoon sun casts long shadows across the ground, mirroring the darkening thoughts now clouding my mind.

Isolde nods. Her expression is solemn and her eyes reflect a depth of sorrow and urgency that she didn't have last time.

Jinx and Trudie share a confused expression but wait to see what's about to unfold. Perhaps they sense the tension or they don't want to spook the witch standing before us.

"What are you doing here, Isolde?" I ask, voicing the question that's been thrumming around my brain.

I cross my arms over my torso and wait.

How did she know where to find us?

Has she been following us?

Isolde steps closer, and I brace myself for what's coming.

It can't be good.

In fact, every instinct in me is saying this is bad. *Very* bad.

Isolde pauses, her gaze sweeping over us and then settling on the horizon where the sun's light is beginning to wane.

"This isn't the place to discuss such weighty matters," she says, glancing around. "Follow me. There's a spot not far from here, shielded from unwanted ears and eyes."

Reluctantly, Stone and I exchange another look, our decision unspoken but mutual.

We follow Isolde, with Jinx and Trudie trailing a few steps behind. I can tell their curiosity is piqued but they're also cautious. Even Jinx, who ordinarily loves the chaos seems reserved enough to allow everything to unfold in due time.

As we walk, the terrain shifts subtly, the desert sands giving way to a small grove of Joshua trees that cast eerie shadows around us. Isolde stops at a clearing encircled by rocks that seem almost deliberately placed, forming a natural barrier.

"Here," Isolde says, gesturing for us to sit on the flat stones. "We can speak freely."

Jinx plops down, her eyes wide with excitement. "This feels like the beginning of either a very good story or a very bad horror movie."

Trudie gives Jinx a gentle elbow nudge, then turns to Isolde with a serene smile. "This is quite a peaceful location, really. Nice choice."

"Oh, brother," Jinx mutters, rolling her eyes. "Kiss ass."

Despite myself, a small smile floats to my lips as I return my gaze to the witch.

Isolde doesn't return our smiles. Instead, she takes a deep breath, as if preparing herself for what she's about to reveal.

My insides feel like a live wire, readying for more bad news.

"I've come because I made a grave mistake," she begins, her gaze locking with mine. "Are you certain you wish for these two to hear what I have to say?"

Her gaze flits to the demons.

"Anything you have to say, you can say in front of them," I respond, tilting my head to the sisters.

Isolde tips her chin in acknowledgment. "Alright. As you wish."

Jinx snickers under her breath. "Where are we? Medieval times? Enter the twenty-first century with us, would you?" she scoffs. "As you wish? Who says that sort of thing these days?"

Isolde's dark green eyes could burn a hole into Jinx's head, but she exhales and returns her gaze to me.

"Ella, Stone," she begins, her voice a soft but firm whisper, as if carrying a weight too heavy for her alone. "What I'm about to tell you does not come easily to me. I've wrestled with this truth—with the prophecy that has haunted my lineage for generations."

She pauses, taking a deep breath that seems to draw the evening chill deeper around us.

My skin prickles with goosebumps. "We already know about the Luna Scrolls and the prophecy."

Isolde's eyes narrow and she shakes her head almost imperceptibly. "Luna Scrolls?"

It's my turn to be confused. "That's—it's not where you received your prophecy?"

She shakes her head. "No, ours is an ancient prophecy—only surviving through my lineage's memories. It's so feared, no one has dared put it to paper. "

"What? Why?" I blurt out, standing up to pace.

"It speaks of the Moon's Chosen—two souls bound by the celestial dance of light and shadow. However, it says they will unleash chaos—an upheaval so profound that it could fracture the very essence of our supernatural world. It could unravel reality and I..."

Stone's jaw sets so hard I can almost hear his teeth grind.

"And you think we're these *Moon's Chosen?*" he asks, his voice low. "This has to be some sick joke. What a convoluted mess."

I rake my fingertips over my forehead, unable to find words.

"Yes," Isolde confesses, her eyes drifting between Stone and me. "And I thought I could prevent it—prevent you from realizing the full extent of your powers together. But then, something curious happened. As I watched you from the shadows, I began to see the two of you not as harbingers of destruction—but as potential saviors. It was a peculiar set of circumstances and one I just couldn't seem to wrap my head around. However, when I tried to alter the decision of the coven—"

"Coven?" Stone practically growls. "What did your coven do?"

But I think we both know.

Isolde's expression is sympathetic as she shifts her gaze to the ground. "As I'm sure you've both discovered, the curse you've been afflicted with—it was meant to keep you apart—to keep your bond from solidifying. But I see now, I may have been wrong."

"*You* cursed them?" Jinx huffs, an almost appreciative tone in her voice.

Trudie clutches to the front of her shirt and gasps.

"Wrong?" I echo, the word tasting bitter on my tongue. "You cursed us based on a prophecy that no one even bothered to write down? And now you just... changed your mind?"

Her face is a mask of regret. "I acted out of fear. The signs were there, and I thought I could alter the path and save us all from—" She sighs. "But there's more I didn't understand—about you—about the bond you share. There's a power in it that I underestimated."

"But you—*you* warned us about the Breath of Selene. You put us on this path. We're here right now because of you," I blurt out, unable to wrap my head around everything.

"I know," she says softly. "I felt it was my job to correct what I could no longer stop. My hope was that you'd acquire the Breath before you..." She stops, biting the side of her lip. "You'd waited so much longer than I expected. I thought if I put you on the path, I might be able to convince my coven to rescind the curse. But they wouldn't listen to reason and—"

The air between us thickens with her admission, heavy with the scent of the desert air.

"I've messed everything up and now Andres is planning a secondary attack the night of the Supermoon. He intends on taking your territory—you already know this. But now, he thinks you are distracted, weakened by this quest. I don't believe he knows of the prophecy, but he senses your vulnerability."

Stone and I exchange a glance. The pieces are falling into place.

"And how do you know this?" I say through gritted teeth.

"Witches talk," she says with a shrug.

"I thought Andres was looking for the Breath of Selene, too? You all but implied it the night we met you," Stone interjects, his voice carrying a low warning.

She inhales a big breath and exhales it just as quickly. "I lied."

Jinx lets out a low, "Ooooh. I need popcorn."

"W-what?" I breathe out, steam practically escaping out my ears.

"The two of you acquiring the Breath is paramount to your transformation. The only way to make things right was to put you on the path," she admits. "Having a potential enemy hunting for it was my way of ensuring you'd go quickly."

"Christ," Stone mutters, pinching the bridge of his nose.

"Both?" I ask. "I mean, I know Stone's behavior is odd but I feel fine. Do you mean because of our bond?"

"Have you not felt it? You cannot be together and cannot be apart. The curse was designed to drive you mad," she says, her words petering out as she glances between Stone and me.

I glance over my shoulder to Stone, wondering if he has any idea of what she's saying because I'm confused as fuck.

However, there's a dawning recognition in his expression.

He nods, letting loose a sardonic chuckle. "That's why..."

I look between the two of them, agitation building. "Anyone wanna fill me in?"

"When you are together, Stone feels the effects," Isolde begins.

"And when we're apart, I regain clarity," he offers. "But *you*..."

"What about me?"

But realization practically slaps me across the face.

When Stone was gone, I just about lost my damn mind.

I raise my hands to my lips. "Oh, shit."

"And there it is," Jinx chuckles. "Geez, woman. I figured it out the moment the words left her lips. I mean, I bow to the master because that was a genius twist."

She slow claps until she sees the glare I throw over my shoulder at her. Then, she flips her hand over, examining her fingernails.

Trudie reaches out without looking and places her hand over her sister's, forcing Jinx to drop her hands to her lap in silence.

"Is there a way to break the curse?" I ask, not sure I want to hear the answer.

Isolde's gaze shifts from me to Stone and back again.

"There is a way, but you won't like it," she says slowly.

"Well, go on then. The suspense is killing us here," Jinx calls out. .

Isolde's expression flattens, but she says, "You must erase your memories of each other. Without the emotional tether, the curse will unravel. I could help you if that's what you'd like."

A cold dread settles in my stomach.

Erase our memories of each other?

How the hell is that an answer?

The thought of forgetting Stone and all that we've shared sparks a panic sharp enough to cut through the fog of my frustration.

"And there's no *other* way?" Stone's voice is rough, tinged with desperation, but there's an edge to it that tells me he's barely holding onto his sanity without the curse's influence.

Isolde hesitates, then nods reluctantly. "There could be another path—one less certain. There would be no way to control the outcome." Her eyes flicker with a hint of mystery, her voice lowering to a near whisper as if the words themselves were delicate secrets. "The tapestry of fate is woven with threads of potential outcomes—not all visible to the seer's eye.

There exists a path, woven into the very fabric of your bond, obscure and veiled in shadow."

Stone and I lean closer, the cryptic nature of her words drawing us in despite the tension that hums between us like a live wire.

"What does that mean, Isolde?" I press, my patience fraying at the edges.

"It means," she continues, her gaze steady on ours, "that within the labyrinth of choices, a route obscured by the fog of destiny might emerge. This path does not erase but transcends—harnessing the essence of what binds you. Not breaking it but elevating it to a pinnacle not previously envisioned."

"Wow, because that was clearer," Jinx snorts. "Sounds like a bunch of mystical mumbo jumbo. Can you give it to us in plain English?"

Trudie's calming hand finds Jinx's shoulder, but her eyes are on Isolde, filled with a gentle urging for clarity.

I have to admit, I'm thankful for her question because I'm still lost.

Isolde's lips curve into a faint, sad smile. "In simpler terms, it is possible that by fully embracing and integrating the essence of your bond—accepting it in all its complexity—you might find a way to transform the curse from a chain into a key."

"The essence of our bond..." Stone murmurs, turning the phrase over in his mind like a puzzle piece.

"Yes," Isolde nods. "Think of it not as breaking

what is between you, but as *completing* it. A journey through the eye of the storm that reaches calm waters not by evading the tempest, but by navigating through its heart."

I feel a chill as her words sink in, the metaphor striking a chord deep within me.

The risk is immense.

Diving deeper into what has already caused us so much pain and confusion so we don't have to forget one another. Yet, the potential to not just escape our curse but to master it and come out stronger on the other side is equally compelling.

"So, we have to dive into the deepest part of our curse—*our connection*—to possibly come out free on the other side?" I ask, wanting to make sure I understand her correctly.

Isolde nods solemnly. "Precisely. It is a path less trodden because it is fraught with peril and profound challenge. I'm uncertain how long it might take and I would not be able to guide you. But should you navigate it successfully, the rewards could be equally profound."

Stone snorts. "Losing my memories might not be so bad. There's plenty I'd like to forget."

My eyes slam shut. This is going to be on me to lead. "We'll take our chances with the hidden path, Isolde. We'll find a way to fix this."

Isolde regards us for a long moment, something like respect—*or is it pity?*—flickering in her eyes.

"Very well," she says finally. "I will assist you where I can. The road you chose is perilous, but it holds the promise of true freedom. Not simply from the curse—but from the fears that bind you."

As she steps back, ready to lead us from the clearing, Jinx claps her hands together, a wicked gleam in her eyes. "Well, this just got a whole lot more interesting. Lead the way, witchy. Let's see what kind of chaos we can conjure up together."

Trudie offers us both a warm, reassuring smile, the calm to Jinx's calamity. "You'll figure this out."

I shoot her a soft smile, hoping it relays some semblance of confidence.

Together, we follow Isolde. The low-hanging sun casts long shadows that stretch out before us like dark, tangible echoes of the journey ahead.

I pull out my phone, the signal flickering weakly. "I need to call Marta and Alanna. They have to be on high alert."

My thumb hovers over the call button, and a shiver of foreboding runs down my spine.

The Breath of Selene, the looming threat of Andres, the cryptic path to breaking the curse—it all converges into the kind of trouble that promises not just revelations, but also potential devastation.

CHAPTER 21

FATE DRAWS NEARER

STONE

S tone's thoughts churned with unease as he paced the confines of Ella's hotel room, each step a battle against the curse's invasive pull. The atmosphere was charged with an electric anticipation—an invisible storm brewing between them as they prepared for their critical journey back to the Integratron at nightfall.

This was more than a mission—it was a gauntlet thrown by fate, demanding they confront their destiny head-on.

The room was littered with maps, books, and various esoteric objects that Isolde had insisted would help shield them from the worst effects of the curse.

So far, Stone had to admit, the worst impulses were being kept at bay. But how long it would last was anyone's guess.

Stone packed the objects carefully into their backpacks, his hands trembling slightly—a physical manifestation of the curse's insidious whispers.

Thanks to his awareness, he felt it then—the curse clawing at his mind, trying to sow doubt about Ella—about their path forward.

He clenched his fists, focusing on the tangible weight of the backpack to ground himself.

Ella watched him with a frown, her eyes narrowing slightly as she picked up on his discomfort.

"Is it getting worse again?" she asked, her voice laced with concern.

Stone paused, meeting her gaze. He wanted to reassure her, to tell her he was fine, but the truth was far from it.

He wanted the damn curse gone.

"It's constant," he admitted, rubbing at his temples. "Like whispers just out of reach, pushing me to doubt everything. But I'm managing. At least I haven't said anything too asinine while I have Isolde's trinkets. We have too much riding on this to let it win."

Ella stood, walking over to him. "Do you think Isolde is the betrayal Diana warned us about?"

Her question was a whisper, almost drowned out by the hum of the air conditioning, yet it cut through Stone's awareness like a blade.

"How the hell would I know?" His voice echoed harshly against the walls.

Ella recoiled slightly, the hurt evident in her expression before she masked it with a curt nod.

Instantly, he regretted the bite in his words, a testament to the curse's tightening hold over his stupid mouth.

Of course, he had to jinx himself.

"Right. I—" she hesitated, biting her lip, then continued with forced calm, "I'm just trying to make sense of everything."

Stone sighed, running a hand through his hair as the curse mocked him with a whisper of satisfaction. He stepped closer, reaching for her hands, needing to bridge the gap his words had created.

"I'm sorry, Ella. I didn't mean—"

He struggled to articulate the chaotic vortex of dark tendrils that wormed their way through his thoughts. It pushed him toward isolation—a way to feel sane in the middle of this bullshit, even though he knew now was when she needed him the most.

Ella squeezed his hands, her own trembled, betraying her worry.

"I know, Stone." Her voice was resolute, her determination clear despite the shadows that flickered across her face.

Stone gritted his teeth, feeling the curse coil tighter. Her acceptance and the way she was able to push down her own hurt to be understanding dug at him.

"If we can't control this thing, Ella... if it keeps

pushing us to the brink," he said, his voice fluctuating between desperation and a harsher tone he couldn't quite soften, "Maybe we need to consider what Isolde offered. At least as last, damn resort."

Ella paused and her expression tightened. "Erase everything? All that we are to each other?"

Her voice was laced with incredulity and hurt, reflecting the sting of his words.

"I don't know—" Stone snapped, more sharply than he intended, a wave of frustration pouring out. He caught himself, seeing the hurt again flash across Ella's face, and exhaled slowly, struggling to modulate his tone. "I mean, maybe it should be an option—if all else fails. I hate the idea as much as you do, but if it comes down to losing our minds to this curse or forgetting..."

The room fell silent as the gravity of the situation settled between them.

Ella shook her head. "I can't. I can't do that, Stone."

"It's not what I want, Ella. But what if it's the only way to save what's left of us? If we wait too long and there's nothing left to save?" His voice cracked with the admission.

Ella met his gaze, her eyes searching his.

"Let's not decide anything now. Not yet." She exhaled heavily. "We focus on finding the Breath of Selene first. Then, we fight this curse with everything we've got. Only then, if we're out of options... we'll consider it."

"Okay." Stone nodded, the tension in his shoulders easing slightly at her words. "We fight first. We find the Breath. And maybe, just maybe, we won't need to make that choice."

Ella reached out, her hand finding his, a silent vow passing between them. Despite the curse's efforts to divide them, this connection, this touch, reaffirmed their unity—a pledge to face the coming challenges together.

"Are you ready to try again?" she asked, her eyes flickering to the door. "Because it's time to go."

He swallowed hard and nodded silently.

"Okay, come on."

As they left the hotel room, Stone wondered if they stand a chance. Could they defy even the darkest of fates?

As they waited for the others, Stone noticed Ella checking her phone more frequently than usual. Each silent glance seemed to tighten the lines around her eyes—a sign of worry she didn't verbalize.

"You've been checking your phone a lot," Stone remarked, trying to keep his tone neutral despite a stirring of frustration. "Anything you need to sort out before we leave?"

Ella looked up from her phone, her expression briefly revealing the strain she felt before she masked it with a nod. "Just trying to reach the kids. They haven't checked in today, and it's... I'm sure it's nothing. They're probably just busy with Alanna. They've been having a good time with her."

The momentary lapse in her usual composure was enough for Stone to gauge the depth of her concern. Everything was starting to pull her down and she was trying hard to hide from it. Perhaps even from herself.

As they met the others in the parking lot, the atmosphere felt charged with anticipation. Would this next trip make or break them?

"Cheer up, team. We're about to break into a high-energy super dome, not join in a funeral procession," Jinx chided, eyeing Stone and Ella with a grin that bordered on irreverent.

Ella forced a small smile, but Stone knew it did nothing to quell her inner turmoil.

"Just gearing up to face the unknown," she said, trying to match Jinx's lighter tone.

"Don't worry, Ella. When we get there, we'll set up wards. There will be strong protections and even stronger wills. There's power in that combination," Trudie said, reaching out and patting Ella's arm.

"Thanks, Trudie," Ella responded, releasing a sigh.

Isolde, holding a small satchel in her hands, nodded. "The Integratron is a place of profound energy currents. These will help stabilize some of the forces around us," she explained, handing out a few last-minute additions to their gear.

Each one of them was given a stone with ornate

carvings on them. Stone's was a dark hematite with a spiral on it. He slipped it into his pocket next to the other objects he'd been given

As the group packed away their gear and reviewed the plan one last time, Ella's phone buzzed. She glanced at it quickly, her expression unreadable as she slipped the device back into her pocket without a word.

Stone noticed the tightness in her movements, the slight furrow in her brow deepening—a sign she was still waiting for that crucial message from her kids.

"Alright, let's do this. Remember, stealth is key. We get in, do what we need to do, and get out before anyone's the wiser," Trudie said, as a soothing smile graced her lips.

The group nodded, rallying around the plan.

They had been close to the Breath of Selene the last time. There was no reason to think they couldn't get in and out. Especially with the help of a witch cloaking their movements.

The group piled into Jinx's car and drove back to the Integratron, the desert landscape sprawling endlessly around them. The conversation focused on the task at hand, but Stone could tell that Ella wasn't fully present.

It wasn't until they reached the outskirts of the Integratron that Ella's phone vibrated again.

Stone watched as a flicker of relief passed over her face as she read the message.

"All good. They were helping Alanna make dinner and she has a no-tech rule when they eat," she murmured almost to herself, the tension visibly draining from her shoulders. "I should probably enforce something like that, come to think of it."

The simplicity of the update seemed to ground her, bringing her back fully to the moment and the dangers that awaited them inside the Integratron.

"That's good," he said, even as the curse tried to darken his mood.

Ella nodded, tucking her phone away with a more genuine smile. "Yeah. All the talk of Andres trying to make a move has me on edge. Especially when I'm not there to protect them. You know?"

"Let's focus then," Stone said. "We've got a mysterious object to try and retrieve. Then, we can get back to them."

"Can't wait," Ella whispered, letting her gaze float out the window.

As Jinx maneuvered the car to the parking lot of the Integratron, Stone's unease escalated into a palpable sense of dread. Each step closer to their destination felt like a tug-of-war with the curse and he wondered why.

"Everything okay?" Ella's voice cut through the tension, her concern evident as she met his gaze.

Stone forced a tight-lipped smile. "Yeah, just... feeling the pressure, you know?"

But Ella could see through the facade, her eyes

narrowing with understanding. "Still feeling the effects?"

Stone hesitated, not wanting to taint the plan or the steps ahead.

"Yeah," he finally confessed, his voice barely above a whisper.

Ella reached out, her hand finding his, offering a silent anchor amidst the chaos. "We'll get through this, Stone. I have a good feeling about this."

But even her words of reassurance couldn't silence the nagging fear that gnawed at Stone's resolve.

What if he said or did something that jeopardized their mission?

What if the curse's influence proved too strong to resist?

What if this time, the curse even stretched into whatever magic the Integratron seemed to hold over them?

With a heavy heart, Stone steeled himself for the challenges ahead. He prayed that their bond would be strong enough to withstand the darkness closing in around them.

CHAPTER 22

FACE YOUR SHADOWS

ELLA

"Are you sure you want to stay out here?" I ask, turning to face Jinx and Trudie.

They've opted to keep watch while Stone and I go inside and try to access the strange mental place we were in earlier today.

It's Jinx who speaks up. "Girly, as much as I hate to admit it, I think having us in there will just amplify Stone's curse. You don't need more chaos. You need to keep your collective cool."

Trudie nods. "She's right. Our energies could overpower yours. It's imperative the two of you make your connection and see what you can see."

Beside me, Isolde's hands move with practiced grace, tracing intricate sigils in the air around the Integratron. The symbols glow briefly, casting eerie shadows on the desert floor as evening settles on the landscape.

Finally, she drops her hands and nods at her handiwork. A visible shimmer floats across the surface of the Integratron, like heat on asphalt as it envelops the building.

"It's done. This will shield us from external influences and amplify your connection to the astral plane," she explains, her voice a soothing murmur against the howling wind. "The space inside is yours to control."

The power emanating from each sigil is palpable, even to me.

"Thank you, Isolde. We'll take it from here," I say, turning to Stone.

He nods, his expression set with determination but his eyes betray a flicker of anxiety. Or perhaps uncertainty.

I can relate.

Stone steps away from us, making his way to the Integratron's door. With a careful push, clearly not wanting to damage the structure more than necessary, the door gives way with a soft groan.

"Ready?" Stone asks, turning to me.

I take a deep breath and nod.

We need answers. We *need* to find a way to obtain the Breath of Selene and get our asses back to Black Crater. I intend on bringing the fight to Andres before he can try a second attempt at my territory.

Having the Breath of Selene will give us an edge.

Stone pushes open the door all the way and we

enter—the coolness of the building is a lovely contrast to the desert heat outside.

I'm here for it.

Sweat has been pooling in the small of my back for the past few minutes and it's starting to drive me insane.

Inside, the air is thick with the scent of old wood and the more subtle, indefinable trace of ancient magics. The remnants of the sound bath we engaged in earlier seem to linger here, too. Like somehow the frequencies live on in a perpetual loop.

Without a word, we position ourselves in the center of the building, under the large domed ceiling we were told was built to concentrate celestial energies. We face each other—our knees touching.

The contact makes my heart thump unevenly, but I need to get over my own apprehension and allow myself to settle into some sort of mindfulness.

But without the distraction of the sound bath and the others in the room, being in here alone with Stone brings a flood of nervousness to my awareness.

Trying to dispel it, I reach out, taking Stone's hands in mine. His eyes dart up, finding mine with a hint of confusion hidden in their depths.

"We need to do this as one," I explain, wanting him to be on the same page.

His lips press into a thin line, but he offers a curt tip of his chin.

Closing our eyes, we begin the breathing exercises

Isolde taught us, synchronizing our breaths as we slowly sink into a trance-like state. It takes ages.

The transition is subtle at first.

The sounds of the desert fade, and a gentle, pulsing light thrums just outside of my awareness. I settle into it, allowing it to lull me into a sense of peace and calm that I don't feel in my waking life.

Suddenly, it's like we emerge in a landscape that seems to stretch infinitely, the ground beneath us shimmering with a translucent quality. I glance upward, trying to orient myself. Above, the sky is a tapestry of swirling colors—not quite night... yet not day, either.

Between.

Somewhere the fabric of reality thins.

Stone and I step forward, each movement echoing with a surreal clarity in this boundless expanse.

Ahead, the Breath of Selene hovers majestically over an altar carved from what looks like moonstone, radiating a silvery glow that casts long, ethereal shadows across the ground.

It's more beautiful than I could have ever imagined. The crystalline orb shimmers with a light that seems alive and pulses in rhythm with my heartbeat. Like it's a part of me and I'm a part of it.

We approach the altar together, our steps hesitant yet drawn by an undeniable force. We're on mission. Here for a reason.

Called.

The closer we get, the stronger the pull—like a tide tugging at the very essence of our beings.

"Wow," Stone whispers, his voice filled with awe as we stand before the altar. He sounds more like himself as he utters, "Every time—it's incredible."

A soft sigh escapes my lips as I nod. "It really is."

Reaching out, I expect to feel the cool touch of crystal, but my fingers pass through it, stirring the air where it should be solid. I turn to him, my eyebrows tugging in.

Without a word, Stone steps forward, his hand meeting the same fate. A ripple of confusion passes over his face.

"Why can't we interact with it?" My voice is tight with disappointment, the reality of our situation settling in.

We're here, yet not fully.

Not enough to touch—to claim what we've come so far to find.

No...

Stone furrows his brow, lost in his own thoughts.

"We're not whole," he muses. "Our physical bodies aren't here, just some other version of us. That has to be it. We can see it, even feel its energy, but we can't interact with it."

"So, we're ghosts?" I half-joke, but the humor falls flat, swallowed by the vastness of this place.

"More like echoes," Stone corrects gently. "Our consciousness is here, projected, but our bodies remain behind. We need both to manipulate physical things here. But... I don't understand. How do we bring our full selves into this plane?"

I circle the altar, tracing my fingers through the air where the Breath should be solid.

"Maybe it's about balance? Could it be that we're too chaotic right now, especially with everything going on? The curse, the prophecy, our fight against Andres..." I muse out loud.

Stone nods slowly. "Possibly." He paces a little, each step deliberate as if he's measuring the astral ground beneath us. "We might need a counterbalance. Something that can bring a little calm."

I nod, considering his theory, but then a chill sweeps through the astral plane—unusual given the lack of physical weather here.

"We need to figure this out quickly," I urge.

As we stand on either side of the altar, Stone's gaze fixes on the shimmering crystal that seems so close yet untouchable. "There's something we're missing— something crucial that would allow us to obtain it. It's like it's on the edge of my awareness, but I just... can't..." His eyes go distant as his words peter out.

As we ponder the missing pieces to this puzzle, the ground beneath us subtly shifts. It begins as a faint tremor—almost like the softest heartbeat quickening under our feet.

I pause, feeling the vibrations grow stronger, more insistent.

Stone stops and looks around, his body tensing.

"Do you feel that?" he asks, his voice low.

I nod, barely able to conceal my growing anxiety. "Something's changing," I reply, my gaze sweeping across the surreal landscape that seems to be turning against us.

The serene beauty of the place is morphing into something more sinister—a manifestation of something far from peaceful.

As we stand, the sense of change intensifies. The ground now visibly ripples, waves of energy distorting the air around us. Shadows lengthen and twist, forming shapes that are almost human—shifting as if stirred by an unseen wind.

"It's like this place is reacting to our presence... or our frustration," Stone murmurs, his eyes narrowing as he tries to understand the phenomenon unfolding around us.

Instinctively, I walk to him and his hand finds mine, his grip tight and reassuring despite the uncertainty.

Before either of us can comment further, a deep, resonating growl echoes through the space. It's a sound so profound and terrifying that it vibrates through my very core.

From the shadows, a form emerges, coalescing into a dark figure.

Goosebumps erupt over my nonexistent skin and I fight back a gasp.

It's a creature born from nightmares. Its body is a swirling mass of dark mist—eyes glowing a fierce, malevolent red. As it approaches, the air around us grows colder, the energy heavier—denser somehow.

This being—this *entity*—it feels like a direct challenge. A barrier meant to keep us from our goal.

Stone's grip on my hand tightens, and he positions himself slightly in front of me.

"What do you want from us?" he demands, his voice steady but edged with the tension that claims us both.

The creature's form seems to pulse with the shadows, drawing them tighter around itself as if cloaked in the very essence of the astral plane's darkness.

Instead of a spoken response, its intentions flood into our minds—a cold, invasive whisper that feels like it's trying to suffocate our thoughts.

"You are intruders here. Leave this plane or be expelled by force."

I step beside Stone, unwilling to hide behind him.

"We were called here by the Breath of Selene. We're not leaving without understanding why. Why are you trying to stop us?" My voice is firm, pushing back against the fear that this creature instills.

The entity's response is a low growl that vibrates through the astral ground, its eyes narrowing as if annoyed by our resistance.

"You carry nothing but disturbance. Your presence

unbalances the sacred equilibrium. Prove your worth or be purged from this place."

Stone tries to pull me back as the creature advances, a dark wave of energy emanating from it. As the entity moves closer, its form becomes more defined and terrifying, and the atmosphere thickens with a palpable malevolence. The shadows around us swirl faster, as if feeding off our anxieties and fears.

"You seek what is protected. Only those worthy may claim it," the voice thunders through our minds—a statement that feels like a judgment.

Suddenly everything becomes all too clear.

This isn't just any encounter.

It's a trial—a test of our worthiness to claim the Breath of Selene.

And perhaps it's interwoven with the prophecy.

Stone and I exchange a glance, understanding dawning between us both.

This trial, it's not something we expected, nor something we can flee from. We have to face it, here and now, on a plane we barely understand.

Fuck, I should have done some research.

"What do we need to do?" I ask the creature, my voice projecting confidence I barely feel.

The creature's eyes burn brighter.

"Show that you can transcend your limitations. Face your shadows and balance the chaos you bring to this realm. Only then can you proceed."

CHAPTER 23

TO RISK EVERYTHING
STONE

In the heart of the astral plane, somewhere in the echoing vastness, Stone and Ella faced the shadowy figure that seemed both guardian and gatekeeper.

There was something about it that was oddly familiar to Stone, but the creature's malevolent red eyes bore into them.

He'd have to question it later.

Stone felt the weight of the creature's demand settle over him like a cloak of lead.

How could he face his darkness when he didn't even fully understand it himself? Especially not when a curse was boring its way inside him, making it impossible to know how deep his darkness truly goes.

Hell, he didn't even know which darkness was his anymore.

Beside him, Ella's posture stiffened with determination, her eyes reflecting the flicker of the same resolve that hardened in his chest.

They had to face this—they both knew it. But how?

With a small nod, Ella offered Stone a silent agreement to face whatever came next. Somehow, they'd have to do it. What other choice did they have?

However, the first trial emerged from the shadows like a specter of unspoken truths and half-acknowledged fears. It took form as a dense, oppressive fog that seemed to whisper their deepest insecurities as it separated him from his mate.

Stone's heart pounded as his vision was consumed and then he faced a scene he hadn't dared revisit in his mind.

The forest around him blurred into a nightmarish tableau, focusing sharply on the moment he had first laid eyes on Ella.

The memory, raw and unfiltered, replayed with visceral clarity. He had arrived at the crash site, heart pounding with the urgency to find Doug—only to stumble upon a scene that would redefine his entire existence.

There she was.

Ella was struggling against the fading strength of Doug, whose life was slipping away even as he inadvertently passed on his legacy of power.

Stone had sensed the shift in authority—the alpha status transferring in a pulse that resonated through the air he breathed. Yet, his mind had been captured by something else entirely—the immediate and overwhelming connection he felt for a woman he'd never met before.

The fog around him thickened, echoing with the sounds of that afternoon—the distant screech of birds, the rustling of leaves, and Ella's gasping breaths.

The creature's voice echoed through his mind, *"Confront your truth, Stone. Face the darkness within your desire. What is the secret here you've refused to face?"*

Stone struggled internally, his instincts as a protector clashing with the raw, almost predatory desire that had surged through him the moment he had made contact with Ella. It had surprised the hell out of him and it had taken every ounce of strength then to pull back from it.

No, he wouldn't give that desperate urge a voice—or even realization.

He couldn't because he...

The waves of connection he felt that day slammed into him and he rocked back from it. The way his body had responded—every nerve ending on alert. The rush of blood to his dick and the way he had to do something—anything to ensure she hadn't noticed.

He had wanted to claim Ella.

Then and there.

From the moment he had been in her vicinity, a desire so potent and immediate had consumed him, and... it had *terrified* him.

A part of him knew what it had meant. How could it not?

Yet, he had never confessed this—not to Ella, not even to himself fully.

He had always overshadowed it by the subsequent turmoil and responsibilities that had enveloped them both. There had been so many things that needed to come first.

Besides, the last thing he wanted to do was scare the hell out of her. She was human coming into a supernatural world, for fucksake.

Stone stood motionless, the memory of that fateful afternoon flooding through him like a relentless tide. He could almost smell the crisp air—could feel the tension and raw energy that had crackled around him, igniting something intense and primal.

The scene played out before his eyes, over and over and over like some sort of Groundhog Day from hell.

It was as vivid as if he were there again—not just a phantom in this spectral realm.

How could he stop this loop?

It was torture.

Every time around, his body reacted to her proximity. He didn't know if it was his physical body or this astral version—but it felt real as fuck.

He slammed his eyes shut, willing the blood flow to back off.

Nothing worked.

Around him, the fog deepened, its tendrils curling into shapes that mirrored his turmoil.

The creature's challenge echoed in his mind, a relentless whisper, urging him to confront the desires he'd buried deep beneath layers of duty and restraint.

"What is the secret you've refused to face?" the voice boomed again, more insistent this time.

Stone's jaw clenched as he wrestled with the implications of that day.

The magnetic pull, the instant bond he felt with Ella was something far deeper than mere attraction or duty.

It was a call of *mate to mate*—a connection forged in the heat of crisis that had overwhelmed his senses, demanding recognition.

Fuck, it demanded *submission*.

And he had *rejected it*.

Oh, god.

He had rejected its calling.

He shook his head, trying to dispel the vision, but it clung to him stubbornly.

"No," he muttered under his breath, his voice barely audible above the howl of the shadowy winds swirling around them.

As the winds howled, the fog continued to thicken, pressing against Stone with the weight of his unacknowledged truths.

He felt it in every fiber of his being—the undeniable force of what he had tried to bury for her.

His wolf.

The primal essence of who he was at his core had been stifled—silenced by him to lean into the comforting acquiescence of his human side—*for Ella.*

Stone had always known he was not just a man, but a creature of profound instinct and elemental needs.

He knew his strength.

His power.

And he relented it all.

Yet, here, in this trial, he was being forced to confront the fact that he had been denying the very core of his being for months.

He wasn't just a man—one who could live with human rules and emotions. He was also a wolf—a wolf who was bound by supernatural rules about love and fate.

A wolf who had found his *mate.*

The creature's voice pierced through the tumult, relentless and sharp as a knife's edge. *"Your denial—your refusal to embrace your true nature will be your undoing. How can you be worthy of the Breath of Selene, when you deny half of who you are?"*

Stone staggered, his form nearly buckling under the intensity of the confrontation. It was like he had been slapped across the face.

How could he be trusted with the Breath of Selene?

Maybe he couldn't—*shouldn't.*

His breath came in ragged pulls, his heart

pounding as if trying to break free from his chest. The mirage of the forest around him seemed to close in, the trees bending toward him, their branches like fingers accusing him of his denial.

"I was trying to be what she needed," Stone gasped out, the admission tearing from him with the force of a confession long held back.

The raw, primal part of him—his wolf—had always been there, simmering just beneath the surface, and in that first overwhelming moment with Ella, it had surged forward, demanding to be recognized—*to claim.*

But he had silenced it, terrified of what it meant to let that part of him loose. Terrified of scaring Ella, of driving her away before they had a chance to understand what was happening between them.

The creature's laughter was a cold, harsh sound that filled the space around him. *"Fear of your true self is no virtue, Stone. To lead, to truly connect with your mate, you must be whole. You must accept all parts of your being. Only then can you face the challenges ahead."*

Stone clenched his fists, his nails digging into his palms.

The truth was a bitter pill, laced with the pain of self-recognition.

The creature was right—and he hated that fact.

He *had* been living half a life—giving Ella half a mate, protecting their pack with half his strength.

The air grew heavier, the weight of his denied

nature bearing down on him as if to crush the very breath from his lungs. Each thought that raced through his mind was shadowed by a darker echo—a whisper of the primal instinct he'd tried to cage.

It had been necessary.

He swore it had been.

But what if...?

"I need to breathe," Stone gasped, the words lost in the roar of the shadowy wind that seemed now not just around him but within him, swirling through his veins with icy fingers.

He stumbled forward, his knees weak, each step an effort against the thickening fog that wrapped around him like chains. The edges of his vision darkened, the world narrowing to this confrontation with himself—with the wolf that was part of his very essence.

In that suffocating darkness, Stone's internal battle raged fiercer. The instinctual pull to embrace his full nature clashed violently with the man who had promised to protect—to restrain himself for the good of those he loved.

"How can I be what she needs if I let the wolf take hold?" he thought, despair threading through his resolve.

The creature's voice, now almost a growl, filled the space. *"By denying your nature, you deny her the mate she deserves. You weaken both yourself and your bond. Face what you are—embrace it, and rise stronger. Or sink into the abyss. Your choice."*

It was a challenge and a prophecy—the words striking at the very core of Stone's fears and desires. He couldn't deny the truth in them, the undeniable fact that his refusal to accept his dual nature might be the one thing holding them back.

"What if she can't accept me for who I am?" he wondered aloud.

The question hung in the dense air of the astral plane and made him sick to his stomach.

The idea that Ella might be repulsed by his animalistic side ripped at his heart, cracking it open like nothing ever had before.

He couldn't lose her.

He couldn't...

The fog pulsed with his heartbeat, tightening as his doubts grew, yet loosening when he edged toward acceptance. This place—it was good at creating physical manifestations of his inner turmoil. It was a battlefield—not with weapons but with his own fragmented self.

Leaves whirled around him as the shadowy landscape of the astral plane twisted and turned with his indecision.

The voices of the forest grew louder—a cacophony of past and present merging into a relentless assault on his senses.

Stone continued to clench his fists, the muscles in his arms tensing as he fought against himself. The desire to let go, *to embrace his wolf,* battled against his need to protect Ella from the intensity he knew resided beneath the surface.

"I can't let go. *I can't,*" Stone whispered, his voice cracking as the words spiraled away into the wind.

Each breath became harder to draw, the air thick with the scent of pine and the cold bite of unresolved truths.

The creature's eyes seemed to burn brighter, its gaze unyielding. *"Denial is a cruel kind of torture. Don't you agree?"*

The words hammered at him with the force of a gale, challenging every barrier he had erected.

This wasn't just about facing his wolf, he realized.

It was about trusting Ella to face it with him.

Could he risk the bond they had by revealing his secrets?

The fog darkened further, swirling into a vortex that seemed to draw him deeper into the mayhem of his fears. The edges of his vision blurred further, the world reduced to the immediate terror of the trial.

He could feel the darkness nibbling at his soul. The threat of being lost to this place was a tangible force pressing against his every thought.

Stone's resolve wavered, the lines between man and beast— protector and destroyer—blurring in his mind.

"Is this what it means to be whole? To risk every-thing in the hope that she might understand? Might accept me?" he called out, his heart a drumbeat of dread and determination.

He had never done this before.

Never thought he'd have the chance.

He thought he'd be alone forever.

"Only one way to find out," the creature responded with a sardonic chuckle that echoed against the confines of his mind.

But what if she couldn't?

As the creature's presence loomed larger, its figure almost blending into the encroaching darkness, Stone's breaths became shallow gulps.

The realization that he might never escape this astral prison settled over him with a suffocating finality.

CHAPTER 24

PUNISHMENT

ELLA

I stand, or at least I *think* I'm standing, in a space that feels both vast and suffocating. Gone is the scenery of the forest and the altar where the Breath of Selene resides.

Instead, it's a blank slate of dense fog.

The air around me is thick, charged with a tension that makes my skin crawl.

Ahead, the shadowy figure waits—its presence oppressive and its gaze piercing.

Stone's not by my side now. I assume this is my battle to face—my fears to confront.

The heavy mist rolls around me, each tendril whispering doubts and taunting me with my deepest insecurities. It's like it can pull them straight out of my subconscious.

"Are you ready to face your truth, Ella?" The crea-

ture's voice isn't a sound—it's a physical force that vibrates through me.

I swallow hard, my throat dry.

"I have to be," I whisper back, unsure if my voice carries any weight here.

As the words leave my lips, the fog lifts, forming a vague, shifting tableau. Abruptly, a scene materializes from the mist, so vivid it's as though I'm living it all over again.

I'm back to that critical moment—my first encounter with Stone.

Blood streams down my arm, the fresh wound from Doug's bite throbbing painfully. The forest is chaotic, filled with the scents of pine and danger—and there stands Stone. He enters the devastating scene like a guardian rushing to the rescue—in his swim trunks.

His presence is both startling and immediately comforting—a strange contradiction that confused me then as much as it does now.

The memory of his eyes meeting mine for the first time sends a jolt through me. They were filled with concern but underscored by an intensity that had seemed to see right through me.

Like he had glimpsed into the very core of my soul.

Before I can understand the meaning of this scene, it shifts.

Now, it's the day Stone burst into my house and fought off the attackers pretending to be my movers. I watch as he advances with lethal precision to protect me—his actions driven by an innate force I hadn't fully understood then.

The memory of how safe I felt, even in the middle of my terror, washes over me, stirring a mix of gratitude and a deeper, more unnerving connection. Something I hadn't even realized was there until this moment.

It was a stirring—a remembrance of some sort.

Like deep down, I knew he was more to me than simply a Good Samaritan.

Next, the fog conjures the intimate, startling moment when he first shifted in front of me. He had been trying to get my attention—needing to help me understand what was coming for me.

His transformation from man to wolf was both terrifying and awe-inspiring. His white wolf was—*is*—so beautiful.

The scene unfolds as if peeled from the pages of my life, not a mere replay but a raw reliving.

I'm standing in my bedroom with the chaos of moving boxes strewn around. My heart thrums wildly in my chest as Stone, no longer a majestic white wolf, reappears in front of me as a man.

The sudden shift from beast to human didn't give me the respite I might have hoped for back then—instead, it added another layer of intensity.

He's there, in the flesh, bare and unshielded, his presence filling the room with an electric charge.

God, he's gorgeous. Even now, I recognize it. Revel in it.

My breath catches—not just at the sight of him so exposed again, but at the rush of memories that flood through me. His naked vulnerability juxtaposes sharply against the palpable strength that emanates from him —the kind of paradox that drew me in deeper.

Then and now.

Of course, then we had kissed. Briefly. It was just a taste.

His lips had brushed against mine gently, hesitantly, as if he felt overwhelmed by the force of our connection and was unsure how to wield it.

I *so* related.

That kiss, soft yet fraught with the tension of unspoken promises and restrained desires, had been a spark. I remember the heat, the undeniable pull toward him, feeling simultaneously scared and exhilarated.

Hell, I thought I was losing my damned mind.

I pull back slightly in the memory, watching as we part—both of us breathless and unsure.

It had been a moment of raw yearning, and it had terrified me—not because of the supernatural elements that had begun to infiltrate my life, but because of the sheer intensity of my feelings for Stone.

Feelings I wasn't ready to admit, even to myself.

Feelings I shouldn't have even had at that point.

Not if I was a sane woman.

The fog shifts again, revealing more instances where I had held back. Each scene plays out with painful clarity—moments laden with the raw sexual tension between us. Moments where I could have reached out, could have accepted the bond, and allowed him in. But each time, I hesitated, scared of the implications—scared of how it would change my life and the lives of my kids.

There's the time I'd been warned about other Alphas who might try to claim me if the bond wasn't consummated. Yet, I'd dismissed the warnings as overprotective—not fully comprehending the super-natural world and the depth of our connection.

On and on they go.

Little moments where I could see the pained expression in Stone's eyes, but I still fell into his patience, his loyalty, and love.

I pushed aside the calling and reasoned with myself as to why.

And then the scene shifts to one of the most painful memories as of late—the night of our planned bath date. I had been so excited, so ready to finally let go and embrace whatever was between us after our shared experience through our mental bond the night before.

But then Troy had happened, dredging up old pains and doubts, and I had completely stood Stone up, spending the night getting drunk and venting to Jinx instead.

The pain of that evening returns with a vengeance, a sharp sting of regret for what might have been. That night could have changed everything—could have been the beginning of truly accepting the bond and seeing where it led.

Instead, I let fear and the past rule me.

The fog around me thickens as the memories continue to unfold, each one a sharp reminder of the walls I've built around my heart.

I've been hiding behind these walls, using my past hurts and fears as bricks, laying them one by one until I've built a fortress to protect myself and my kids. But in doing so, I've also kept Stone out—kept out the one person who has shown me nothing but dedication and care.

God, I'm so stupid.

In the mist, the memories slow, focusing on that missed bath date and the realization of what I had done the following morning.

The creature's voice breaks through the cascade of memories, deep and resonant, echoing in my mind, *"You have pushed him away, time and again. Yet, he remains. Why do you fear this bond, Ella?"*

The question hangs heavy in the air, and I feel the weight of it in my chest.

My fear... it's always been about losing control—about being hurt again.

After Troy, after feeling so foolish and so used, the idea of opening up, of allowing myself to depend on someone else so completely... *it terrifies me.*

But as the scenes play out before me, I see the cost of my fear. Stone's face in each memory is filled with understanding and patience... but also a hint of sorrow. There's a silent wish for something more hidden in those green depths.

Something I've denied us both out of a misplaced sense of self-preservation.

The realization hits me hard—like a physical blow to the gut. This isn't just about protecting myself. It's about fear of what life would be if I truly let someone in again. It's about the challenge of accepting a love that could consume and redefine my entire existence.

"I've been punishing us both," I admit aloud, my voice wavering slightly.

The words feel like an acknowledgment of a deeply buried truth, one that's painful yet liberating.

As the words tumble from my lips, the fog seems to react, swirling around me in a gentle caress, almost as if it's urging me to delve deeper into this revelation.

The creature's presence, once daunting, now feels more like a guide—a sentinel on my journey of self-discovery.

What is this place? A magical truth realm?

"I've been so focused on not repeating my past mistakes, that I didn't see that I was making new ones," I continue, my voice gaining strength as the weight of my admissions anchors me more firmly in this surreal landscape. "By guarding so fiercely against hurt, I've denied myself the chance to truly live. To truly *love*."

The mist shifts again, scenes flashing faster now, as if eager to show me the breadth of what I've missed. Stone's laughter on a sunny day in the park with the kids, his hand reaching for mine across the dinner table, his eyes alight with passion and hope.

Each memory punctuates the stark contrast between what could have been and the cold distance I imposed.

"Each moment I held back, I told myself I was being prudent—*responsible*. But what I was really doing was letting fear steer my life. Not just my life, but Stone's too, and my kids'," I confess, the heaviness of my previous choices pressing down on me.

The creature's voice surrounds me, not with judgment, but with a clarity that cuts through the fog. *"What will you do with this understanding, Ella?"*

The question lingers in the air, echoing around me as the scenes start to slow, settling on that last night—the missed bath date.

Tears prickle at the edges of my eyes as I remember the hurt that flickered across Stone's face when I finally found him so I could apologize.

"I need to make it right," I whisper, the fog around me thinning as if my resolve is pushing it back.

With a deep, cleansing breath, I look up, finding

the shadowy figure before me less intimidating, and more comforting at this point.

"I'm ready," I declare, not just to the creature, but to myself. "I'm ready to face this. I'm ready to fully embrace the bond, and fight for a future where I don't just survive, but thrive. With Stone by my side."

The creature nods, and a path clears through the fog, leading forward.

As I take a step toward the path, ready to confront whatever awaits with newfound courage, the world around me starts to blur.

The dense fog that had enveloped my every moment begins to dissolve as if melting away under the force of my decision.

But the shift is too sudden—too unexpected.

Instead of transitioning to another scene of revelation or the chance to confront Stone, the astral plane collapses entirely—dragging me back to a jarring reality.

I blink against the harsh, abrupt return to the physical world. My body recoils slightly on the cold, hard floor of the Integratron. The wooden beams of the ceiling swim into focus above me, stark and unyielding against the backdrop of my disorientation.

I was so close. I could *feel* it.

What happened?

Stone is already sitting up next to me. His expression mirrors my confusion as his wide eyes scan the room.

"What happened?" he asks, his voice rough.

I push myself up, feeling every muscle tense and unyielding, as if they too protest the sudden return.

"I don't know," I reply, my mind racing through the last moments in the astral plane—the revelations, the acceptance, and then... this unexpected ejection.

It doesn't make any sense.

We sit there, side by side, in the silence of the Integratron, the weight of unfinished business pressing down on us.

The air feels thick, charged with a tension that speaks of interrupted processes and incomplete transitions.

"Did we do something wrong?" Stone's question hangs between us, tinged with insecurity.

I shake my head, more out of confusion than certainty.

"It felt like I was just getting to something... *important*." My words trail off as I try to grasp the elusive threads of enlightenment that had seemed so within reach just moments before.

"We were kicked out," Stone concludes, his tone flat, stating the obvious which does nothing to alleviate the sense of failure that starts to creep in. "But why? We weren't done."

The quiet of the Integratron feels oppressive now. I look around, half-expecting to find an answer etched in the shadows.

"Maybe it's part of the trial?" I speculate, grasping

at straws, trying to find a sliver of sense in what feels like an arbitrary end to our profound journey. "Or maybe we weren't ready for what comes next."

Stone nods slowly, his gaze still distant. "Or we missed something crucial. Something that was supposed to guide us further?"

Frustration bubbles up within me, mingling with the remnants of revelations that now seem so distant.

The need to understand—to return and complete what we started, feels like the most important thing in the world.

CHAPTER 25

TETHERED

STONE

S tone stood abruptly, the frustration that had been simmering within him finally boiling over after yet another failed attempt to access the astral realm.

Three tries, and *nothing*.

Not a goddamn thing.

The curse's grip tightened, coloring his frustration with a bitter edge, making him want to punch a hole through the stupid Integratron's wall. He was at a breaking point and if he didn't get away from Ella now, he was afraid of what he could do to her.

"This is fucking pointless," Stone's voice echoed off the stark walls of the Integratron, his tone harsher than he meant it to be. He glanced down at Ella, who remained seated on the floor, her expression carrying more than just weariness. "It isn't working, and banging our heads against the same wall isn't going to change that."

Ella looked up at him, hurt flickering through her eyes, quickly masked by a subtle frown. "So, what? You're just going to walk away? Give up? Is that what you're proposing?"

Stone felt a pang of guilt for his harsh words but the curse made it hard to back down or soften his stance.

Even the charms Isolde had given him stopped working.

They were probably sick of this bullshit, too.

"Maybe I am," he snapped, feeling trapped and cornered—not just by the room, but by his own swirling emotions. "It seems the more logical option when nothing we do is making a damn bit of difference."

Without waiting for a response, Stone turned and strode toward the door. Every step felt heavy, and each one echoed like a gavel in the quiet of the Integratron. He didn't want to leave like this, but part of him believed it was the only way to break the cycle of their failures.

The fresh air outside hit him like a slap, sobering up his thoughts a little, and making him question his abrupt departure.

Or was it the distance from Ella?

He had spent the past few hours trapped in a

building designed to amplify energies—and his were growing more volatile by the minute.

Stone strode past Jinx, Trudie, and Isolde, their faces etched with concern.

He didn't have the energy to meet their eyes or explain. It wouldn't end well if he did.

Instead, his need for solitude outweighed the polite niceties of group dynamics.

Besides, they were big girls. They could handle it.

The desert air was cool, the sky above splattered with stars, offering him a vast, open canvas to cast his frustrations upon.

As he stood alone, taking deep, deliberate breaths, the calm of the desert night began to seep into his bones. The curse's stranglehold loosened slightly with each inhalation of the crisp, night air.

Behind him, the door to the Integratron opened and closed softly.

Stone didn't need to look back to know Ella had followed him out. But instead of joining him, her voice, low and strained, floated over from where she stood with the others.

"We can't seem to stay in the astral plane long enough to do any good," Ella explained, sounding as defeated as he felt. "Every time we think we're getting somewhere, we get kicked right back out. I don't get it."

Stone listened, his back still turned to the group,

the isolation allowing him to eavesdrop without interruption.

He heard Isolde's soothing tone reply, "The astral realm isn't just about willpower or desire. It's about balance and readiness. Both of you must be in alignment, or it rejects you."

"I'll bet money the curse is throwing off the balance. You need to present a united front and it's cracking you apart," Jinx chimed in with her usual bluntness.

"But in the astral realm, it feels like the curse is gone. It's like we're us again and we..." Ella began.

"That's not possible," Isolde states softly. "The curse will be with you regardless."

Ella sighed. "No, we're normal there. Stone is—"

"When you were in the astral realm, was everything coming up peaches and roses? Or was there anything there that made you sit up and take notice?" Jinx asked.

There was a silence that extended between them before Ella admitted, "There was a darkness. It—it sort of took over for a while."

"The curse," Trudie added softly, the healer in her always sensitive to the undercurrents of emotional and spiritual energies. "It took on form."

"What? No, that's not—"

"It is," Isolde stated, her concern evident even to Stone.

"But if felt like it was helping me. At last, toward the end." Ella's sigh was audible even from a distance. "Great. So, do we need to break the curse first? But if so, how? We've tried everything we know. God, this sucks. I thought dealing with asshole Alphas and my ex were bad."

Stone's fingers clenched into fists at his sides. The conversation was a stark reminder of his failure—not just in controlling this curse when they were together, but in protecting Ella from the fallout.

He was the weak link, and his continued presence seemed to only endanger their mission further.

As the group continued to discuss potential strategies, Stone felt a flicker of something shift inside him —resignation, perhaps, or maybe the first sparks of a necessary epiphany.

He couldn't keep fighting like this. Not if it meant he was putting everything at risk.

Stone turned slowly, his resolution hardening in the quiet desert night.

"What if we just... *forget?*" The words slipped out, laden with desperation and a hint of surrender.

He proposed the drastic option almost as a whisper, his voice carrying to the group behind him, echoing slightly in the cool air.

"Forget? What exactly are you suggesting?" Ella's voice carried a mix of confusion and alarm.

Stone swallowed hard. "Forget each other," he

clarified, the idea sounding just as radical to his own ears as it did in the open air. "Isolde mentioned it was an option. If the curse is fueled by our connection, and our memories, maybe erasing them would allow us to push through. Then we could obtain the Breath. We'd have the others here to help us remember the mission, even if we don't."

Silence descended for a moment, heavy and thick.

Jinx broke it first, her tone unusually subdued before a wry smile cracked her face. "Man, that's some soap opera level amnesia plot right there. What's next? Do we find out Ella has an evil twin?"

Despite the gravity of the situation, Stone couldn't help but snort. The absurdity of Jinx's humor in such a dire moment was both inappropriate and oddly fitting.

Trudie interjected gently, "It's a serious suggestion, Jinx. But maybe we should consider all other options before we turn to the magical equivalent of a hard reset."

Isolde nodded thoughtfully. "Erasing memories... it's irreversible. Once done, there's no going back. You'd have to rebuild your connection to each other."

Jinx's eyebrows shot up. "The last thing we need is to wipe the epic saga of Stone and Ella, only to rewrite it because we missed a loophole in the curse."

Trudie stepped closer, her eyes lighting up. "Maybe there's another way to approach this. The

Integratron is designed to amplify energies, right? What if Jinx and I join you and hold a balance circle inside? Maybe we can stabilize the energies enough to counteract some of the curse's influence."

Ella turned to Trudie and tilted her head slightly. "What do you mean? How would that work? I thought you were afraid to join us because of your energies?"

"I was—but sometimes, it's a matter of intention. If Jinx uses her chaos magic and I use my harmony spells, we might be able to create a balanced energy field inside the Integratron. It won't cure the curse, but it could give you both the stable environment you need to try entering the astral realm again. Think of it as... *neutral ground,*" Trudie explained, her voice calm and soothing. "I told you when I met you—I felt like I was meant to be here. Be around whatever was happening. Maybe this is it?"

Jinx nodded, her demeanor serious for once. "Ah, hell. It's worth a shot. Chaos and harmony, working together to keep this crazy curse at bay while you both dive deep. It's like setting up a magical buffer zone. Nice job, *goody-goody.*"

Trudie rolled her eyes, but her lips slid into a smirk.

Stone, who had been ready to abandon all hope, felt a flicker of it reignite.

This plan didn't require forgetting—didn't involve irreversible choices. It was a chance, however slim, and that was enough to pull him back from the brink.

However, the idea of going back inside the Integratron, only to fail some more had him rethinking things.

"And if it doesn't work?" he muttered, his voice heavy with skepticism.

Ella stepped closer and touched his arm. "Then we try something else. But we have to try, Stone. We can't give up now—not when we might have a real solution. *Please.*"

Stone looked back at the Integratron, the dome of the building looming like a silent soldier in the night.

He drew a deep breath. The desert's chill air was sharp in his lungs, but the fight slowly reignited within him. "Alright, let's do this. But if I start to lose it again..."

"Oh, don't you worry about a thing, Drama King. We'll pull you back," Jinx cut in, her tone serious, yet edged with her typical bravado. "We're not going to let the curse win. And we're certainly not going to let you implode. Chaos magic has its perks, you know. I can take it as well as I can give it."

Her wink did nothing to quell the panic starting to rise in him.

"Fine," he muttered.

With a reluctant grunt, Stone allowed himself to be herded back toward the Integratron by Jinx, who clapped him on the back with a little more force than necessary. "Come on, Grumpy. Let's go balance out your bad vibes."

Inside, Trudie and Jinx quickly set up the space, drawing intricate sigils and arranging candles they pulled out of nowhere, it seemed, in a meticulous pattern.

Once again, the air inside felt thick, charged with potential energy as Trudie began to chant softly, her voice weaving through the air like a calming song.

Stone stood in the center of the protective circle with Ella beside him. The hairs on his arms stood up as Jinx began her part of the spell. The air crackled with chaotic energy that somehow didn't clash with Trudie's harmony, but instead, complemented it. It created a strange sort of balance that Stone could feel seeping into his bones.

As the energies around them stabilized, Stone felt a momentary peace—a respite from the constant battle within himself. He glanced at Ella, who met his gaze with a determined nod.

"Ready?" she asked, squeezing his hand.

"As I'll ever be," Stone replied, tightening his grip on her hand, wishing he felt more sure than he did.

With a deep, collective breath, they sat down on the floor and closed their eyes. Stone focused on returning to the astral plane—the gateway they needed to reach.

This time, the entry was smoother, the resistance they had felt their last few attempts seemed to be dampened by the buffer of balanced magic.

The astral realm unfolded before them, clearer and more stable than it had been before.

Like the last time they made it in, Stone felt free of the curse. For now, it also felt like the darkness that had tried to convince him to share his truths with Ella was nowhere to be found.

They moved together through the astral landscape, each step measured and cautious as they hunted for the Breath of Selene.

Perhaps Ella was right. Maybe being kicked out was a part of the trials?

Stone and Ella approached a shimmering boundary that appeared to mark their path forward.

Before they could continue down it, the echo of the shadowy figure's earlier words hung thickly between them.

It resonated inside his mind and pulled him up short.

"Show that you can transcend your limitations, face your shadows, and balance the chaos you bring to this realm. Only then can you proceed."

The words, once a distant challenge, now felt like a direct accusation aimed at Stone.

The sinking feeling in his gut grew as he considered what lay ahead. He had refused the trial—refused to give in.

Hell, now that he had more clarity, maybe *that* was the reason they were kicked out.

The truth of his trial—the raw, almost predatory

pull he had felt toward Ella and the overwhelming desire to claim her that he had fought to suppress—wasn't something he wanted to share.

But he might have to.

Standing at the edge of what felt like a precipice, Stone realized with a heavy certainty that they would not be allowed to move forward without confronting the truth of their trials.

The shadowy figure's demand was clear, and the barrier before them was not just a physical obstacle but a metaphorical one, too. It represented the walls he had built around his darkest secrets.

His heart pounded louder in his chest, each beat echoing the creature's words about facing shadows and balancing chaos. The secrets he had buried were not just shadows—they were storm clouds threatening to burst.

He knew that revealing these truths could change everything between him and Ella.

The fear of her reaction—of disgust, fear, or even *rejection*—clawed at him. Yet, the understanding that honesty was the only way forward pressed heavier on his spirit.

"Ella," he began, his voice rough with the weight of his confession as he turned to face her. "The last time, in the trial... there were things I faced. About myself—about us. Things I haven't shared and I think I need to."

Ella's eyes widened but he knew he had to push through this.

He had to let it go and hope for the best.

The boundary to the path ahead remained, shimmering slightly as if reacting to their conversation. It was a silent challenge, urging Stone to step forward with the truth.

CHAPTER 26

HARD TRUTHS

In the hushed expanse of the astral plane, surrounded by a dreamlike landscape that magnified every emotion, Stone felt an intensity he'd seldom allowed himself to settle into.

If he did, who knew what the outcome would be?

He stood close to Ella, the surreal light casting otherworldly shadows around them. It intensified the raw, visceral feeling that surged inside him.

Here, in this place, he could no longer hide from his deepest truths and that scared the hell out of him.

He turned to Ella, feeling his heart race with a combination of dread and an overwhelming love that demanded expression.

"Ella," he began, his eyes locked onto hers, hopefully conveying the depth of what he was about to reveal. She needed to know this connection to her was more than just physical. It was everything. *She* was everything. "There's something I've never told you—something about the first day we met. It's a truth I've struggled with because... honestly, it scares me." He huffed a humorless laugh.

"What do you mean?" Ella's expression was attentive, her presence a steady comfort that slightly eased the tightness in his chest.

She reached out, gently touching his arm, encouraging him to continue.

"The day Doug died," Stone continued, the memory vivid and sharp in the back of his mind, "I was thrown into chaos, rushing to handle the aftermath of the accident. I was so angry—so hellbent on revenge because I knew what Silas was doing—what he'd already done. But when I saw you, everything else just... *stopped*. It wasn't just concern for a stranger caught in a terrible situation. It was more profound—*fucking instantaneous.*"

"What was?" Ella asked, shaking her head.

Stone worked his jaw back and forth, then he breathed out his truth in a rush. "I felt an overwhelming urge—a need to *claim* you as mine. In all senses. In, *fuck*—" he paused, struggling to articulate the complexity of that moment. "It terrified me, Ella. It terrified me because my attraction to you wasn't normal. It was a primal pull so strong that it felt like an imperative from the core of my very soul. Nothing else mattered—but I..."

She watched him with those big, soulful brown

eyes of hers, allowing him to continue without interjecting. Stone didn't know if that made it easier or worse to continue.

He reached out, rubbing his knuckles across her jaw as he remembered the internal conflict of that day. "You were human, with no idea about our world or its rules. And there I was, feeling a bond that our kind experiences only with a true mate. The part of me that knew what you were to me wanted to burn the world down and claim that bond anyway." His voice lowered, each word laden with the weight of what he had suppressed. "But I fought it. I fought those instincts because I couldn't just act on them—not without scaring you. And certainly not without pulling you into a reality you were unprepared for. It would have been more like rape at that moment and I couldn't—" A tear slid down his cheek as his voice gave out.

"Stone, I knew something significant happened that day, too. It was like a switch had been flipped inside me. I didn't understand it then, but I felt... drawn to you in a way that went beyond anything logical. It was compelling, *powerful*, and it scared me as well because I didn't know what it meant. I mean, like you said, I didn't even know yet what I was about to become."

He nodded and dropped his hands to hold hers between them. It felt like the connection he needed to ground himself to this moment—to their shared truths.

Her gaze held his and he searched for signs of judgment or retreat. Instead, he found only an open acceptance.

"Why was this so hard for you to share with me, Stone? Why hold it back if you felt it so strongly? Especially after I understood what we were to each other. After—" she breathed out, still maintaining eye contact with him.

Stone felt a rush of emotions at her questions—relief, love, and an old, lingering fear.

"I held back because I thought acknowledging it might push you away. You were dealing with so much. If I admitted how deeply I wanted to claim you—how much I felt like you were mine from that first encounter, I thought it might make you see me as something... less than what you wanted. And I couldn't bear that. I've never felt anything this powerful, Ella."

Ella squeezed his hands, her warmth seeping into him.

"Stone, the fact that you felt that way and fought it —that you respected me enough to give me time to understand—to catch up... It doesn't push me away. It pulls me in closer. I see the man you are—one who respects, despite his own desires. That's not something lesser—it's something *far* greater. I'm incredibly proud of the fact that we've been connected this way. I'm so sorry if I made you question that."

Her words washed over him, soothing the raw edges of his confession. Stone felt a shift—a loosening of the tight knot of fears that had bound his heart for too long.

"You didn't, Ella. I always felt connected. But"—he dropped his gaze to their joined hands—"I've been so afraid that revealing the depth of this instinct... would be too much. Unfortunately, holding it back has been a barrier between us—one I don't want anymore. I need you to know, I *wanted* to claim you that day in the forest. I never meant to reject our bond..."

Ella nodded, her eyes shimmering with unshed tears and something else—understanding, maybe even admiration. "We've both been holding back, haven't we? Maybe it's time we stop letting fear dictate how we live and love."

"Yes," Stone whispered, feeling a newfound strength coursing through him. "I don't want to hide any part of myself from you. Not when every part of me already belongs to you."

Without a word, Ella closed the distance between them, her hands reaching up to cup his face gently. Her eyes searched his for a moment, a silent communication passing between them.

Then, she pulled him down and pressed her lips to his and it was everything he needed.

The kiss was soft at first, hesitant as if testing the

waters, but it quickly deepened as if it released pent-up emotions too powerful to contain any longer.

Encouraged by Ella's boldness, Stone felt a surge of liberation that loosened his last tethers of restraint. Her touch, warm and insistent even on this strange plane, ignited a response deep within him that was raw and pure.

Something elemental awakened by her acceptance of him and desire *for* him.

With her encouragement echoing in his senses, Stone allowed his hands to roam over her back, drawing her closer still. He needed to feel her—allow her to *feel* his need for her.

Each touch reinforced their connection and grounded him in the here and now.

Though, how they could do any of this in the astral realm, he had no idea.

Something to ponder another time.

Stone felt the heat of Ella's skin through the fabric of her clothes—a heat that matched his own rising temperature. He'd burn up if he couldn't have her.

Ella moaned against his lips and it just about unraveled him. They needed to lose their clothing—now.

The need he'd only spoken of rushed back to him like a tidal wave.

He needed to claim her. To be *inside* her.

They needed to repair their bond.

Take the reins back and accept it.

The sensation of Ella's lips against his became the focal point of his world as he ripped at her shirt, wanting it gone.

She gasped at the sudden burst from him, but her eyes blazed with the same desire burning through him as they broke their kiss momentarily.

Then, she was doing the same to his clothes.

His wolf howled inside, singing its praises of *finally* being allowed to unleash.

To claim her wolf as his mate.

To claim *her*.

Now.

Here.

Forever.

The primal urge he had battled against for so long was now welcomed and reciprocated.

How did this happen?

How did he get so lucky?

He kissed her with a hunger that was honest and unguarded—a physical manifestation of all the emotions he had bottled up for so long—and thank fuck, she did the same.

Her hands worked his pants, dropping them to his feet.

He deepened their kiss, allowing the powerful, primal wolf side of him to rise and be felt fully as she sprung him free.

Stone's hands explored her with a new boldness, removing Ella's jeans, and then tracing the contours of her sexy hips. He lingered for a moment before dragging his hands up to her breasts. When she shivered under his fingertips, he smiled against her mouth.

God, why had he been so afraid to give in to this?

He drew her in against his body—needing her contact against his cock.

The connection sparked a wildfire of emotions, each one burning away the shadows of past fears as his body came alive.

But it wasn't enough.

There needed to be no space left between them.

They needed to become one.

The ethereal light of the astral plane seemed to pulse in rhythm with their escalating heartbeats, reflecting the primal energy that flowed between them. It was calling to them—egging them on.

Celebrating with them.

He knew whatever came next, it would not be just a physical union—it would be a spiritual amalgamation of two souls who had fought through shadows to find their truth in each other's arms.

They were truly fated.

The raw energy that Stone unleashed was met with an equally passionate force from Ella, proving that she was not just accepting but embracing the full might of his wolfish nature. And maybe... accepting her own.

Their movements were fluid and natural, as if each

knew instinctively how to answer the other's silent calls.

Because they did.

As they continued exploring this newfound depth between them, the atmosphere thrummed with power. The astral realm, with its boundless expanse, felt like the only place vast enough to contain the magnitude of their connection.

Both stripped naked, Stone lifted Ella effortlessly, her legs wrapping around his waist. Then, he moved to the stone altar where the Breathe of Selene had once hovered appeared.

With no sign of the glowing crystal orb, the altar pulsed with an eerie light, and seemed to call to them —its surface a promise of unity and strength.

Laying Ella gently on the smooth surface of the altar, Stone gazed down at her with a reverence that transcended the physical. Here, they were not just two beings consumed by desire—they were the embodiment of a profound bond that had weathered trials and transformations.

The altar was not just a place of offering but a foundation of their new beginning—a witness to the purity of their union.

As Stone positioned himself at her entrance—the sense of completion overwhelmed his senses. His brain fired off so many feelings, and sensations, and there were none that he could hang onto. His brain was short-circuiting with the pleasure.

He entered her slowly, reverently—each movement a sacred rite.

Ella's gasp of contentment was a sound more beautiful than any chorus, and as he began to move, their bodies found a rhythm that was both ancient and new—primal yet fucking *perfect*.

With each thrust, waves of energy pulsed around them, the light from the altar rising in intensity, mirroring the incoming crescendo of their passion.

They were meant to do this. They were meant to fit like this.

Always.

CHAPTER 27

MOON WOLVES

ELLA

H oly shit, the intensity of our connection is blowing my mind.

It swells around us, an almost palpable force in the quiet of the astral realm. In some ways, it's so similar to the last time we did this.

But in other ways, this time is so much more profound.

Like somehow, being here, on this plane, taps into a vast expanse of our souls that we didn't even know existed.

At least, I didn't.

Our confessions hang in the air—mingling with the charged energy that envelops us as we move in tandem. I never thought I could love him more intensely, but hearing how he fought his darkest, most primal instincts—*for me*—tears down the last of my reservations.

Not even the curse could take that from us.

His every touch now feels like a vow—his kisses like promises etched into my very skin.

This man *and* his wolf will protect me until his dying breath.

And I'll do the same for him.

The power of his revelations, the weight of his restraint—it's all here between us, making each movement, each connection, feel more pronounced.

I truly thought the last time we did this it was powerful.

But this...

His touch sparks more than desire. It ignites a fierce need to match his honesty—to give him all of myself without restraint or fear.

As his hands explore, claiming every inch of my body in ways I've only imagined, I feel the urgent need to open myself up to the full extent of our bond.

My hands roam across his upper body, mapping the landscape, with a reverence that sends shivers through my core and straight back to him. Each caress sent between us is both a question and an answer—as if one of us is asking for permission and the other is granting it without hesitation.

Back and forth.

Over and over again.

The energy around us pulses, growing with each touch, each breath shared in the quiet intimacy of this place. We are connected—not just physically, but in a way far more expansive than either of us has even begun to understand.

Soul level.

The reality where we are feels both distant and intensely present. Like we've stepped out of time and into a space made just for us.

"Stone," I whisper, my voice breaking on his name as he shifts, aligning our bodies in perfect synchrony.

God, he feels so good.

He slows, resting his forehead against mine. His breaths are hot and ragged as he pauses long enough to pull back, his eyes searching mine, waiting.

"I love you," I whisper, my hands sliding up his back, feeling the powerful muscles tense and shudder under my touch. "And I claim you as mine. Only you. *Always.*"

With a growl that rumbles from deep within his chest, he thrusts forward hard and fast, unhinging completely.

I welcome the pressure, the exquisite fullness as he slides in and out of me. While not slow, it's a deliberate movement, filled with so much emotion that tears prick at my eyes—not from pain, but from the overwhelming sense of becoming one with this man— *my mate.*

My *soul* mate.

Yes, we are meant for this.

We are meant to bond.

Meant to transcend into this place of total worship for one another.

Our connection deepens, the bond between us weaving tighter with each thrust. It's as if each movement is a stroke of a painter's brush, coloring in a masterpiece that only we will ever fully understand or appreciate.

The pleasure inside me builds but it's not just a physical sensation. It's also an emotional crescendo that fills the vastness around us. My heart expands, stretching beyond my body as it embraces him.

His kisses are deep and consuming, tasting of passion and the faintest hint of the wildness that is his nature. My nature, too.

Every touch seals his vows to me, not spoken, but felt—a covenant made in the heat of our union.

Everything narrows to just this—*just us*—and the intensity of what we share drowns out all else. There's no room for fear or doubt here—not with how he fills me so completely, touching parts of my soul that were once shrouded in darkness.

"More," I gasp, clinging to him, my nails digging into his shoulders as I urge him deeper.

He responds with a fervor, his movements becoming more urgent, more insistent as our bodies ride one another. And as we reach the precipice, the energy around us crests like a wave poised to crash on the shore.

Once again, the bubble of light—our bond begins to consume all that I am.

All that I'll ever be.

His.

The palpable energy that extends from the center of our hearts once again reaches out, braiding itself together.

Any shred of the darkness that tainted our bond—any sign of the curse—is dispelled. It shatters across the fabric of this reality like dust on the wind.

His name spills from my lips in a litany—a prayer as ancient as time itself, as our bond seals fully, *completely.*

My climax hits me like a meteor striking the earth—*explosive* and *radiant*—scattering light across the canvas of the astral plane.

Stone is right there with me—his release is a force that binds him to me, heart and soul.

I hear his thoughts of love—of complete adoration as if they're my own. And maybe at this point, they are.

We're the same.

We're *one.*

The sound of his climax resonates through every fiber of my being, searing itself into the recesses of my mind. I want to hear it again and again. Into eternity.

It's the sexiest sound ever made.

For a moment, we hold each other, breathless and awed by the magnitude of what we've shared.

It's undeniable—our bond is sealed, unbreakable, and sacred.

It thrums with an ebb and flow of energy that centers me—like the world was always off-kilter until this.

The curse is nothing more than a distant memory. How? I don't care. I just know *this* is how we are meant to be.

This moment is a testament to the journey we've endured and the battles we've fought—both within ourselves and against the darkness that sought to divide us.

As I lean forward, resting my head against Stone's chest, listening to the steady beat of his heart, I know that this is only the beginning.

We've crossed into a new realm—one where our love is both the shield and the sword.

And together, we are invincible.

Just as I begin to relax with Stone still wrapped around me—still *inside* me—the air around us pulses with a new, peculiar energy.

It's different from what we just experienced.

This is soft, pure, and resonant—like the humming of a divine chord.

Stone and I pause, our breaths caught in unison as we feel the presence of something ancient and powerful drawing near.

Suddenly, the Breath of Selene materializes, hovering in the air directly above us. It shimmers with a boundless energy that pulsates with the heartbeat of the universe itself.

Stone's grip tightens around me, his body tensed in awe. "Ella, do you see—?"

"Yes," I breathe out, unable to tear my gaze from the crystal.

Then, the Breath of Selene dissipates, spreading into countless particles of light that drift toward us like celestial snowflakes. As they touch our skin, a surge of warmth floods through us both.

The particles seep in and thanks to the heightened state of our bond, I can feel them weaving through both our veins, pulsing with our blood, and melding with the very essence of our beings.

Fully integrated, a shockwave of power erupts from within us, radiating outwards in a brilliant wave of light that fills the astral plane, turning shadows into mere memories.

Somehow, this energy binds us even tighter, reinforcing our already solid bond with a strength that feels as old as time itself.

"It deems us worthy," Stone whispers, his voice filled with wonder and a hint of awe.

His words resonate with truth—a confirmation from the Breath of Selene itself.

It *has* deemed us worthy. It's chosen us to carry its legacy—to wield its power.

I nod, overwhelmed by the honor and the responsibility that comes with this acceptance.

The realization that we're now guardians of something so ancient and powerful fills me with a sense of purpose and determination—and an unshakeable belief in the truth of the prophecy Clementine shared with us.

We *are* the Moon Wolves.

Without warning, the astral plane dissolves like mist under the morning sun.

One moment, Stone and I are entwined in each other's naked bodies and the revelation of our souls' union, and the next... we're lying side by side on the cold, hard wooden floor of the Integratron.

The contrast is so stark and abrupt, that for a heartbeat, I can't breathe.

My body still hums with the echoes of our connection, yet here we are, fully clothed—and distinctly separate.

I catch Stone shifting uncomfortably beside me, a quick, subtle maneuver to adjust his jeans, clearly trying to disguise his body's physical reaction to the intense connection we'd just experienced in the astral. His face is tinged with a flush I can't say I've ever seen him wear before but I'm determined to make it happen again.

"Well, Stone," Jinx chuckles, her voice rich with amusement, "looks like you've lived up to your name in more ways than one."

Stone's gaze shifts to me and I just smirk and shrug sheepishly.

What can I say?

I'd be more likely to agree if I opened my mouth.

Trudie drops her arms, releasing the circle. Her cheeks turn a shade of pink as well, and her gaze flits between us with a mix of amusement and embarrassment.

"The energies were certainly powerful today," she adds, her voice a whisper—perhaps in deference to the sanctity of what had just occurred. Then, she raises her right hand, fanning her face.

"Yeah, it was... uh," I attempt, shaking my head.

Evidently, words still elude me.

Stone and I manage to regain some semblance of composure as we stand, still slightly dazed by the sudden shift from the astral to the physical.

"I gotta say, whatever you two were doing, I was pretty sure things were going well. I was getting all hot and bothered over here, and I haven't been bothered with that kind of hassle in over a decade." Jinx gives us a conspiratorial wink, her humor helping to cut through the last tendrils of awkwardness hanging in the air.

Trudie, ignoring her sister's admission, clasps her hands together, her eyes bright with curiosity. "So, what happened exactly? Other than the obvious."

Stone and I exchange a glance, the significance of our experience still resonating deeply between us. Just as inside the astral plane, I feel our connection so profoundly, that I can't even tell where one of us ends and the other begins.

"We've obtained the Breath of Selene," Stone says at the same time, I say, "We... *bonded.*"

Trudie and Jinx both look at us with wide eyes.

"It was..." I begin.

"Ack, no details, please," Trudie says, covering her ears but Jinx looks like she's more than willing to get down and dirty.

I smile at them both, shaking my head. "There was something else... the curse, it felt like it just... lifted."

Stone picks up the thread, his tone reflective. "We don't know exactly how or why, but during our bond, something shifted. The darkness that was part of the curse—it just faded away, like it was never meant to be there in the first place."

Trudie's brows knit together in thoughtful concern. "The curse lifting spontaneously is unusual. That's not something that happens without significant power or intervention. We should get Isolde in here. She'd be able to confirm for us."

Jinx chimes in, her eyes serious but with an underlying spark of excitement. "That's got to mean something big. You two are probably more important than you realize."

"We're beginning to realize that," I whisper, thinking again about the prophecy and so much is beginning to make sense.

Just as we're about to discuss the wider implications of her words, the door to the Integratron swings open with a force that startles us all. Isolde steps through, her face etched with lines of urgency and concern.

"Oh, thank goodness. You're out of the astral realm. I hope that means good news because Stone, Ella, we have a serious problem," she declares sharply, catching her breath as her eyes lock onto ours. "Andres has made his move—he's returned to Black Crater and he's not alone. We must return—*now.*"

CHAPTER 28
OVERLOAD

ELLA

Panic claws at my stomach as Isolde's news ignites every protective instinct I possess.

I need to get back to protect my children and my pack.

"Andres at Black Crater already? We still have days before the Supermoon Are you sure?" My voice is sharp, channeling the urgency of an Alpha and mother.

Isolde's expression is grim as she meets my gaze. "I was maintaining the wards outside when I got a call—my coven has scouts in Black Crater. They've seen him, Ella, and he's not alone. They're setting up something big—fortifications. It looks planned and serious."

Stone's jaw tightens, his stance protective beside me. "Who's with him? Did they see?"

I sense he's thinking about the local packs and

trying to determine who would be brave enough to ally with Andres.

"Details were hard to come by without compromising their position, but it's clear he's not alone. There are significant magical signatures," Isolde explains, her phone clutched tightly in her hand as if it's a lifeline. "My assumption is they still have witches employed."

"We need to move—*now,*" I state flatly, the decision firm in my mind.

Every second we delay could be disastrous.

"You'll never make it in time by car." Jinx shakes her head, her jaw clenched tight. Then, she turns to her sister. "What about teleportation?"

Trudie nods slowly. "Right, teleportation could work, but who can we call? Marcus is out—he still hasn't forgiven you for that New Orleans incident."

Jinx rolls her eyes. "Damn. And I owe Lucia money."

"Of course, you do," Trudie says, planting a hand on her hip. "What about Victor?"

"Isn't that old bastard dead?" Jinx scrunches her brow, her lips twisting to the side.

While they bicker, Stone and I exchange looks of confusion and growing impatience.

"Can someone explain what's going on? *Teleportation?* Is that even a thing?" I demand, frustration coloring my tone as we stand there, wasting precious minutes.

Jinx, catching the urgency—and the confusion—in my voice, waves her hand dismissively. "Yeah, it's a thing. Not common, but for emergencies, it's perfect. We just need someone who won't botch it."

Suddenly, Trudie's phone rings.

Her eyes flare as she checks the screen. She answers quickly, her expression shifting from concern to surprise.

"Yes, Diana, we're all together," Trudie says. She listens intently, nodding as she paces a small circle. "Yes, it's urgent. We were just discussing how to... Really? He can? That would be incredible." Her face brightens as she glances up with a mixture of astonishment and gratitude. "Thank you, Diana. We'll be ready."

Before Trudie can even end the call, a shimmering ripple distorts the air in the center of the Integratron. The fabric of reality seems to fold in on itself, and with a soft pop, a figure materializes.

He's an older gentleman, his wavy white hair neatly trimmed, framing a face that bears the marks of many years but with a twinkle of youth still evident in his eyes. His suit is impeccably tailored, and the bright pink undershirt he wears underneath adds a quirky contrast that seems to match his off-center demeanor.

"Ah, splendid," the man exclaims with a grandiose sweep of his hand. His voice carries a melodious accent that hints at ancient origins. "You must be the lovely individuals Diana mentioned from her vision. My name is Kyros, and I am happily at your service."

Stone and I exchange a glance, both taken aback by the sudden appearance of this man and his flamboyant introduction.

Kyros claps his hands together, looking between us. "Well, don't be shy. Who needs to be whisked away, and where to? Diana mentioned Black Crater, Oregon. A bit of a tricky spot, but nothing I can't handle. I've studied the Google."

The Google?

I shake my head, unsure if it's actually all that wise to go with him.

Stone steps forward. "I'll go first."

Shit, looks like we are.

I place a hand on his arm. "No, Stone. I'm the Alpha. It's my responsibility to lead. I should be the first to arrive."

"But you don't know what you'll return to. I should—"

"No," I reiterate, infusing my tone with just enough power.

The room fills with tense energy as Stone and I stand, locked in a silent battle of wills.

"Ah, a spirited debate—how delightful," Kyros chuckles, then quickly sobers. "However, my dears, there's no need for dispute. I can take you both simultaneously. It might be a tad more... exhilarating than usual but fear not. You're in capable hands. I've even done it once before."

Jinx coughs. "Once?"

Kyros, puffs his chest, clearly flustered. "Well, ordinarily, I prefer to travel with only one other, but I assure you—"

"Are there any... side effects we should be aware of?" I ask, my voice cautious as I consider the potential risks.

God, am I even considering this?

I guess I am.

Kyros nods sagely, his expression turning serious. "Indeed, the journey can be jarring. Some experience nausea and disorientation. More than once I've seen people lose their lunch. It's the price of bypassing the usual constraints of space and time. But worry not, I'll ensure you arrive as gracefully as possible."

As the weight of the situation presses upon us, I turn to address Kyros directly, "Can you take all of us at once?"

Kyros hesitates, his eyebrows knitting together in concentration. "I wouldn't recommend it. Ideally, I would prefer to take you and the gentleman first, then return for the others. It's the most efficient method without overtaxing the magical boundaries and ensuring everyone's safety."

Stone nods in agreement but looks to me for the final decision.

"Okay," I agree, wishing there was another way because this sounds bonkers. "Let's do it."

Isolde steps forward. "I'll go next. My abilities might be necessary if you run into any magical traps or barriers when you return."

Jinx crosses her arms and gives a rueful smile. "And *I'll* be driving. Trust me, teleporting is not in the cards for me—not after last time. Nearly ended up inside a tree. My chaos energy will blow your circuits, Kyros. My car's fast, and I'll bring Trudie and the gear. We'll be there as quick as demonly possible."

Trudie nods, clearly relieved at the arrangement.

Kyros claps his hands decisively, the sound echoing slightly in the tense air of the Integratron. "Very well. Would you two please come closer? I require physical contact to maintain a stable connection."

Stone and I step forward, positioning ourselves beside Kyros. He instructs us to hold his hands, creating a physical link between the three of us.

Kyros's expression is serious despite the faint twinkle of mischief in his eyes. "Focus on your desired destination. Visualize it as clearly as you can in your minds."

Taking a deep breath, I close my eyes and picture the Sacred Grove in Black Crater—its stone circle embedded in the middle of the woods. The visualization comes so naturally, that it's almost like tapping into the astral plane.

I can smell the mossy scent of the stones and hear the whisper of the wind through the leaves. Beside me, I feel Stone's grip tighten, a silent affirmation of our shared resolve and focus.

Kyros nods once, apparently satisfied with our preparations. "Very well."

There's no chanting, no grand gestures. Instead, Kyros simply closes his eyes, and the world shifts beneath us.

The sensation is immediate and disorienting—like being sucked through a narrow, bending tube at an impossible speed.

The next moment, we're standing in the Sacred Grove, but the transition isn't gentle. The abrupt stop leaves both Stone and me staggering, clutching at each other for support as waves of nausea wash over us.

Because of the connection to Stone, it's like I'm experiencing motion sickness times two.

My stomach churns violently, and the world spins dizzyingly around us. It takes every ounce of willpower not to collapse or succumb to the urge to vomit.

It doesn't work. I fall to my knees and hurl up my dinner.

As the initial wave of nausea begins to subside, another sensation takes over—my senses are suddenly, painfully heightened.

The moonlight is too bright, the colors too vivid. Sounds are magnified to an overwhelming cacophony.

Somehow, the rustling leaves sound like thunder, and the distant nighttime sounds are unbearable. The usually comforting smell of the forest is now a potent mix that borders on sickly.

Stone groans beside me, his hands pressed to his temples.

"Everything is... *too much,*" he mutters, his voice strained and way too loud to my ears. It's like he's yelling but I know he's not.

I nod in agreement, unable to speak as the chorus of the forest assaults my ears.

Kyros, who seems only mildly affected, watches us with concern. "The side effects of teleportation can be quite intense, especially when combined with your already heightened senses. It will pass, but you must try to focus, to ground yourselves."

We don't have time for this.

The thought brings a clawing panic through my chest.

How long will this last?

Drawing in a shaky breath, I try to heed his advice, focusing on the literal ground. I bend over, away from the vomit, and rest my head against the cool stones.

"I will return post haste with Isolde," Kyros says so softly it's almost a whisper. Yet inside my head, it vibrates like standing beside a firetruck's horn blast.

With a soft pop, Kyros vanishes, leaving Stone and me to contend with our disorientation and heightened senses.

As the world stabilizes, a chill sweeps through the air—not from the evening, but from a tangible sense of dread that seems to seep from the very stones of the Sacred Grove.

Stone and I reach out to support each other as we stand cautiously. Our senses strain against the heightened awareness that makes every shadow a specter and every rustle a potential threat. It seems like our breathing is the loudest sound, rasping through the encroaching silence like a harsh whisper.

"Stone," I whisper, clutching his arm, my voice trembling despite my effort to sound calm. I fight the urge to puke all over again. "Do you feel that?"

He nods slowly, his eyes scanning the darkened forest. "Something's circling us... I can feel it—hear it. But I can't see anything. It's like it's just out of sight."

"Something's not right," I murmur, scanning the dark perimeter of the grove. My voice sounds too loud in my ears, almost echoing off the stones that encircle us.

Stone nods, his expression grim. "Keep your guard up."

We move cautiously toward the edge of the stone circle, our eyes scanning every bush—every rustle in the grass.

That's when we hear it—a soft, taunting whisper that seems to come from all around us.

"Moon Wolves... so mighty, yet so easily fooled," the voice mocks.

I clench my fists, trying to locate the source of the voice, but it's elusive, moving like smoke on the wind.

"Show yourself—" I call out, my voice ringing with the authority of an Alpha. The sound has my mind whirling from the intensity of it. It's like I've drunk too much and can't think straight.

The only response is a low, malicious laugh that curls around us like a cold embrace.

The sacred forest that would normally comfort me now looms beyond the Sacred Grove—ominous under the moon's watchful eye. The air thickens with palpable tension as if this site breathes in uneasy anticipation.

Suddenly, the ground beneath us seems to pulse, sending a shockwave of energy that rattles through my bones. For a moment, it's like my skull is being split apart.

Stone stumbles beside me, reaching out to steady himself against the stone wall.

Before we can regain our bearings, a series of bright, disorienting flashes ignite around us—like lightning striking too close. Each burst of light momentarily blinds us, and in those brief flashes, shadows dance at the edge of my vision—ghostly figures that circle and vanish as quickly as they appear.

The echoes of taunting voices fill the air as their words twist around us in a cruel symphony.

"Moon Wolves... so mighty, yet so easily broken," they jeer, each syllable dripping with malice. "Nothing more than flashy words. They mean nothing. *Are* nothing."

The voices multiply, surrounding us in a cacophony of scorn and mockery, pulling at the edges of my resolve. The motion is so disorienting, that I grab hold of my stomach and slam my eyes shut.

Then, everything stops—the flashes, the voices, the sense of movement.

Silence crashes down with oppressive weight, and in the stillness that follows, a chilling scream cuts through the night.

It's a sound of pure agony—one that freezes my heart and roots me to the spot. Despite myself, my eyes fly open.

The scream fades into a haunting echo, and as it does, the moonlight gathers and focuses on one point in the center of our sacred circle.

There, in the heart of the Sacred Grove, as if spot-lighted for a macabre show, lies a body.

Even in the dim light, I know exactly who it is.

It's Clementine.

CHAPTER 29

BOW DOWN

STONE

The moonlight's serene glow is cast over the Sacred Grove, its silvery beams belying the chaos that has unfolded under its watchful gaze.

With his head still swimming, Stone knelt beside Clementine, his sister's lifeless eyes staring up at the stars she once believed held answers.

A guttural growl of sorrow escaped him, reverberating through the grove like a somber wind. Seeing her like this—it had a sobering effect, ushering out the last remnants of disorientation left from their teleportation.

Why would anyone do this?

Was it just to get back at them?

But the truth unraveled itself like a lotus flower.

"She died protecting the Luna Scrolls," Stone

murmured, the words thick with grief, despite their revelation.

The weight of her belief in the prophecy—*that it would save them*—felt like a heavy chain around his heart.

His hand trembled as he reached out to close her eyes. The simple gesture was a silent farewell to a life intertwined deeply with the fate of their pack.

Ella knelt beside him, tears silently tracing down her cheeks as she gazed upon Clementine's still form.

After a moment of shared mourning, Ella's posture stiffened, her expression shifting into one of resolute command. With a deep, steadying breath, she reached out with her mind—her Alpha command resonant and clear as it echoed telepathically to every member of the pack.

Everyone, get to the Sacred Grove. Now.

As Stone sensed the pack members beginning to heed her summons, a slow, sarcastic clap sliced through the quiet night.

Stone and Ella turned sharply to see Andres emerging from the shadows with an insufferable smirk playing on his lips.

"Well, well, if it isn't the great *Moon Wolves*, brought to their knees over a legend," he mocked, his voice smooth and contemptuous.

Stone's grief twisted into fury, his hands balling into fists at his sides. Before he could move, Ella placed a calming hand on his arm, her touch a silent command for restraint.

We need time for the others to arrive. We'll have our asses handed to us with this disorientation, she said, reaching out to him through the bond.

She rose to her feet, facing Andres squarely. "If you think so little of these *'legends,'* why bother with us at all?"

Andres's smirk widened as he stepped closer, his gaze flicking dismissively between Stone and Ella. "Let's call it morbid curiosity at this point."

As Andres stared at them from the shadows, his words lingered with Stone like a bad aftertaste.

The Sacred Grove remained tense—the air thick with the scent of unease and freshly disturbed earth. Before Stone could voice his lament, a familiar disturbance in the air rippled behind them.

With a soft pop and a slight wobble, Kyros reappeared in the center of the Sacred Grove with Isolde.

Kyros's grandiose demeanor momentarily faltered as he caught the tension in the air and took in Clementine's body.

"Oh dear, did we miss something crucial?" he asked, his eyes wide with concern.

Isolde stepped forward, her mouth agape. "What happened here?"

Stone had no words for her to explain what she was seeing. He couldn't believe it himself.

As Isolde dropped down beside Ella's feet to

inspect Clementine, Andres's laughter cut through the tense air, drawing all eyes back to him.

"Oh, how touching," he mocked, ignoring Isolde's question entirely. "The fancy *Moon Wolves* have enlisted a solitary witch and an old man to their cause. Truly, revolutionary."

Despite her travel sickness, Ella's stance remained unyielding as she faced him.

"I wouldn't underestimate either of them," she countered firmly, her voice carrying the weight of her authority.

Andres's smirk only broadened and it made Stone's stomach roll. He was up to something—something big.

"Perhaps. But compared to the entire coven at my disposal, I think I'll shake in my Chelsea boots another day," he taunted, his eyes gleaming with scorn. ."

Isolde's posture stiffened. Though her hands rested on Clementine's shoulder, her gaze never wavered from Andres.

"Underestimating what others can do is a common mistake of the arrogant," she retorted, her voice cool and controlled.

"Is that so?" Andres said, his gaze cooly landing on Kyros. "And what can you do? Other than parlor tricks?"

With a shudder, Kyros glanced around, his nerves visibly fraying.

He caught Stone's gaze before blurting out, "Perhaps I should—yes, I think it's best if I leave you all to it. Magical confrontations are not quite my cup of tea, if you will."

Before anyone could respond, Kyros vanished with another pop, leaving behind a faint scent of ozone and a trace of his quirky presence.

Andres's mocking laughter echoed through the grove, raking over Stone's nerves. He clenched his fists, trying to contain the beast within that urged him to shift and attack. He sensed the same fight going on inside Ella, too.

They needed a plan.

The first of their pack members began to arrive, slipping through the trees with quiet, lethal grace, their eyes alight with the glow of their wolf forms.

Stone kept his gaze locked on Andres, who seemed unfazed by the growing number of werewolves entering the fray.

"What I find annoying is that you really think you're worthy to rule this territory," Andres chided, his voice smooth and condescending. "You were a fucking *human*, Ella. Black Crater should be under the control of someone who can *actually* protect it. Who understands what that even means."

Ella's energy vibrated from her as her eyes flashed a fierceness that reflected her inner wolf with their multicolored light.

"We've managed just fine without you," she retorted with a low growl.

Andres chuckled, his eyes sweeping over the pack members that were quickly forming a protective crescent around their Alpha.

"Look at this. A ragtag group of moon chasers, all clinging to ancient prophecies and a few dusty old scrolls. Do you even understand what you're guarding? Or are you just playing with fables?"

Stone felt the pack's collective anger simmering just beneath the surface, ready to erupt. Yet, they held back, standing firm behind their Alpha waiting on her order. Their discipline was a testament to the unity and strength they've built over the past few months.

Stone's heart filled with pride, despite mourning their loss at the same time.

Andres stepped closer, his tone smooth, almost reasonable. "Think about it, Ella. I said it before and I'll say it now. Hand over the territory. Let someone with the resources to manage it take over. You can keep your titles—your rituals. Just fall under my jurisdiction. It's a generous offer, really."

Ella's eyes narrowed, the rumble in her throat deepening.

"We are not subjects to be ruled, Andres. This is our territory. We won't surrender it," she declared, her voice resonating through the sacred site.

Stone felt a gnawing panic rising within him as Andres's words echoed in his ears, each taunt slicing through the tension like a well-aimed arrow.

This was the same rhetoric Andres had spouted

last time they faced off. Yet now, there was an undeniable confidence in his demeanor—a cockiness that hadn't been there before.

What had changed?

Why did Andres seem so sure of himself this time?

As he scanned the clearing, Stone's gaze lingered on the faces of his pack members—their energy full of both resolve and unease.

They were ready to fight, to defend their territory, but Stone couldn't shake the feeling that they were missing a crucial piece of the puzzle.

Suddenly more alert, his eyes surveyed the woods around him. He could sense Andres' pack and other magical beings—the witches most likely—but there had to be more.

Something that was about to tip the scales.

He could *feel* it.

Andres seemed to revel in the tension he was creating, his eyes gleaming as he surveyed the growing number of Black Crater werewolves.

"You think your little gatherings and your ancient prophecies will save you?" he jeered. "You're living in the ancient past, Ella. The world is changing, and I have the means to change with it—*to control it*. With the Luna Scrolls now in my possession, I'm certain the power they describe will be mine to command."

Ella remained stoic, but Stone could sense the ripple of concern that passed through her. Andres's mention of the scrolls wasn't just a boast—it was a declaration of an advantage he believed he had.

But was that it?

Stone's thoughts flashed to the cryptic nature of the Luna Scrolls, the deep magic they were rumored to contain. Not only did they detail the prophecy, but the vision for the future where the supernatural community was united under one ruler.

Did he actually believe *he* was it?

"Your confidence is misplaced, Andres," Ella shot back, her voice strong despite the uncertainty that Stone knew she felt. "Having the Luna Scrolls and understanding them are two very different things."

As their pack tightened around the Sacred Grove, the unity among them was palpable. They were more than just a pack—they were a family, bound by blood, loyalty, and a shared dedication to their land and legacy. Each member radiated a quiet strength that bolstered Stone's resolve.

Andres scoffed, shaking his head. "You rely too much on loyalty and tradition. But I'm offering you a way out before this escalates further. Think about your pack, Ella. You can avoid unnecessary bloodshed."

Stone fought back a snarl.

They were not just defending territory—they were defending their way of life, their history, and their future.

Andres's words, though menacing, also betrayed

his desperation. He wanted Black Crater's territory for the symbolic defeat it would represent.

If Black Crater bowed to Andres, others would follow because he had both the Luna Scrolls and the Moon Wolves under his command.

The air thickened as Andres's mocking laughter faded, the tension palpable under the serene moonlight. Stone's muscles tensed, preparing for any sudden move, but Andres remained casual, almost carefree, his eyes lingering on Ella with a cool, sarcastic gaze.

Ella's jaw ticked, but she didn't say the words that appeared to be on the tip of her tongue.

"You really should consider my offer," Andres continued, that stupid smirk never leaving his face. "It's only a matter of time, Ella. Resistance is just prolonging the inevitable."

"Are you deaf, Andres? We will never bow to you," she declared. "It'll never happen."

The standoff continued, each moment stretching longer. The silence was punctuated only by the soft rustle of leaves in the gentle night breeze.

The pack's collective energy was a tightly wound spring, ready to snap at the slightest provocation.

Unfortunately, Stone knew it was exactly what Andres wanted.

Just as the tension seemed unbearable, Andres turned and tipped his chin toward the darkness behind him. "Very well. Don't say I didn't warn you."

As if an invisible cloak was dropped, another figure emerged from the darkness, stepping into the moonlit grove with a presence that sent a chill straight down Stone's spine.

A growl bubbled up from the back of his throat as he actively fought the urge to shift and rip his throat out.

Silas slinked into view, his arrival unannounced but his timing impeccable—as if he'd been waiting for the perfect moment to make his entrance.

That's when Stone realized that's exactly what had happened.

This—*this was what Stone had been sensing.*

Silas's eyes locked with Ella's, and a slow, sinister smile spread across his face.

"Andres has been trying to persuade you with words," he said, his familiar voice cutting through the night. "But I believe actions speak louder than any threat or promise."

Without another word, two figures were pushed forward from the shadows. As moonlight illuminated them, Stone watched in horror as Asher and Avery were unceremoniously pushed forward into the clearing.

Asher stumbled slightly, catching himself with a wide-eyed look of confusion and fear. His hand instinctively reached for his sister, who clung to him, her smaller body shaking.

Avery's eyes were huge in the pale light, darting

around the clearing in a desperate search for something familiar—something safe.

When they landed on Ella, her lips parted as if to speak or cry out, but no sound came—only a silent, trembling gasp that spoke volumes of her fright.

Asher's jaw set, a determined frown forming as he tried to mask his own fear. His gaze met his mother's across the clearing, and in that brief glance, a flurry of unspoken messages passed between them—reassurance, fear, *defiance.*

Despite their grim situation, Asher squared his shoulders, standing a little taller, his protective instincts palpable even in his own vulnerability.

Isolde stood up, then gasped, her voice low as she whispered, "Oh, no."

Stone watched, his heart clenching at the sight of the kids so cruelly used as pawns.

How the hell did they find them?

Next to him, Ella gasped, and then a fierce snarl tore from the depths of what felt like her soul.

The grove fell deathly silent, every wolf holding their breath, their eyes fixed on the children who stood trembling under Silas's grip.

Andres looked around, his smile never faltering. "So, tell us again how you'll never bow down."

CHAPTER 30

BERSERK

ELLA

My heart is about to burst from my ribcage, each beat a loud echo in the eerie stillness of the Sacred Grove.

Asher and Avery stand there, terrified, under Silas's looming shadow.

How? How did they get my children?

Panic claws at my throat, thick and suffocating.

I can't breathe, can't think, except for the wild, spiraling terror that they have them—my kids, my heart, *my fucking family.*

The stones spin around me, the faces of my pack blurred and distant, as one thought hammers through the chaos: I need to save them.

But *how?*

Silas's voice slithers through the air, cold and triumphant. "Not so cocky now, are you?"

His taunt is a physical blow, and I stagger under its

weight, my gaze locked on my children's pale, scared faces.

I barely register Stone's hand on my shoulder, his presence a grounding force.

"Ella, we need a plan," he whispers urgently.

But all I can think is—*Alanna.*

What the fuck happened to Alanna?

She was supposed to protect them. She swore—she'd burn the world down for us.

How did this happen? Is she okay?

Oh, god. Did they—

My gaze drifts to Clementine's body and bile pricks at the back of my throat.

Despair gives way to a burning anger, a fierce, protective rage.

I force my mind to pivot—to strategize.

We can't just attack. The kids are right there, in the line of fire.

Bartering?

What do we have that Silas wants more than to see us crushed?

My mind races through options, discarding them as fast as they come.

What if I pretended this was no big deal? Could I convince Andres and Silas it's not killing me inside that they have my kids?

Troy is a part of Andres' pack—or at least he will be when the Supermoon hits.

He's their dad.

And even if we didn't see eye to eye, he'd still fight to protect them, right?

I wish I could believe it.

But...

"God, how did this happen?" I curse, letting the thought slip out loud as I rake my fingertips through my hair.

Suddenly, a new figure is dragged forward from the shadows—*Alanna.*

A knot forms in the middle of my throat.

Her appearance is disheveled, her eyes red and swollen with guilt and grief. She stumbles just like Asher, almost falling before righting herself, her gaze meeting mine.

The betrayal in her eyes is clear, and her lips tremble as she tries to speak.

The betrayer.

The one close to me.

Diana's words come back to haunt me in full force.

"El... Ella, I'm so sorry," she chokes out, her voice a whisper of despair.

Her confession is a knife twisting in my gut. *How could she?*

Behind her, Andres smirks, clearly enjoying the scene unfolding before him.

"Oh, don't you worry. She put up a good fight, but everyone has a weakness," he says with a cold laugh. "Isn't that right, Alanna?"

"Fuck you," Alanna spits back.

"Such a firecracker, this one." His gaze shifts back to me, his smirk widening. "See, we found her brother. In a group home, no less, helpless without her protection. It's fascinating what people will do when you threaten the right leverage."

His words have a double meaning and they're not lost on me.

Not at all.

My heart pounds even harder, fury mingling with my fear.

How dare they use her family against her?

How dare she betray *mine?*

"And now, Ella," Andres continues, stepping closer, his voice dripping with venom, "let's return to the discussion at hand. The question is still yours to answer and I have a feeling you'll choose differently now—but let's see." He winks at me as if he already knows my answer.

My nostrils flare and I swear, if I were a dragon, I'd be breathing fire right about now.

Andres claps his hands in front of him. "So, what will it be? Will you concede your territory, or will your children meet an untimely end?"

He snaps his fingers and a sea of his allies flood the space behind him. His pack—some in human form, some as wolves are convened, as well as god knows how many witches.

The weight of his ultimatum hangs heavy in the air. I glance at Asher and Avery as they cling to each other, their eyes wide with fear. Asher shakes his head vehemently.

The sight fuels my resolve.

"No," I whisper at first, my voice gaining strength. "We will not bow to you. We will not surrender."

I fight back a sob and I shake my head.

As I turn to Stone, seeing the same determination mirrored in his eyes, I say through the bond, *We need a distraction.*

Just as I send the thought, a crackle of energy slices through the tense air. With a pop and a sharp gust of wind, Kyros appears right behind us. Right beside him, Jinx and Trudie materialize—a manifestation of my wish.

Kyros, on the other hand, doesn't stick around to help. Instead, he chirps out his alarm and vanishes again.

"Looks like we arrived just in time for a little bit of chaos," Jinx chirps, her voice slicing through the heavy silence like a knife.

Without waiting for an answer, Jinx grins widely, her eyes alight with chaotic energy. She snaps her fingers and immediately, the bizarre effects of her powers ripple through Andres' and Silas' ranks.

Andres' pack members begin inexplicably tripping over their own feet, shoelaces knotting together magically. One particularly large werewolf suddenly yelps as his belt buckle snaps open, his pants pooling around his ankles.

Another pack member tries to shift, only to end up a small wolf pup.

Confusion turns to chaos as more of Andres' pack struggle with similar embarrassments. Another finds his eyes glued shut, blinding him, while someone else's feet stick to the ground, rendering him unable to move forward. Instead, he falls face first, nearly breaking at the ankles.

As this mayhem unfolds, Trudie focuses her efforts on Asher and Avery. She extends her hands, sending waves of calming, harmonious energy toward the children.

Isolde backs her play, melding some sort of magic with Trudie's.

Avery's sobs quiet almost instantly, and Asher's rigid posture relaxes slightly under the soothing influence of their magic.

Just as I'm about to shift to protect my kids, Alanna's eyes suddenly widen with panic, a raw and fearful energy brewing within her features.

Her voice breaks through the confusion, laced with urgency and fear. "Ella, I can't—" she cries out, her words cut short as her body begins to tremble violently.

Behind her, three witches have their hands raised and heads down, clearly affecting her somehow.

Before anyone can react, Alanna's form expands grotesquely, her muscles bulging and bones elongating. With a guttural roar, she transforms into what I can only assume is her Berserker form—an uncontrollable force of rage and destruction.

"Shit. Alanna, no—" My heart lurches as she begins to rampage, indiscriminately targeting anyone in her path—friend or foe.

My pack, caught off guard, scrambles to avoid her wild swings and powerful lunges.

Stone leaps into action.

With swift movements, he guides younger pack members out of Alanna's destructive path, his commands sharp and clear above the chaos.

He throws himself into the fray, a calm force in the storm, working to steer the confused and frightened toward safety.

Somewhere nearby, I sense Marta doing the same.

But I can't focus on any of it. The only thing in my sights—the only thing that matters—*is my kids.*

The chaos created by Jinx suddenly intensifies as Alanna tears through the ranks, her massive form causing even Andres' well-disciplined troops to falter.

The Sacred Grove erupts into pandemonium, the lines between ally and enemy blurred amidst the confusion.

Fueled by Trudie and Isolde's magic, Asher grabs Avery by the shoulder.

"Run to Mom—*now!*" he shouts, pushing her toward me with all his might, as he turns and slams his elbow into the middle of Silas' stomach.

Avery, propelled by her brother's urgency, dashes

across the clearing and into the Sacred Grove, her form dodging flailing limbs and magical mishaps caused by Jinx's chaos.

As she reaches me, I envelop her in my arms, her body trembling against mine.

But my relief is short-lived.

As I pull her close, I look up just in time to see Silas seize Asher. His hand clamps down on Asher's arm, dragging him back before he can follow his sister.

"Asher—" My voice is a sharp, desperate cry as Silas pulls him away.

Asher struggles against Silas's grip, his eyes wide with fear as his gaze locks with mine.

Then, from the ranks of the enemy, Troy steps forward.

My heart fills with a fleeting hope, praying he's there to save our son. But the cold reality sets in as Silas turns to him with a silent question.

Troy, his expression torn between duty and regret, nods.

Without hesitation, Silas clamps his teeth into Asher's shoulder. The sound of his pain-stricken scream pierces the night, echoing through the grove.

The energy of the grove changes and I feel the distinct shift of the powerful supernatural force that sweeps my son's life out from under me.

"*No!*" My scream is raw—torn from the depths of my being.

The world slows down around me, the noise and

chaos fading into a dull roar. I drop to my knees, still holding Avery tightly against me, my eyes are fixed on Asher as he stumbles back, his face contorted in agony as he clamps a hand over the wound.

Andres' cruel laughter fills the air, his voice mocking and cutting through the cacophony around us. "So, Ella, will you reconsider now? Your pride or will your son become your enemy?"

Tears blur my vision, and a hollow feeling gnaws at my chest. My son, my brave boy is now a pawn in this twisted game.

The thought of him, forced into a life he never chose, under the thumb of Silas and Andres—and his fucking father—fuels a rage deep within me. But right now, my heart is breaking, shattering into pieces with every labored breath he takes.

How did this happen?

We're supposed to be fucking Moon Wolves? We have the Breath of Selene embedded inside us.

How the *fuck* did this happen?

Alanna, still in her Berserker frenzy, crashes through the underbrush, her roars becoming distant thunder as she rampages farther away from us. The ground shakes with her every step, a stark reminder of the chaos we are enveloped in.

Andres watches the unfolding disaster with a smirk, his eyes gleaming with malice.

"You see, Ella, everything has a price," he calls out

over the noise, his voice eerily calm amid the chaos. "And everyone has a breaking point."

His words, meant to taunt, instead solidify my resolve.

I rise, Avery clutched tightly to my side, her small body shivering against mine. I meet Andres's gaze, my own eyes steeled with determination.

"You think you've won," I spit the words out, my voice steady despite the turmoil swirling inside me. "You think because you've cornered me—because you've hurt my son, that I'll bend. But you underestimate the strength of a mother—of an Alpha protecting her pack. Isn't that right, Silas?"

My Alpha power rolls through the words, scattering the birds from the trees, as I turn my attention to Silas.

To his credit, he has the good sense to flinch.

Stone, who has been fighting his own battles, now steps up beside me.

The pack, though scattered and rattled, regroups around us, their faces set in grim determination. They are my family, my strength, and together we form a barrier of resolve.

Andres laughs, but it's a sound devoid of true humor. "Very well, Ella. Since you are so determined to play the martyr, I'll give you time to consider the gravity of your situation." He waves a dismissive hand, signaling his forces to retreat. "Think about what you stand to lose," he throws over his shoulder as he begins to withdraw, his pack moving with him like shadows melding into the night.

Silas, holding a still-struggling Asher by the arm, gives me one final, penetrating look. "The clock is ticking, Ella."

With a tight grip on Asher, he follows Andres and Troy, disappearing into a magical darkness that slowly envelops the grove.

The silence that follows is oppressive, filled with the heavy breaths of my pack and the soft sobs of Avery. I pull her closer, kissing the top of her head, whispering reassurances while my mind races with plans, with the need for vengeance, for rescue. All the while, my heart is breaking into pieces.

"We'll get him back," I promise her, promise myself.

The words are a vow that I intend to keep.

The Sacred Grove, once a place of peace and power, now feels like a battlefield, marked by loss but also by a new resolve.

We are bruised but not broken.

As the last echoes of chaos fade into the night, I stand, Avery in my arms, surrounded by my pack.

By my friends.

By my mate.

This battle may be lost, but the war is far from over. Andres and Silas have underestimated the strength of a mother and the bond of my pack.

No matter the cost, I *will* find a way to save my son.

I'll protect my territory.

And I will reclaim what has been taken from me.

They'll regret ever starting this war.

This fight has only just begun.

TO BE CONCLUDED...

READY FOR MORE?

Thank you for joining Ella and Stone on their journey in *Midlife Wolf Bond*. The adventure is far from over! Be the first to know when the next thrilling installment, *Midlife Wolf Reign*, is available for preorder.

Stay Ahead of the Pack!

Sign up now to receive exclusive updates, sneak peeks, and special offers straight to your inbox. Don't miss out on the epic conclusion of the Accidental Alpha series.

JOIN THE WAITLIST NOW

(Sign up here: subscribepage.io/Midlife-Wolf-Reign)

Keep the excitement alive and ensure you're the first to dive into the next chapter of this unforgettable story!

MIDLIFE WOLF REIGN
ACCIDENTAL ALPHA · BOOK 5

Midlife Can Burn...

Ella Breene thought midlife was supposed to be about finding peace and maybe a good stretch of knitting. Instead, she's knee-deep in a supernatural showdown that could make or break the balance between realms. And let's not forget, she's still got PTA meetings and grocery runs to juggle.

With the Breath of Selene coursing through her and bonded to her hunky, fated mate Stone, Ella must now figure out if these new powers are just a magical energy boost or something far more explosive. But who has time to meditate when her teenage son, Asher, has been bitten by an enemy pack? The clock is ticking down to the Supermoon—his birthday, no less—when he'll shift into a werewolf and fall under the control of the rival Alpha. Permanently.

Ella's maternal instincts are on overdrive, and she's ready to tear through anyone—or anything—that stands in her way. Between Stone's steadfast support and their combined powers, they're a force to be reckoned with. But first, they've got to figure out just what those powers are, and fast.

As the final battle looms, Ella knows one thing for sure: midlife crisis be damned, she's not losing her son without the fight of a lifetime. It's time to show everyone why you don't mess with a mother, a mate, and an Alpha all rolled into one.

Midlife Wolf Reign is the thrilling conclusion to the Accidental Alpha series, where humor, heart, and high-stakes magic collide. Join Ella as she embraces her destiny, battles fierce enemies, and proves that even in midlife, a mother's love is the fiercest power of all.

READY FOR MORE?

Thank you for joining Ella and Stone on their journey in **Midlife Wolf Bond**. The adventure is far from over! Be the first to know when the next thrilling installment, **Midlife Wolf Reign**, is available for preorder.

Stay Ahead of the Pack!

Sign up now to receive exclusive updates, sneak peeks, and special offers straight to your inbox. Don't miss out on the epic conclusion of the Accidental Alpha series.

JOIN THE WAITLIST NOW

(Sign up here: subscribepage.io/Midlife-Wolf-Reign)

Keep the excitement alive and ensure you're the first to dive into the next chapter of this unforgettable story!

A Note from the Author

Thanks so much for reading **Midlife Wolf Bond**, Book 4 in the *Accidental Alpha* series.

This series will be continuing with *Midlife Wolf Reign*.

Join my Patreon to read my books as they're being written (including this series!), get exclusive merch, and to get more news and book-related nerdery from me.

Thanks for being here!
xo Carissa

CAN'T WAIT FOR MORE ACCIDENTAL ALPHA?

If you're waiting for the next installment of Accidental Alpha, check out Carissa's other series.

The Windhaven Witches

Secret Legacy

Soul Legacy

Haunted Legacy

Cursed Legacy

The Diana Hawthorne Series

The Final Five (prequel)

Oracle

Amends

Immortals

Ruins

The Pendomus Chronicles

Trajectory (prequel)

Pendomus

Polarities

Revolutions

Stand Alone Titles

Awakening

Merciless

Contemporary Romcoms (as Carissa Knight)

Dirty Plans

Dirty Books

Dirty Developments

About the Author

Carissa Andrews
Sci-fi/Fantasy is my pen of choice.

 Carissa Andrews is an award-winning and international bestselling indie author from central Minnesota. Her books range from paranormal and urban fantasy to science fiction dystopia. Her plans for right now include the continuation of her acclaimed *Diana Hawthorne Supernatural Mysteries* and a new series called *Accidental Alpha*. As a publishing powerhouse, she keeps sane by chilling with her husband, five kids, and their husky pup, Aztec.

For a free ebook and to find out what Carissa's up to, head over to her website and sign up for her newsletter:
www.carissaandrews.com

patreon.com/carissaandrews

bookbub.com/authors/carissa-andrews

goodreads.com/Carissa_Andrews